Anit

Her angel's face
As the great eye of heaven shined bright,
And made a sunshine in the shady place;
Did never mortal eye behold such heavenly grace.

The Faerie Queen (1596) Book1, canto 3, st. 4

PROLOGUE

She hurt so much. There was so much blood on the sheet and she reached a hand up to pull on the chain that shackled her to the bed every day. She had never felt anything like this before.

Daddy had been so rough with her and she instinctively knew that if he came to her again when he got home from work she would not be able to stand the pain. She didn't know about death. She didn't know about anything because Daddy had kept her locked up for all her life.

She felt she wanted to wee and looked at the bucket that was already full at the side of her bed. She fought against the feeling because she knew it would hurt even more if she let her wee go. Eventually, she could wait no longer and clinging on to the chain that allowed her to move as far as the two buckets she dragged herself off the bed.

She bent over the bucket and screamed as the red-hot urine burnt the cuts and scarring inside her. She clung on to the chain letting it bite into her hand, focussing on that pain instead of the burning one.

That was the point when she realised that for the only time since she had taken that first tiny step, she wasn't connected to the chain. She stared at the handcuff on the end of the rusty links and began to tremble.

She had a vague recollection of Daddy coming to her and looking down at her before he went to work and saying something about no chains today then but she had been so spaced out with the painkillers he had doped her with, the horrific pain they didn't touch, that his words hadn't registered.

But now they did.

She managed to pull on three pairs of socks and some pants, pulled her thickest cardigan out of the suitcase that held the few clothes she had and carefully opened her bedroom door.

There was no sound and she went down the stairs one careful step at a time expecting to hear Daddy's voice at any time. She didn't know when he would be home from work but she did know fear.

In the small hallway she paused for a moment, listening. The pain washed over her and she knelt down, waiting for it to pass. She moved to the front door but it wouldn't open. Slowly, she walked towards the kitchen door. It was open and she couldn't see any movement inside.

The room was empty and she moved, trancelike, towards the back door. She tried to open it but it was locked just like the front door. She knew nothing of keys, of how to unlock doors and she stared wildly around the room unsure of how to get out of the house.

She pushed a chair towards the sink unit and climbed onto it to try and open the window but that too was locked. And then she saw the frying pan on the draining board. She picked it up and hit the window with it. She remembered how glass broke; Daddy had been very angry with her when she had dropped her drinking glass and it had shattered. She hadn't been given another drink for three days.

Nothing happened with her first tentative strike and she knew she would have to hit it harder and cope with how much that would hurt her. The second hit caused the crack to appear and the third hit sent a large shard flying through and on to the garden outside the window. She smashed some more pieces out and then had to use her hands. She started to crawl through and felt her skin burst open in many places. As she tumbled outside and landed on her back, she lay still for a long time. Internally and externally, the pain was excruciating. She couldn't move. When the throbbing temporarily subsided, she placed a hand on the wall and rose to her feet. She didn't see the bloodied imprint she left on the white painted wall. She knew she had to go, and quickly.

She set off across the fields at the back of the house and didn't stop until she was too tired and in too much discomfort to go on. It was dark and she was on a small dirt track that ran along the back of some houses. She took advantage of the night sky and bent down for a wee, stifling the moan that involuntarily escaped her.

Most of the gardens had sheds. She tried the first two and couldn't open the doors but the third one opened with a squeak. She slipped inside and opened the little curtains covering the window. The moonlight gave her vision and she saw a chair with a big cushion on it. She curled up on the chair and slept soundly until the cold woke her.

She then used the cushion to cover her tiny body and slept a little more but as dawn broke, she knew she had to leave her sanctuary. She placed the cushion back in the chair and ignored the blood that was clearly evident. She could do nothing about it.

No one saw her as she left the shed. Her socks were torn and barely covering her soles but she knew nothing of shoes. Daddy only got her socks because he said she couldn't go out; she had an illness that stopped her being in fresh air.

As she walked along, she thought about the illness. She seemed to be okay. Daddy must have been wrong. Daddy just wanted her to stay in the house.

She walked a little further until she saw a small road with houses on it. At the same time, she was aware of something trickling down her leg and she looked down. There was blood, a lot of blood. She stumbled and cried out.

She moved as quickly as she could and saw a house with a red door.

She crept up to it and listened just in case Daddy knew where she was. She knocked on the door.

BOOK ONE
1995
ANGEL

CHAPTER 1

Lauren stood at the graveside without speaking. This annual pilgrimage on Christmas Eve was almost unbearable for her and she held tightly to Pilot's hand as he gently squeezed his wife's fingers, letting her know his understanding was complete.

But it wasn't. How could it be complete? She had lost both her parents within a very short of space of time, her mother in particularly horrific circumstances. And Lauren hadn't known of Amy's traumatic life until after her death, sheltered from all the details by the love of grandparents and a close-knit Cornish community. To be told that Amy had been raped as a child by the man her mother had eventually married had been hard to hear and had gone some way towards Lauren accepting that the coldness of Amy towards her had been caused by what she had suffered.

It was cold, very cold. There had been the promise of a white Christmas but it hadn't snowed yet. He hoped it wouldn't, they were too close to having the baby for complications like snow-blocked roads to enter the equation.

Pilot released her fingers and knelt to place the Christmas wreath on the grave. He stayed in that position for a moment praying quietly under his breath and then lifted his face to his wife. His short dark hair had fallen over his forehead and she leaned forward to stroke it back. His brown eyes showed his love. He stood up slowly and kissed her.

'Okay?'

She nodded and rubbed the huge stomach that carried their soon- to-be-born first child.

'I'm fine, just a few twinges from standing for so long. He's not playing football so much today, but he's feeling mighty heavy.'

'He? You're convinced, aren't you?' Pilot said with a smile. 'It could be a girl, you know.'

She shook her head. 'Order the blue wallpaper, Pilot, order the blue wallpaper.'

They both looked at the headstone for one last time, the black letters telling them that John and Amy Thornton resided therein and that this was their third Christmas without them. She guessed that in the beginning their love would have been strong, if indeed Amy had ever been capable of real love. But she knew that at the end of John's life, his love had been for Dawn Lynch.

They visited one other grave at the far side of the cemetery. Lauren's grandfather Jack had died before she was adopted and she had only ever known Brenda and Ken as her grandparents. But Jack had never been forgotten.

Pilot knelt and placed their second wreath on the grave then stood and pulled Lauren to him.

'They would all have welcomed this baby, you know.' He spoke quietly into her blonde hair as he leaned to kiss the top of her head.

She sighed. 'I know. Such a waste, none of them lived long enough to have a full life. Amy, Dad – both dead at such a young age. And still nobody brought to account for her murder.'

He smiled. 'Have faith; one day they'll get Treverick or whatever he's calling himself now. He might even be dead. He's got to be turned sixty, I would have thought.

And your Dad managed to pack a lot into his life, whether it was a long one or not.'

She turned to him with a slight frown on her face. 'He...' and then she laughed. 'Oh, you're right. Of course, you're right. Two separate families, twelve books published, Josh and me.'

'You miss Josh?'

She nodded. 'I do, but he's coming over with Dawn after the baby is born. You know, it was so, so painful when your Mum and Dad and Nan and Granddad sat us down to tell us the full story of Amy and Dad but it answered so many questions and gave us Dawn and Josh. Without Josh, I would have been an only child but now I have a stepbrother who is so like my Dad, it almost breaks my heart. I thought it only happened to other people, this business of one man having two families and managing to keep them apart, but oh no, my Dad became an expert at it.'

He noticed her use of her mother's Christian name rather than Mum but made no mention of it. Lauren wasn't healed yet.

'Your Dad only became expert at it because Dawn knew he had a family before her. She always made him put that first. But for all that, he had a good life.'

She rubbed her stomach again and he looked closely at her. 'Ready to go?'

She nodded and he took her hand to help her between gravestones. At six feet, he was so much taller than her five and a bit and he helped her further by almost carrying her over the last few yards to the car. The temperature was dropping and both of them shivered, moving quickly. The comforts of Hillside Cottage seemed infinitely preferable to their present location.

They headed for the iron gates that led to where they had parked the car, neither of them noticing the man in the workman's overalls who leaned on a spade watching them.

Chapter 2

Occasionally staring out of the window at the view she knew her Dad had loved so much, Lauren moved around the room. Her father's deliberate choice of this room for his office had been driven by the vista of the garden and even though the room was no longer used as an office, John's presence was always there to comfort her. The view on this dark night had the added benefit of an outdoor Christmas tree with decorative lights. Mesmerised, she stared at the flashing, twinkling column of light.

Following the death of Amy, Hillside Cottage had passed to Lauren and six months later, shortly after their return from honeymoon, she and Pilot had moved in. They had set aside a small room upstairs for the new baby and the intermittent pains in her lower back told her they would be meeting the child pretty soon.

With a due date of 22 December, he or she was already two days late and she was almost at the point of telling Pilot that the pains were starting to become a little more serious.

'Cup of tea?'

She heard him call and turned from the window to answer him. The gush of water caused her simply to say,

'Oh!'

He popped his head around the door and waved a teapot at her. She stood looking down at the floor and he dropped the teapot with a crash.

They arrived at the hospital excited and scared at the same time with Pilot considerably more edgy than Lauren. They had rung his parents, Pat and David, before setting off and had in turn rung Lauren's grandmother Brenda and her husband Ken who had rung Aunt Freda, so everybody who was important in their lives was at the hospital with them, supporting them by just being there.

By midnight, implacable Freda was attempting to calm down the men folk and Brenda and Pat were biting nails.

Freda sent David and Ken to get coffees and all three women began to talk at once.

'It's...'

'When...'

'Should…?'

They looked at each other and laughed.

'This baby will be here when it arrives,' Freda smiled. 'And I'm sure it can't be much longer now. £1says it's a girl,' and she placed a coin on the coffee table.

'Do you know something we don't know?' Brenda asked her sister-in-law, accusation in her voice. Freda had worked for the local doctor for many years of her working life and they had remained very close friends.

'Certainly not,' said Freda. 'Just a feeling.'

'Well, Lauren thinks it's a boy.'

'She's wrong,' said Freda firmly. 'It's a girl. Do you think they'll call it Freda?'

The men returned with the coffees to see the women in shrieks of laughter.

'Is it...?' David asked. 'And happy Christmas everybody! It's Christmas Day!' He raised a cardboard cup of coffee in salute. His first grandchild was so very much wanted and to have the birth on Christmas Day itself was very much a plus in his eyes.

The door opened and a midwife came through.

'Would you like to come and see your grandchild,' she smiled.

'What is it?' Freda asked.

'The parents will tell you. They're through here.'

She pushed the door and Pilot was holding the baby. He held it out to his mother.

'Meet Miss Grace Elizabeth Farmer, our Christmas Day gift. She's absolutely perfect and weighs in at a stonking 8 lbs 11 ozs.'

Looking slightly dazed, Lauren managed a smile for the people surrounding her bed.

Freda leaned down to kiss her great-niece.

'Are you sure you want to call her Grace and not Freda? It's the same number of letters, you know.'

'Sorry, Aunt Freda,' Pilot said, 'Freda Farmer sounded all wrong when we tried it, so we had to discount it and go with Grace.'

The silliness continued until four o'clock in the morning when Lauren was finally left alone with her new-born daughter.

She pulled the plastic crib as close to the bedside as she could get it and lay for a while stroking the tiny head before falling into an exhausted, deep sleep.

In the hospital, car park, a lone figure watched three cars depart.

The following day, Pilot was back at the hospital for three o'clock visiting. Lauren had had a good night's sleep and looked much improved, her pallor had gone and her skin and eyes were glowing. She was clearly a very happy person.

Her blonde hair was pulled back in a pony-tail and Pilot tugged on it.

'What's this then? This isn't like you!'

She laughed. 'When it's loose, Grace clutches on to it when she's feeding. It's better like this at the moment.'

'So, how is our little sweetheart?' he asked, bending over to kiss Lauren.

'She's absolutely fine,' Lauren said drily, 'but she hasn't got stitches where no stitches should ever expect to be had. I have.'

'You poor darling' Pilot sympathised. 'Can I hold her?'

Lauren laughed. 'She's ours. We basically can hold her whenever we want. That's how it works. Just keep her blanket round her. She had a visit from Father Christmas this morning. He brought her that little pink teddy in her cot. Oh, and the good news is we can go home tomorrow morning.'

Pilot picked up his daughter and moved around the maternity ward, chatting quietly to her all the time. Lauren watched for a while, smiling, and then drifted off to sleep in the middle of hearing the words *pink wallpaper*. It had been a long night and she had had very little sleep for the two nights prior to the birth.

Pilot woke her gently at about four thirty pm to say he'd be back later with his Mum and Dad. Lauren sat up with a struggle.

'I need to feed her,' she muttered. She gave Pilot a kiss. 'Just go, I'll see you later.'

As he left, Pilot saw the nurse on her way to help Lauren with the breast-feeding. He blew a kiss but she didn't see it.

Grace fed well, and by six o'clock both Mother and baby were dozing. Then Lauren became aware of a doctor in a white coat touching her shoulder.

'Mrs Farmer? I have to take baby for her Guthrie test. You can come with me if you want but most parents don't like to see their babies having blood taken from the heel.' His Scottish accent penetrated Lauren's sleepy brain and she smiled at him.

'No, you see to her. Just bring her back when it's over.' She closed her eyes once more.

At 6.30 pm Lauren felt another touch on the shoulder.

'Is she back? Was she good?'

'What?' Pilot sounded puzzled. 'Where's Grace?'

'Oh, sorry.' Lauren tried to sit up without causing pain to herself; Pilot helped her, reorganising pillows behind her to make her more comfortable. 'A doctor came and took her for a Guthrie test. It's the test where they stab them in the foot. Remember them telling us about it at ante-natal class?'

Pilot nodded.

'Yes, they have it at five days, don't they? She's not even one day old yet! Bit premature, aren't they?'

He moved away towards the nurses' station and asked where Grace was, explaining a doctor had taken her for a Guthrie test. There was instant pandemonium. The nurse hit the panic button, and the hospital was put into lock down.

Pat, David, Brenda, Ken and Freda, along with the new parents, sat around Lauren's bed all night waiting but there was no news.

Grace had disappeared.

Chapter 3

2003

'Olivia! Stop running! You'll fall!' Lauren shouted at the four-year-old in a vain attempt to stop the headlong flight down the grassy slope.

'You'll never get her to stop,' Pilot said with a grin, cradling a very sleepy Noah in his arms. He felt Noah stir and whispered *sssh* to him.

'Don't worry,' Lauren smiled. 'He's getting ready for a feed. Pass him to me and you go chase Olivia.'

He passed the tiny baby over to his wife and moved to follow Olivia down the slope.

'Don't let her out of your sight, Pilot,' Lauren warned quietly as she knelt down on the grass.

He shook his head. 'Never.'

The baby's tiny head turned towards his mother's breast and she unbuttoned her top.

'Come on then, little man, feed time,' she said softly and hugged him tightly before helping the tiny mouth on to her nipple. At two weeks old, Noah was still struggling with knowing exactly where his food came from. Lauren couldn't remember Olivia ever being like that.

She heard Olivia giggling as her Daddy caught up with her and a smile that sometimes had to be forced came readily to Lauren's lips. 'Okay, Noah, time for lunch. And don't hang about, the health visitor is coming to weigh you this afternoon and I want you to have put loads of weight on. So, drink up, big boy.'

She felt the familiar drag on her breast and then breathed a sigh of relief as Noah began to suck. No tantrums today, just a contented baby.

Olivia and Pilot came back up the hill towards her and Pilot said he'd go back to the house and bring down some drinks. Olivia flopped down on to the grass beside her Mummy, whom she looked so like. Her long blonde hair and deep blue eyes mirrored Lauren but the little girl was already showing signs of growth that would take her over Lauren's adult height.

'Tired,' Olivia said.

'Too much running around,' Lauren responded. 'Maybe we can have a nap later, do you think?'

The little girl gave a solemn nod and put her head on her mother's lap. Within two minutes, she had drifted off into a light sleep.

Lauren wanted to wrap both of them in cotton wool and protect them for all of their lives. She wanted no part of the outside world to touch them and Lauren did not know how she would cope with the fact that Olivia was due to start nursery after the Easter holidays. How could she could handle the enormity of her child being away from her and outside her watchful protection?

The police had never had any idea where Treverick, her mother's killer, was. Indeed, they had never had any concrete proof that he had been the one to snatch Grace. Back in 1952, when he had been eighteen-years-old, he had raped a small child called Amelia Andrews - more than rape her, he had destroyed her. He had destroyed her mind and he had destroyed her body. His intention had been to rape her and, if he'd been caught, to kill himself. Caught very quickly, he hadn't even managed to kill himself – the bullet he fired from a rifle had grazed him enough to knock him out but had done no damage beyond a scar. If it had been a shotgun and not a rifle, the end result would have been very different. Hearing the shot, the police had found the house where he was hiding and he had been virtually gift-wrapped. When he had recovered, he had confessed and sent to prison. But not for nearly long enough. And that's where everything had begun.

Lauren had never doubted for a minute that he had taken the tiny baby. She did not know what he had taken her for.

Pilot returned with their drinks and sat down beside her.

'Ok?'

She nodded. 'He fed well. Let Olivia sleep, we need to be going back to the house in about quarter of an hour for the health visitor. Daren't be late for her - it's that look she gives you when she disapproves of something,' she laughed.

He nodded his head. 'Oh, I know. I clearly remember *the look* when I placed Olivia in her crib on her tummy! If she only knew that Noah seems to be following the same sleep pattern...'

'Do not tell her!'

'Well I won't if you won't...'

They finished their drink in the early spring sunshine until some clouds crossed the sky. Lauren shivered.

'The temperature's dropping a bit. Let's head back up to the house.'

Pilot gently woke his daughter and gathered everything up, placing it all in the pram basket. Noah was the one now fast asleep and Lauren carefully settled him in the pram before pushing it up the slight incline.

It was quiet as they entered the front door and Olivia went to the corner of the lounge that accommodated her dolls house. She opened the front of the house and took out all the little people before replacing them in different rooms.

Lauren could hear her chatting to the tiny wooden dolls as she rummaged in a drawer to find the birth book and notes. She placed them ready on the coffee table. Noah was still asleep so she sat on the settee and let her mind temporarily slow down.

And Grace wandered into it. She had known her first child for less than a day but every day at some point and at several points in the Christmas season, she thought about her daughter. They had no idea whether she was alive or dead, although there had been a scare within a couple of months of Grace's abduction when a newborn's body had been found. They had both had to give DNA samples because the police said the corpse was a couple of months old. That had been a really low point in their lives. But the DNA had proved it wasn't Grace and they had breathed again.

Hope had faded now and she was starting to believe the unthinkable. Treverick had taken the baby and killed her. The police had nothing to go on, there had been no sighting of the bogus doctor and while several of the police officers privately thought it was Treverick, there was no proof at all.

Lauren enjoyed the quiet moments thinking about her firstborn. Tears fell at Christmastime, but the rest of the year was peaceful as she enfolded her tiny daughter into her memory bank. She heard the doorbell and stood, fixing the smile on her face that would welcome the health visitor.

Noah was pronounced fit and well with healthy lungs that he used to great effect. He had gained a few ounces after dropping a little of his birth weight and everyone was happy except the health visitor who really didn't like urine on her uniform.

Full of apologies for his wayward son, Pilot escorted her to the door. He returned to the lounge and he and Lauren doubled up with laughter.

'Bet she sends somebody else next time,' she spluttered. 'Her face was an absolute picture.'

'Well, by the time of the next visit, I'll be back at work so you'll have to deal with whoever turns up.'

She groaned. 'I don't want you to go back to work.'

'I have to work, my love. It's my publishing company now.'

She kissed him. 'I know. I've just enjoyed having you around the place.'

'Being waited on hand and foot, you mean.'

'That as well,' she conceded, 'but as the brood mare in this family, it's only what I deserve.'

'So, tea and biscuits it is then,' he said with a sigh. 'Nothing but a man-slave, that's all I am, nothing but a man-slave.'

'Yes, Daddy,' said Olivia from the depths of the dolls house.

'And outnumbered by talkative women,' he muttered as he headed for the kitchen.

Lauren was reading a magazine when he returned from completing his latest chores.

'Biscuits are a bit naff,' he said. 'We could do with a shop sometime soon. Shall I go tonight?'

'Might be an idea. Or send the list to your Mum – she said she'd do that for us if we needed anything.'

He nodded. 'I know but it's quicker to do it myself. Will you be okay while I'm gone? I can ask Brenda or Ken to pop over and stay with you...'

'I'm fine.' Her reply was sharper than Lauren intended and she softened it with a smile. 'Really I'm fine. The door will be locked and the panic button has been tested. And can I just point out that Nan Brenda is now 87 years old and hardly up to babysitting me? Or fighting intruders off!'

'Huh! I'd back her against anyone, and she's only 87 in years, not in mind and body.'

Within a week of Grace's abduction, they had installed the panic button, which connected directly to Padstow police. Lauren thanked God every day that the only time it had ever been used was on its six monthly testing. It simply gave her a degree of comfort to know it was there.

She knew that Treverick would be 69 or 70 years old by now but the fact that her own Nan was proof of age being just a number, gave her cause for concern that he could still be actively seeking to destroy the Thornton family. She hoped he was dead. Since the disappearance of Grace, there had been nothing. No sighting, no communication, nothing but grief on their part. He was an ever-present danger to them and they had no idea what he looked like, how he spoke, where he was.

In the end, Pat and David came over to visit with news of their own; Dawn and Josh would be here at the weekend to see the new baby. Lauren welcomed the news; since finding out she had a half-brother and getting to know him, she hated the fact that he lived so far away from them but loved the way they were able to just fly over whenever they felt like it.

The evening finally ended a little after eleven o'clock, with Lauren trying to stifle her yawns.

It had been a good evening: the last one for a long time to come.

Chapter 4

On Wednesday morning, Lauren was standing at the kitchen work surface chopping vegetables when she heard the car. She wiped her hands on the tea towel and moved into the lounge to see who it was.

'Pilot!' Her cry came out as a constricted squeak and she shouted again, this time with volume. 'Pilot!'

He ran from the utility room where he had been loading the washing machine and his eyes followed her gaze.

'It's a police car,' he said. 'Don't panic. Have we forgotten to pay a parking fine or something?'

'They don't send Detective Inspectors for parking fine collection.' Lauren's eyes never moved from the car and its occupants.

'What? Oh...'

Getting out of the car, the man they had grown to trust and who had agreed with them that the abductor was probably Treverick, was accompanied by a WPC who stepped out of the back. The driver remained with the car while the two officers walked towards their door.

Pilot moved quickly and was at the door before they knocked. He held his fingers to his lips.

'Sssh,' he said. 'The noisy one is sleeping.'

'Mr. Farmer, can we come in?'

Pilot was a little put out – he had always been Pilot to Jake Dunbar, the detective inspector who had led the investigation into Grace's disappearance.

Dunbar recognised the expression on Pilot's face and spoke quietly.

'Sorry to be so formal, Pilot, but we are here officially. We need to come in. Is your wife here?'

'Yes, she is.'

'And your little girl?'

'Yes, Olivia's playing in the lounge. Why? What's happening?'

'Is there someone who can look after the children?'

Pilot recognised the tone of voice and rang his mother. She took three minutes to get there and both children were whisked away five minutes later.

The WPC had made tea for all four of them and DI Dunbar produced a file from his briefcase, which he laid on the coffee table. His greying hair gave him a look of authority that, combined with his grey eyes and a height of well over six feet, always made Lauren think he should be in films and not the police.

'I'm sorry to be so secretive,' he said, 'but I am mindful of the fact that you have a small baby, Lauren, and what I am about to tell you is going to change your lives. I needed to speak to you two together without distractions.'

He picked up the file.

'First of all, I need to introduce WPC Sarah Miller. Please call her Sarah. The last thing we need at this moment in time is formality. I apologise for the way we were when we entered your home, but we have rules...'

Both Lauren and Pilot nodded and then looked at each other.

'What's going on, Jake?' Pilot spoke quietly.

'This file is the one we started when Grace was abducted. As you know, we never had any proof that it was Treverick who took her, just gut feelings and those can't be put into a police file. However, we now have proof.'

He watched as Lauren's head dropped and he reached across to touch her hand.

'Stay with me, Lauren, stay with me. Almost two weeks ago, on the 19th March to be precise, we had a telephone call from an elderly couple who said they had taken in a small girl who had knocked on their door in a very distressed state. They guessed she was about five or six years old but they could make very little sense of anything she was saying.'

He watched as Lauren lifted her head and turn to her husband.

'We sent officers immediately to the house and the case was handed to me. I need to say that because of the size of the little girl I did not initially connect her to Grace. We went with her to the hospital and they sedated her for three days. She was in a mess, covered in blood around her genital area, scratches and cuts all over her body and dirty. Her feet were cut to ribbons; she had walked some considerable way without shoes, just socks that offered no protection at all. The doctors and nurses cared for her and then gently brought her back to us. They had taken DNA samples while she was sedated but at this point we didn't have results.'

He paused, searching for the right words.

'When she saw me, she cried. Her first words were *don't let him hurt me again.* We spoke to her calmly, and even at this stage, I felt she was five years old at the most. She was so fragile and tiny. Her language was childlike and her vocabulary limited. I asked her how old she was and she didn't know. I asked her if she knew her birthday and she said, quite significantly as it turned out, that it was when her Daddy started hurting her. There was no doubt what form the hurting had taken; she was ripped to pieces inside. We tried to delve deeper but the child psychologist stopped us. She said enough was enough for that day, and it was. She was allowed to sleep again.'

'It's Grace, isn't it?' Lauren's voice was harsher than Pilot had ever heard it before. 'He's had my baby all this time.' She jumped up from the settee and set about Dunbar. 'I told you, I told you,' she sobbed.

Dunbar held her wrists and pulled her closer to him. 'You have to listen to the full story as we know it, Lauren. You have to listen.'

Pilot stood and held his wife, lowering her back into her seat.

'They woke her again the next day and we tried to get her to open up but she wouldn't talk. She had completely closed down. All we had was what the Wainwrights had managed to elicit from her while they were sending for us. Apparently, she said her Daddy loved her, but he didn't want her to go out of the house because the air outside could kill her. He had told her she had an illness and she had to stay inside with him. It seems that every time he went out for shopping or to go to work, he chained her to her bed. She could reach a bucket, which she used for a toilet and he used to bath her. She said he liked to bath her. She never went out into the fresh air for the whole of her life.'

Lauren moaned.

'This is going to get more painful, Lauren. Be strong. And then we get to last Christmas. He started to have sex with her, told her it was her birthday present. He apparently said to her that when little girls became older they had to do things with their Daddy. She said she didn't like it because it hurt and then two nights before she arrived at the elderly couple's house, he had raped her repeatedly.

Remember all of this is what she told Mr and Mrs Wainwright. She didn't have the right words, obviously, but it was very clear what he had done to her. It was spontaneous because she was so frightened that they would send her back to Daddy. We're optimistic that one day she will say it all to us. That will be when she starts to heal, when her soul starts to heal.'

He stopped for a moment, trying to find the right words. Pilot provided them.

'I'll kill the fucking bastard.'

'Pilot,' said Dunbar, 'believe me, I'd let you. This little girl is so damaged, both mentally and physically, that it is almost a carbon copy of her grandmother. That, of course, is a deliberate action on Treverick's part. It's why he took her. Treverick sees his imprisonment as down to Amy and her family. That's not going to change until the day he dies. On the day she escaped, she was in a dreadful state. He apparently told her he was going to work but he wouldn't chain her up. He clearly thought she was incapable of moving. She is one brave child, I can tell you.'

Again, he paused.

'We had to wait a further two days before we could talk to her again because she began to bleed badly and they had to do major surgery. When we next spoke to her, we knew who she was. The DNA results were back. But we not only knew who she was, we knew who *Daddy* was because when we found Amy in that field the day after he killed her she still had his semen on her and we DNA tested it. We had a match with Treverick for the perpetrator and a match with your DNA that you both supplied seven years ago. She is your Grace.'

The sound that came from Lauren was almost inhuman in its intensity and Pilot held her tightly.

'So she saw her chance and escaped?'

'Yes. She waited some time and then realised she could move around an empty house. She broke a downstairs window because the door was locked and crawled out, which is why she was covered in cuts and scratches. She has no idea where she was, she just ran as fast as she could despite the pain she must have been in and on that first night she told the Wainwrights she had slept in a garden shed. She must have been so cold but she said it had a chair in it with a cushion and she used the cushion as a blanket. She left early the next morning, probably through being so cold and unable to sleep until eventually something inside her had told her she needed to stop. She went to a house with a red door – she said because it looked nice – and Mrs. Wainwright rang us immediately.'

Sarah stood and gathered up the untouched cups of tea.

'I'll make another drink,' she said. 'You've had a shock. You need a drink.' She walked into the kitchen and wiped away a tear. She ached for the young couple that had been robbed of so much.

'I want to see her.' Lauren stood and faced Dunbar, her face implacable.

'You will, but not until the psychologist has explained your side to her. She knows nothing of you, doesn't even know her name was Grace. Treverick named her Angel. No surname, just Angel.'

'Does she look like me?'

'Now that she's clean and had her hair washed and brushed, she's actually very much like you,' he smiled. 'But mentally she's in a bad place. We cannot just spring a new Mummy and Daddy on her without a lot of careful planning.

Physically, she's also in a bad place. Just like your Mum, Lauren, she will never have children of her own. She is undernourished, very tiny for a seven-year-old and she will come back to you but it has to be at the right time.'

And then the tears began to flow.

'I never gave up. I knew she was alive. Pilot, we can love her better.' She turned to Dunbar. 'How soon...?'

'How long is a piece of string,' he responded. 'That side of things is out of my hands, I have no medical training so the experts will decide at what point we can start to reveal who she is, who her family is. My job is to find Treverick but that isn't going to be easy. If he has any brains at all, he will have disappeared by now. And believe me, he does have brains. Now, this is what is going to happen in the immediate future. We are allocating protection to patrol this locality but that can't go on forever. It can, and will, for the near future. Pilot, you have to step up your security. Your children and Lauren need to be protected at all times. Once we find Treverick, you will be able to breathe easier but until then don't take any chances at all. We believe he lived within maybe an eight mile radius of where we found Grace because I don't think in her state she could have travelled further than that but even if we find the house where he kept her for seven years, he's not going to be there.'

Pilot nodded.

'Protection will be in place by tonight.'

'Good. As you know, we have limited funding. Your children need to know who is looking after them, who they run to if there is a problem.' And then for the first time he laughed. 'Although I guess Noah is a little young for running.'

Sarah returned with fresh drinks and they all took one. Lauren couldn't taste it, she couldn't think of anything beyond Grace coming back to them. She turned to Pilot.

'Get everyone back here. I need the children with me. Your Mum and Dad, Nan Brenda and Granddad Ken, Aunt Freda – get them back here. They have to know about this. He could go for any one of us now he's lost Grace.'

'Now you're starting to think clearly, Lauren,' said Dunbar. 'This man is so evil, he's well off the scale. We will be fitting panic buttons at Stonebrook Cottage for your grandparents and at Moorgate Manor for your parents, Pilot. But panic buttons are only ever any good if you're actually there. Everyone needs to up their security in every way until we've got him.'

Pilot took out his mobile phone and organised the family into dropping everything and travelling to Hillside Cottage. He explained that they needed a family conference.

Dunbar put down his mug and spoke quietly to Pilot.

'Do you need me to stay and explain anything? We will be in touch constantly until Grace is back home with you but I need to do my job.'

'No, you and Sarah go. If there are questions I can't answer, then I have your number. It goes without saying how grateful we are for this, but please bear in mind we need to see our daughter as soon as possible.'

The police car disappeared from view as Pat and David's Lexus drove up the drive, followed within a minute by Ken and Brenda in the Range Rover.

Pat was the first through the door carrying her tiny grandson. 'There's a police car looks as though it's taken root at the bottom of the drive. You know why?'

Pilot took the sleeping baby from his mother and passed him to Lauren to put in the crib.

'We certainly do. We're going to make drinks for everyone and if you want anything stronger than tea or coffee please bear in mind there's a police car at the bottom of the drive. Mum?'

'Do I need anything stronger?'

'Probably later...'

'Then I'll have tea. Your Dad will have coffee, no sugar.'

'Dad?'

Coffee, no sugar,' David said with a sigh. 'She's put me on a diet.' He bent down to whisper to a giggling Olivia. 'She's cruel to me, isn't she, Honeybun.' Olivia nodded and skipped over to the doll's house. Time to play.

Pat's greying hair was looking a little tousled and she tried to smooth it with her hand. She turned her huge eyes towards her husband. 'David, do you have a comb? I didn't even stop to pick up my bag.'

David grinned and looked at her. 'You look absolutely fine, still the same gorgeous face I fell in love with all those years ago - a bit chubbier, perhaps, but...'

Pat punched him on the arm. 'Careful, husband dearest, I'm the one controlling your food at the moment. It can be reduced further...'

He rubbed his hand across his expanding stomach area and laughed.

Ken and Brenda walked through the door, concern etched on their faces.

'Do you know...?'

Pilot interrupted her. 'There's a police car at the bottom of our drive. Yes, we know.'

'Oh...' Brenda looked quite disgruntled. 'Can't tell you anything, can I?' Brenda had aged well and she put it down to Ken being some ten years younger than her. She always said that a brown dye skilfully applied to her naturally greying hair worked wonders. And a toy boy for a husband kept you on your toes. Ken, in his blunt Yorkshire fashion, always said she was a bit of a'reight, anyway.

He was looking older; his legs had suffered some damage a few years earlier and Brenda had noticed increasingly that he tried to hide the pain when he stood up. He had lost most of his hair now and never went anywhere without his glasses, but she still blessed the day he had arrived on her doorstep looking for a job.

Pilot did a quick tally of drinks and moved into the kitchen to make them. Everyone sat around talking about anything but what they wanted to talk about; everyone except Lauren. She couldn't speak.

She watched Brenda sit down carefully. She was remarkably fit for an eighty-seven-year-old woman but the aches and pains were becoming more pronounced. Ken held her hand, squeezing her fingers gently trying not to let his own aches and pains show.

Pilot carried in the drinks and steered Lauren away from staring out of the window at the darkening sky, to a place on the settee. He looked at his wife.

'Shall I begin?'

She nodded, knowing that if she tried to tell the twisted story, she would start to cry and they would miss most of it.

'What about Olivia? Shall I take her to her room?' Pat asked.

'No!' The word was almost a scream coming from Lauren's mouth. 'No, she must stay here. She's playing;

she's lost in her world. She won't realise what we're saying.'

David looked at his son.

'Pilot?'

'Grace is alive. She's coming home to us.'

There was an eerie silence in the room and then Brenda said, quite simply,

'Thank you, Lord, thank you.'

Chapter 5

Later that afternoon, Pilot told the family the entire harrowing story, all the time keeping an eye on Olivia. He wanted no nightmares for his second daughter. The people sitting around listening to him waited until he had finished and then continued to sit silently.

Finally, David broke the tension.

'How quickly can we get her home to be mended?'

'We have no idea. We can't even see her yet, she is so damaged and the professionals say no contact yet. She has to hear about us slowly.'

All of them nodded. Not all of them agreed.

'The most important thing at the moment is security. Treverick is going to be angry, angry enough to try and take out any one of us, or even all of us. Dad, I'm going to ring Mark. We need to talk to him to get something in place by tomorrow morning. It's lucky for us that Mark set up his own security company. At least we know him and that he'll put his best operatives on to it. There will be police cars at Stonebrook and here tonight but we need to be upgrading that. I'd like you to be with me at that meeting if you can.'

David nodded. 'Of course, and the cost will be covered by me for all three properties.'

'We may not need to cover costs at Stonebrook.' He turned to Ken and Brenda. 'Ken, when do you exchange on Stonebrook?'

Ken and Brenda had taken the decision to retire and had sold the business within a day of it being advertised. As a result, they still hadn't found their future home and had planned on moving into a hotel in Padstow until they found exactly what they wanted.

'Two weeks.' Ken smiled. 'The new owners would like to move in yesterday, but no, it's two weeks. Why?'

'I want you to move in here. I know you said you wouldn't when we first asked you, but things are different now. It will take away some of the worry if you're here. Please say yes.'

They looked at each other and Brenda nodded.

'Pilot's right, Ken. There is more safety in numbers and they have plenty of room here. It scares me that Treverick knows Stonebrook so well, he could hide in any of the outbuildings and we wouldn't know.' She turned to her granddaughter. 'Lauren, are you okay with that? This is your home, and you haven't said anything.'

Lauren reached across and squeezed Brenda's hand.

'I'll go make up a bed for tonight and then tomorrow we'll sort out a suite of sorts for you so that you have your own space away from the little monsters. This is what I wanted anyway, as you know. I never wanted you to stay in the hotel.'

'Well, that's one worry off the list,' said Pilot. 'Mum, didn't you say Dawn and Josh are travelling over this Friday? Maybe we should put them off?'

Pat lifted her head and fixed angry blue eyes on her son.

'I will not allow that imbecile to force me into putting a hold on my life. I'll explain the situation to Dawn later, and give her the choice, but there is no way I will put her off. And I rather fancy I know what Dawn will say. And I definitely know what Josh will say – he is his father's son.'

Just for a moment – and no one knew others experienced the same moment – everyone held a memory of John Thornton close to their heart. He had been the rock that all of them had leaned on and he had died far too young. But he had died loved by so many people.

Pilot moved into the room that had been John's office and picked up the telephone that the author had used so many times. He glanced down the preset list of numbers pinned to the wall just above the phone and pressed 6.

He listened to the ringing and waited for, at the most, three seconds before hearing,

'Carter Security, Mark Carter speaking.'

'Mark.' Pilot spoke quietly and with a note of urgency.

'Pilot? That you?'

'Yes. Listen. I need a meeting with you as early as possible tomorrow morning. Will you be able to come to Hillside? I can't leave Lauren.'

Mark didn't hesitate. 'Of course, 7am suit you? Or do you want it earlier?'

'No, that will be fine. There will be a police car at the bottom of the drive but I'll warn them you're coming. You still driving the MG?'

'I am. Pilot – what's wrong?'

'I'll fill you in tomorrow with all the details but Grace is alive and in a safe place. We're going to get her back but there are other issues now.'

'There'll be a man there in fifteen minutes. I'll tell him where to spend the night, but he'll not be sleeping. Do you need one anywhere else tonight?'

'Yes. Not at Stonebrook, Ken and Brenda are staying here, but Moorgate needs protection. Mum and Dad will be going home later. There's a police car there, too.'

'Leave the police car issue with me. I'll contact the DI you dealt with and tell him what I'm doing. He'll authorise passes for my men. Was his name Dunbar?'

'Memory as good as ever, Mark,' said Pilot. 'Yes it is. He's still on the case. He was the one who came here this afternoon.'

'Right, leave it with me. The lad who is coming to you tonight is Alan Shimwell. Just do what he tells you to do and you'll be safe. I'll be there at seven o'clock in the morning. Pilot – I'll need to know everything. Every last little detail, understand?'

'Of course ... And Mark, thanks.'

He put down the phone and returned to the others.

'Sorted. Mum and Dad, there'll be someone at Moorgate when you get back, just show him the best place for him to be overnight and make sure he's got access to drinks and suchlike. He'll not be sleeping. Dad, Mark is coming here at 7am for a meeting with us. You'll be here?'

David nodded.

'I will.'

Lauren went upstairs to make up a guest bed for her Nan and Granddad and the group of people downstairs began to disassemble. When she went back downstairs it was to see a tall, fair-haired man, about thirty years old, standing at Pilot's side.

'Lauren, this is Alan Shimwell. He's going to spend most of the night in your Dad's office, but he'll be doing walk rounds as well. I'm going to take Brenda and Ken back to Stonebrook for some clothes, medication and such, but you'll be safe here. We'll bring stuff they're going to need for a couple of weeks and then everything will be coming anyway.'

Lauren's face was ashen.

'Be careful, Pilot. Don't take any stupid chances like going round inspecting the outbuildings. The police can do that. We don't know where he is...'

Pilot's voice was flat, emotionless. 'Lauren, I hope he's there.'

Chapter 6

With Ken and Brenda safely ensconced in one of the front bedrooms, it was late that evening by the time Pilot and Lauren were able to sit down and discuss the enormity of everything that had happened during a very long day.

'So, that's everybody safe for tonight but that doesn't really mean anything – we've seen that Treverick has patience. Until he's caught, we can't live normal lives, Lauren.'

She nodded.

'I know. And when Grace comes home to us, I think it will be harder to keep us safe because I think he will want her back. We can't even move somewhere else. He would find us. The only way we will be rid of him is when he is dead.'

'And you have to know, Lauren, that if I ever get the chance, I will kill him. It will take me away from all of you but then everyone will be safe. I will do it.'

'I know and let's face it, anyone who is part of our family would do the same and take the consequences. But for now, we have to trust Jake. It seems that Treverick is a master of disguise so to be honest we wouldn't know who he was. That's the truly scary part. He completely fooled Amy all those years ago. She had no idea she was marrying her childhood attacker.'

He pulled her closer to him and they sat staring into the flames in the large inglenook fireplace. Again, Lauren had referred to her mother as Amy and not Mum. They didn't speak for a while, each lost in their own thoughts.

They went to bed after saying goodnight to Alan and making sure he had everything he required. He said he was fine, he had a kettle and water and he could manage without anything else. His eyes never left the outside world all the time he was speaking to them and they left him with a deep feeling of reassurance.

Neither of them spoke of the subject they really needed to discuss over and above everything else.

Grace.

Mark Carter arrived exactly on time; he was immaculately dressed as always, his hair still as thick as ever, his dark brown eyes now helped by glasses and sporting one of his never-ending source of silk ties, this time in red. By nine o'clock, they had a plan in place to protect the close-knit family. It was clear Mark enjoyed being back at Hillside. He had spent many years working as personal assistant to John Thornton, years that in the main had been good ones, marred only by Amy Thornton and yet made extra-special by Amy Thornton.

He allowed a glimmer of a smile to cross his features as he remembered her; she had possibly been the only truly wicked person in his life until Treverick had taken top billing, and yet he had loved Amy. The last few months of her life when he had taken on the role of personal assistant to her had been good months, mainly because she had softened as she enjoyed what she perceived as love from Treverick in his guise of Brian Lazenby. He shook his head trying to dismiss the memories. They wouldn't help in the current situation.

Lauren and Pilot were clearly in danger, their children even more so. Until Treverick was either dead or back behind bars, they could never be complacent, never relaxed.

Mark left and went back to his small office building in Padstow. It was discreet. The signage said simply *Carter Security* and yet he had access to twelve highly-trained, efficient male operatives and five female ones. His business had grown by word of mouth, not by open advertising, and he was the planner. He knew exactly which skill sets were needed and once ensconced behind his desk, he had begun to contact the right people.

Once he felt happy with every aspect of the cover required, Mark detailed the security plan into the computer and then checked in with all the associates he had already notified. Without exception, all were already in place.

DI Dunbar arrived at Hillside Cottage unannounced. He hadn't intended to call but felt he needed to see what Pilot had done about security. Within two minutes of his arrival, he realised that his worries and concerns were groundless. Mark Carter was living up to his reputation.

'So, is there any news of Treverick?' Pilot asked quietly. Lauren had disappeared into the kitchen to make them all a drink.

'Not yet. We are going on television tonight with a ten-mile radius map of the Wainwright's home, although that won't be mentioned of course, asking everyone to check if they have had a neighbour move out in the last twenty-four hours. I don't care how many legitimate leads there are, I'm just hoping there will be that one that will show us where he's kept Grace for seven years.'

'And Grace? How is she?'

'No change. She's still sedated and until they bring her round properly, we can't move forward. Pilot, it's not going to be a quick return home to you. You have to accept that.'

'I do. I'm not sure my wife does.'

As if on cue, Lauren walked in carrying a tray of drinks.

'How is my daughter?' she asked, handing round the cups.

'No different. I was just telling Pilot that it's going to be a long slow journey. There is a lot of healing to do, both physical and mental, of course.'

Lauren smiled.

'I can wait. Nothing matters at all now that I know she is alive and that one day she will be here, at home with us.'

Chapter 7

Dawn and Josh arrived at Moorgate Manor in the early hours of Friday morning. Pat and David had risen early in order to welcome their guests and after the greetings were over, the topic of conversation became Grace.

Pat filled them in on all the details as far as they knew them and explained about the stringent security measures put in place by Mark.

'Josh, no going off-piste with this one. Treverick is dangerous, we have no idea what he looks like, where he is, what car he has. The only thing that we do know is that he's going to be in a murderous rage and that we have to be careful.'

'Lauren is my step-sister. Grace is my niece. Pilot is my brother-in- law.' Josh's words were measured. 'I hope I meet Treverick.'

Dawn reached for his hand.

'Leave it to the police, Josh.'

'And what have the police done so far, Mum? He killed Dad's wife and calmly walked out of the picture, set up a new identity, abducted my niece. Tell me, what have they excelled at in that scenario? He needs to be dead.'

Dawn nodded. 'I know. Josh, you're so like your Dad. He would have used the same words. But there's a possibility of underestimating this evil man. We have to be so careful. He's clever and I don't want to lose anyone else to him.'

David interrupted.

'Listen to your Mum, Josh. We have so much security in place now but I do feel that if he wants to get to any one of us, he will be able to do it. Don't rely on your youth, your strength. He's a seventy-year-old man now and he's clever and probably very angry. Be aware. Now, do you need some sleep? We've put you in your usual rooms and we can go over to Hillside later.'

Dawn had changed very little; the attractive face that John Thornton had seen the first time he had met her in David's office was still beautiful. She still wore her hair long and would have easily passed for ten years younger than her true age of fifty-two. Having a son of thirty years gave her age away but she didn't care about such a trifling matter. She was inordinately proud of Josh. He was his father's doppelganger. He shared John's blonde hair, his blue eyes, his sense of humour and his sheer love of life.

As she closed her eyes, her thoughts were on John; she had loved him so much, too much. If she hadn't loved him, she wouldn't still be feeling this pain...

Dawn slept sparingly. Josh didn't even close his eyes. He tried to picture where Treverick could have kept Grace for all those years but came up with nothing. His anger was boiling just below the surface and sleep was out of the question. He wanted to see Lauren and Pilot, renew his acquaintance with Olivia and meet his brand new nephew for the first time.

He took one of John's books out of his bag, rolled into a comfortable position on the bed and began to re-read the words he knew so well. The world had lost a great writer with the early death of his father and Josh was never without one of his books nearby. He read until he heard a gentle knock at the door from Pat telling him that it was ten o'clock and that she'd made breakfast.

The drive over to Hillside was short but Josh was aware of David constantly turning his head, checking who was on the road, who was in the fields bordering the road, monitoring that their security operative was still behind them in his car; it was unnerving.

Their arrival at Lauren and Pilot's house gave both Josh and Dawn a feeling of tranquillity. This had been where John lived when he wasn't at the home he had shared with Dawn and Josh. Dawn knew she would never stop missing him, would never stop loving him and to be where he had been, was something she craved. She had sold their home in Delabole, wanting to make a complete break when she had escaped to the States and sometimes she regretted letting it go.

She walked into what had been Josh's office and simply stood, drinking in the atmosphere that still held something of John. He had completed twelve books in this room, sharing it first with Linda Chambers and then with Mark Carter and she glanced around the room, taking in the ambience. His desk was still in the same place, his bookshelves still held his research material used in pre-computer days and if she closed her eyes...

Lauren entered the room and closed the door softly behind her.

'I know. He's still here, isn't he? It's why we've never done anything with the room. We occasionally just come and stand in it, but it's never used properly.'

Dawn nodded. 'You should, Lauren. It's only a room. John is in here,' and she touched her heart.

'We are going to use it. We've persuaded Brenda and Ken to stay with us. They're selling up at Stonebrook and it's finalised in a couple of weeks. We've asked them to stay with us to make security easier instead of them moving into a hotel as they had originally planned. They haven't found their new home yet. I want to try and persuade them not to bother buying another one but to stay with us permanently. This room would be their sitting room and we can turn the other two rooms on this side of the house into a kitchen and bedroom. They then have the option of a family life with us or they can close off their wing and be alone.'

'You're a good girl, Lauren. I hope Brenda and Ken agree to the plan. At their age, they need help on hand. If you need anything doing while we're here, just shout. We're staying for about a month or more; we have to be home by the end of May at the latest.'

'Then let's hope that Grace is back home with us before you have to leave. It's so scary, Dawn, but I never thought we'd ever see her again. I always knew he'd taken her, but she disappeared so completely, I thought he had killed her. I'm going to ask Jake Dunbar if we can have a photo, even if it's just taken on a mobile phone. It will give me something to hold on to while we wait for the real face to arrive here.'

Dawn gently touched her arm. 'Do you have any idea of the difficulties in front of you? Can I make a suggestion? Talk to Pat. Talk to David. They know more about what your mother went through after Treverick had finished with her. They know how she was mentally. Brenda tended not to see bad things until they became impossible to ignore but Freda is also very knowledgeable about Amy. She saw so much. David and your Dad were the ones who protected Amy at school. David can tell you stuff. Forewarned is forearmed, sweetheart. Talk to all of them. And just maybe your Grace will become whole again.'

The door opened and Pilot said the local news was just starting and to come see it. Dunbar was putting out his appeal for information.

They all sat on various chairs and chair arms in the lounge and watched as DI Dunbar began to speak. He did not mention Treverick by name, merely said that they were investigating child abduction. A map appeared on the screen with a large circle drawn on to it.

'We are looking for anyone who has moved out of a property very hurriedly within the last week. We believe that person will have lived there for a few years but has now moved on. Any names and addresses given to us will be in confidence. Thank you for listening. Please look closely at this map. These are our parameters. Think, and ring us.'

The picture disappeared and the presenter came into view. She repeated what had been said and moved on to the next news item.

They looked at one another and collectively began to breathe again.

'Let's hope something comes of it,' David said. 'We know Treverick won't be there, but he'll have left DNA, possible clues to where he is...'

'You think?' Pilot shook his head. 'Dad, he completely fooled Amy. She actually fell in love with him and she had no idea he was the person who had destroyed her life. He's far too savvy to have left anything behind that will tell his whereabouts.'

Brenda joined in.

'He fooled us all. On the night he killed Amy, I actually remember saying what a beautiful couple they were. He is a very frightening man indeed and the more we think about it, Ken and I are very grateful for your offer of temporary accommodation here. We are too old to be running scared from a monster like Treverick.'

Lauren flashed a smile at Dawn. Temporary accommodation indeed. She leaned over and kissed Brenda's head.

'Nan Brenda, we wouldn't want you anywhere else but here. Tomorrow we make you comfortable in your own set of rooms and leave the clearance of Stonebrook to the furniture removers. I'll ring them in the morning, explain that you've moved out and you want everything packing up and bringing here. We can store it until you decide what you want to do.'

'You're a good girl,' Brenda patted her granddaughter's hand. 'Am I being manipulated?' They all laughed waiting for a response from Lauren who managed a grin.

They decided not to cook or eat out that night but to have a takeaway. Everyone felt on edge and they all felt better for being together. The delivery driver was a little put-out at being stopped by a police car and then stopped at the door by a man in a suit who was clearly in a position of authority, but it gave him something to talk about for a couple of days.

Lauren fed Noah in the master bedroom, as the house was so full. Dawn accompanied her.

'It's best that nobody is alone,' she said. 'That's a little bit of security we can organise on our own.'

Pilot was making tea and coffee for everyone downstairs when the telephone rang.

He said 'Oh, hi,' and listened patiently for a while.

''Thanks for letting us know,' he responded and replaced the receiver.

Several quizzical pairs of eyes looked at him and he confirmed that the caller had been Jake Dunbar and that they had had around twenty calls offering information. Two had looked promising and he would ring as soon as there was further news.

The evening ended soon afterward and their visitors departed for Moorgate Manor. Lauren and Pilot made hot chocolate and biscuits for their own visitors and as Brenda left to go to the temporary bedroom that was

oh-so comfortable, she turned to her granddaughter with a twinkle.

'I could get used to treatment like this. Is that the plan?'

'Nan Brenda, Granddad Ken, go to bed. Love you.'

Chapter 8

The next morning heralded the start of an eventful day. Lauren arranged the moving company to go straight to Stonebrook and empty it. She explained that it was an elderly couple that could do nothing for

themselves and that they would need to take packing cases. It would all need delivering to Hillside by nightfall. Brenda smiled as she listened to her granddaughter tell the person on the other end of the phone how infirm she was. She then knelt on the floor to play dolls house with Olivia. Infirm indeed!

Lauren smiled at Brenda.

'It will all be here and unloaded into the big garage by tonight. I'll get Pilot to move his car and get it cleared but there's not much in it. It will easily take all your stuff.'

'You're wicked, Lauren. We could easily have packed everything ourselves...'

'No!' Lauren sounded angry. 'You take no chances, Nan. I want you to be safe. You cannot go back to Stonebrook. He knows it too well.'

'As well as he knows Hillside, would that be?' Her tone was dry.

'We can protect you here. No arguments, Nan, you're safer here than at Stonebrook.'

* * * * *

Grace stirred for the second time in as many minutes and the nurse checked the machines that were connected to her.

'Sweetheart,' she whispered. 'Can you hear me?'

Grace's eyes fluttered open momentarily and the nurse hit the buzzer on the wall. Within seconds, several people entered the room.

'She's coming round,' she said. 'Without our help.'

Slowly, over the next two or three hours, Grace began to wake up. They made her comfortable, packing pillows around her to support her frail body, and giving her tiny sips of water.

She didn't smile, didn't try to speak; she just looked at everyone who was there as if weighing them up.

As soon as Dunbar received the call that she was waking up, he left the office where they were still taking phone calls after his television appeal, and headed off down to the hospital.

The young PC on duty outside Grace's door made him show his identification badge and Dunbar commended him.

'There's been no trouble then? Nobody trying to get in here who shouldn't be here?'

The PC shook his head.

'Nobody, sir. It's been busy since the little girl woke up, but I've checked everybody as they went in.'

'Good. Don't stop doing that, no matter what.'

He entered the room and looked at Grace. She was clearly awake and clearly saying nothing at all.

'Has she...?' he asked.

'Not a word,' said the nurse.

He moved to the side of the bed and reached for Grace's left hand. She flinched as soon as his hand went near her.

'Don't be frightened,' he said. 'All of us are here to help you, and nothing bad can happen to you ever again. Do you know where you are, Angel?'

She held his gaze for a long time and he was just about to ask her again, when she nodded.

'Good. A hospital is a place where they make you better, and you will get better now.'

She stared at him solemnly. She hurt and she was uncomfortable. He was talking rubbish whoever he was.

In the peace of the side ward, the chime of his ring tone sounded and he quickly went outside the door to take the call.

'We think we've found it, sir.'

He could hear a degree of excitement in the voice speaking into his ear.

'Found it? The house?'

'Yes, sir. It's a detached place, quite small, and he's clearly left in a hurry. Didn't have close neighbours but he did have a dog-walker going past when he was loading up a van with everything he could get in it. Luckily, this dog walker saw your appeal and thought it might be worth ringing it in. His name's Jim Tandy. We suited up and two of us have been in the house. The back door was wide open and the window is broken. The room where he kept the little girl...'

'Angel,' Dunbar interrupted. 'Her name's Angel.'

'Oh, right. Sorry, sir. Angel. Anyway, Angel's room is at the back of the house, which overlooks fields. The chain he used to secure her is still attached to the bed. We're just waiting for forensics now, so we've come outside. Don't want to contaminate anything more than we already have, but I felt we needed to make sure we had the right place. We do, sir, I'm sure of it.'

'I'll be there as soon as I can. Give me the address.'

He went back into the room and took the doctor to one side.

'I'm sending a WPC, name of Sarah Miller, to stay with Angel. I have to go. It looks as though we may have found the property where he kept her hidden for seven years. If she speaks, says anything at all, I need to know what she says. Once Sarah is here she'll not leave her side, but until then...'

The doctor nodded.

'I understand, but don't be too hopeful. She's traumatised and she could be a while before she says anything. You go; we'll look after her, DI Dunbar.'

It took him twenty-five minutes to reach the house. It was situated in the middle of a field; set well back from the road and reasonably well looked after. Dunbar left his car on the road and ducked under the crime scene tape already ringing the entire property. He scrunched his way up a gravel path that had wheel ruts either side of it and reflected how smart it was of Treverick to have the laid the gravel path – he would have heard anyone approaching.

He reached the house. With daylight starting to fade, the arc lights had been switched on. They lit up the exterior white walls of the house, giving off a glare painful to his eyes. He blinked and went round to the back of the property. He saw the broken window first, and then the bloodied child-size handprint on the wall. Confirmation, that was all he had needed.

Anger swept over him, indescribable anger, and if Treverick had been there ... He thought about the Farmers, a young couple having their first child and having her snatched away before she was a day old. He hunkered down and forced his breathing to slow down. He had never been in favour of the death penalty, too many mistakes had been made, but in Treverick's case, there was no mistake.

This man should have died when he was first shot all those years ago.

'Sir?'

He stood and turned to face DC Johnson, the young detective constable who had been on the case from the onset of Angel's reappearance.

'I want to kill him, Andy. I want to fucking kill him, so help me.'

Andy Johnson nodded.

'We all do, sir. Two things – how is Angel and do you want to go inside? If you do want to go in, SOCO ask that you go in through the front door and get fully suited up. They're going to be here a while.'

'Angel is progressing. She's awake but not speaking, unless Sarah can get anything out of her and yes, I do want to go inside. Is that my suit?'

He followed Andy round to the front of the house and spoke quietly to him.

'DC Johnson, I want to put something to you. I want you to be in charge of protection duties for Angel. She's Angel whilst she's in hospital. I realise it's not strictly detective work, but right now I suspect it's the most important job on the force. It will mean a lot of sitting around all day and every day but the bastard's out there and I need someone I can trust. Say no if you'd rather stay out in the field.'

Johnson looked at Dunbar.

'Give me fifteen minutes to get there, sir. Send me my rota when you've worked it out. I'll be okay going through tonight and tomorrow but I'll need relieving tomorrow night. Nobody will go in who shouldn't be in. Don't forget I've seen that room upstairs.'

Dunbar shook the young DC's hand, then put on the white coveralls and boots before going through the front door. He was in a small entrance hall with a room off to the right that looked to be a lounge. To the left, was a similar reception room. Stairs faced him and just beyond the stairs was a door that led to the kitchen and the back door. He climbed to the upper floor and was met at the top by someone wearing an exact replica of his own outer garments.

'DI Dunbar, this is the child's room.' He indicated a room off to the right and Dunbar opened the door with gloved hands. The stench was quite overpowering. There were two buckets by the bed, one full of urine and the other excrement and toilet paper. A half used toilet roll was under the metal bed frame. Attached to the bed frame was a chain, soldered to the bed at one end and with a locking handcuff at the other. The chain was short and would only have allowed Angel to reach a bucket, and no further. With the bed on the opposite wall to the window, she would not have been able to see out, and nobody would ever have seen her.

'Have photographs been taken?' he asked.

'Yes, sir. This room has been processed. We've moved on to the other bedroom now.'

Dunbar looked around the room and prayed that Treverick would die before this ever had to come to trial. He could not imagine the reactions of Pilot and Lauren to the pictures that would have to be shown in court of the circumstances under which their daughter had spent the first seven years of her life.

He moved on to the second bedroom. It held a double bed, the bedding in the process of being removed for forensic examination. It was filthy. This was a much bigger bedroom and had an ensuite facility. It was very different to the ensuite facilities he had provided for his young guest.

He stayed for quite a while on the upstairs level, memorising everything, setting the details into his mind.

When he returned downstairs, he looked around once more, writing things down and committing visually to memory. In the kitchen, there was still a chair placed in front of the sink unit; Grace had clearly used it to get to the window prior to smashing it. There was blood on the window-sill and blood on the floor outside the house, as well as the clear handprint on the wall. He couldn't begin to imagine how frightened the little girl must have been.

'Sir!' He turned as he heard someone shout for him. 'Sir, we think we've found the shed where she stayed that first night. It's about a mile and a half from here, over in that direction.' The officer pointed across the fields at the back of the house.

'Someone has just rung in to say they've just been in their shed and there's blood on the chair, on a cushion and on the floor. We've sent someone to take a look, sir.'

Dunbar nodded.

'Give me the address, I'll go there now.'

He realised what a remarkable young lady Grace was; from the amount of blood on the floor alone, she must have been bleeding quite heavily. It had been a cold night with temperatures barely above freezing and she really couldn't have slept much. He thanked God that she had shown sense the next day and gone to the Wainwrights for help.

He looked around the small shed, careful to touch nothing. The 8' x 6' building was now surrounded by crime scene tape. He realised the evidence collected here would have no direct link to Treverick but his mantra of leaving no stone unturned had served him well over the years. The shed would be thoroughly checked.

He decided to go over to the Wainwright's house the following day. They had already given a statement but he wanted to see them himself. He got into his car and set off for Hillside Cottage.

Chapter 9

The two officers sat patiently in the police car at the bottom of the Farmer drive. As Dunbar stopped to speak to them, he saw the headlights of a car, a Lexus, heading towards him. He waved at the occupants, and David pulled up just behind the police car.

'Do you need us?' David asked. 'Is there news?'

'It might be handy if you went back to Pilot's – I can tell everyone at the same time. Are Ken and Brenda still there?'

David nodded. 'Yes and loving being looked after.'

Dunbar smiled. 'Good. This has been hanging over Brenda for most of her life. Let's hope we can give her some peace in her life at the latter end of it.'

'You've found him?' David was quick to ask the question.

'No. He's running. But go back to Hillside and I'll fill you all in on what has been quite a busy day. Just don't let your guard down, any of you.'

He bent to see who was in the back of the car and smiled.

'Welcome home, you two. It's good to see you both again. You here to stay this time?'

Dawn laughed. 'No. We have our life in St. Louis now. But we're here for a while. We don't really know how long, yet.'

'I'll see you all up at the house. Thank you, David,' and Dunbar climbed back into his own car. He headed up the drive, leaving the Lexus to do a three-point turn on a very small lane, before driving back up the drive it had just been driven down.

He stood with his back to the fireplace, now just holding dying embers. He felt sick that he didn't have better news for the expectant faces in front of him; he began to speak.

'We've found the house in which Grace was kept.' Dunbar cast his eye around the room. 'It was nothing like the home she should have had.'

Pilot took hold of Lauren's hand.

'It was a small detached property with no immediate neighbours. He chose well. It seems that Grace never went outdoors.' He paused for a moment, not wanting to go on but knowing that they had to hear it from him. 'She lived her entire seven years in the tiny back bedroom of the house, and was constantly chained to the bed when he wasn't there.'

Again he paused, giving them chance to digest his words. 'The bedroom was filthy. There were two buckets, one full of urine and one full of excrement. He clearly didn't empty them very often. I'm sorry to have to be so graphic but it's better you hear it from me than hear it for the first time in court. Because we will get him, I promise you that.'

Lauren was sobbing and Pilot held her tightly. He couldn't cry. He could only store the anger that he hoped to use one day.

'There was no lock on the bedroom door. I should imagine she never even tried to get out of the bedroom, not until that final day. We found the broken window she escaped from and she ran across the fields at the back of the house. She just ran. You have to remember she did not know where she was, and she spent the first night in a shed that wasn't locked. We have found that shed. There was a fair bit of blood in it. The next day she ran again and fortunately went to the Wainwright's door.'

Lauren's tear ravaged face lifted and she looked at him.

'How is she now? Does she know anything of us yet?'

'She is starting to come round now. Sarah is with her but there has been no communication as yet. In fact, we have had nothing from her. The only reason we know what happened is because she told the Wainwrights. They didn't have the restrictions that have been placed on us. They questioned her and she answered. We can't do that because if she is ever to recover from the appalling events that have happened so far in her young life, she has to be treated with kid gloves.'

Everyone started to talk at once and Dunbar held up a hand. 'Whoa! I have told you everything I can. Anything else that there may be I cannot tell you. Don't forget this will go to court one day and we don't want any technicalities getting him released. One day you will know the full story and you'll all be able to move on. To be perfectly honest, we're only at the very beginning of this investigation and we know very little ourselves. Make sure you're always safe, don't go anywhere on your own and we'll get through it. What I will say is that Grace showed bravery that no seven year old should ever have to show. You should be very proud of your little girl, very proud indeed. For now, we have to leave her with the medical profession but they'll get her back to you as soon as they can.'

Everyone accepted this. They followed Dunbar out, waved him off and went back into the house.

Pilot offered all their remaining visitors a drink but David said they would head off home again. They needed to digest what they had heard and get some sleep. The

Hillside residents watched the car disappear down the drive then went back inside, locking the door behind them.

Pilot said good night to Alan, once more on night duty, and headed for the stairs. He paused on the landing and looked out across the fields towards Stonebrook, a sight that in the past had always comforted him. Ken and Brenda had played a large part in his own life.

The telephone rang at the same time as he registered the blue flashing lights.

He ran into the master bedroom and snatched up the receiver. 'Yes?'

'Pilot, it's Jake. Stonebrook is on fire. Do not move from that house. Make sure every window and every door is locked. I've despatched two cars to give you additional protection. Go and tell Carter's man.'

'I'll ring Dad. Jake ... is it bad?'

'I think so. There are three engines here now. It's not just the house, it's the outbuildings, everything. Malcolm is here, he rang it in, saw the blaze from his own place. I've spoken with him and he's safe. I should have kept the surveillance on here. I should have...'

Pilot interrupted him. 'There's nothing there to protect, Jake. It's just a house, no contents – they're all in my garage – no people because Ken and Brenda are here and Malcolm doesn't live on the premises. He's got his own family home.'

Pilot felt sick. They had never even considered for a minute that Malcolm, the man who had started work at Stonebrook when he was only sixteen, could be in any danger. Even if he wasn't, he was angry with himself for not having thought about it.

'Go ring your Dad, Pilot. Do not come over here. Leave this to the professionals.'

Pilot put down the receiver and turned to go out of the bedroom. His way was blocked by Lauren, Ken and Brenda.

Ken spoke.

'It's Stonebrook, isn't it? We can see flames and blue lights.'

Pilot nodded. 'It's everything, Ken. The house, the outbuildings, everything. Malcolm...'

'Malcolm?' For the first time, Brenda looked terrified.

'Malcolm is fine, Brenda. Don't worry. He saw the flames first, rang it in and then went to see what he could do. He's there at the moment but I think Jake will be sending him home any time now. There's nothing we can do. So let's try and get some sleep, we'll deal with it all tomorrow.'

Emotions were mixed as they tried to follow Pilot's instructions. They all knew sleep wouldn't come easy. Ken put his arm around Brenda and together they went back to their room; they had no idea what would confront them but they were together.

Pilot went back downstairs to tell Alan but he was already on the phone to his boss. His face was creased in concentration, his foot tapping in anger. He had started to get to know this family and they didn't deserve this.

'Thanks, Mark,' Pilot heard him say. 'They are all safe here. Ring me if you need me to do anything else.'

Chapter 10

There was a heavy police presence next morning as they all assembled at Stonebrook. The cottage itself had taken the worst hit – it would need demolishing and rebuilding. Astonishingly the outbuildings from the outside didn't look too bad. Malcolm held Brenda's hand as they looked at what had been her home for so many years, first with Jack and then with Ken.

'I'm so sorry I couldn't save it for you,' he said to his employer. 'So sorry.'

'Don't be silly, Malcolm! It's just a building. Nobody was hurt and he didn't know we had already moved everything out just a few hours earlier.'

'He?'

Malcolm was clearly puzzled and she initially thought to laugh off her words by saying nobody thought of arsonists as female but then thought better of it.

'We're pretty certain it's Treverick, Malcolm. You have to be aware. I don't think you and your family are in immediate danger – I think it's me and mine he has the issue with, but just be careful.'

Ken walked towards them. He had been to inspect as much as the fire service would allow him to inspect and his face was grim.

'We have to take it off the market, Bren. There's no way the Barkers will want it now. We've decisions to make about what to do.'

'We'll talk about it when we get home,' she said. 'We can't make any judgment calls while we're here. Our first issue is sorting out the insurance. Then we'll know where we stand.'

Lauren heard her say home, and knew she was referring to Hillside. She breathed a sigh of relief. She needed Ken and Brenda close to her. She thanked God for the bullying tactics she had used with the removals firm to get them to move everything that day; Brenda still had her treasured possessions including the blue flowered chair decorated by Amy at the start of her furniture restoring career.

They all walked back to Hillside together, taking their time, allowing for Brenda and Ken's advanced years. The burnt-out cottage had shaken them all but Lauren suspected that in Ken's case it was the sight of the ruined crops and flowers that had upset him the most.

He clung to Brenda almost ferociously. His mind was clearly racing along the lines of what if ... what if they hadn't moved to Hillside, what if they hadn't moved everything out, what if the Barkers had already been in residence. He was more scared than he cared to admit.

Freda joined them later. She had been to visit a friend in Looe and when they had managed to get hold of her, it was much too late for her to return. She had driven straight to them that morning without going home first. Freda was now almost ninety and still wore the tweeds and brogues that had been part of her for so many years. Her strident voice cut through many a conversation and as she walked into the house, she was cleaning her glasses.

'We're running scared,' she said as she entered the lounge. Her stocky figure stopped and she looked around at everyone. 'What on earth are we playing at letting that little turd dictate our lives? '

Brenda laughed. 'I knew everything would look better when you arrived. Freda, the man is a maniac. He's not dictating our lives, but we have to respect the fact that we have no idea what he looks like, where he is, what he's planning next.'

'Huh!' She said. 'Is there anything left of Stonebrook?'

'Very little of the house. The business is still there or will be after some new planting, the outbuildings seem ok – I don't think they'd got going properly before the fire brigade arrived but the house had. Ken is going to ring the Barkers later and explain that we're not going ahead with the sale. For the moment we're staying here.'

Lauren interrupted.

'And we would like you to stay here as well, Aunt Freda. You're no safer than we are. The police, as far as I know, haven't allocated protection to you so we need to do it. And the safest place is here.'

'No!' Freda was adamant.

'Then stay with us,' said Pat quietly. 'We've loads of room and you know how much Josh enjoys your company. Please, Freda. We can't leave you on your own. Josh, talk to her!'

'Freda, we need you with us. No arguments,' said Josh. 'We'll go and get whatever you need and you're to come back with us. Besides, you're the only one I can have a sensible conversation with around here. This lot are all a bit flaky for me.'

She looked disgruntled. 'Are you all going to be like this with me?'

There was a chorus of yeses.

'Two weeks maximum,' she said. 'After that, I'm going home. And, young Josh, it's Aunt Freda, not Freda.'

'Yeah,' he said, emphasising the slight American drawl that had entered his speech since Dawn and he had emigrated to the States, 'that's fine by me, Freda.'

Dunbar was furious with himself. He could have put a police car at Stonebrook for a couple of nights; he shouldn't have listened to the Farmers when they had said they would keep Ken and Brenda safe. Yes, they had kept them safe but Treverick was clearly in close proximity and if a car had been on surveillance at Stonebrook, just maybe...

He sighed. It was going to take more than luck to get this dangerous man off the streets and give closure to the Farmers. He pulled up outside the hospital and went in to see if there had been any progress with Grace. He hoped he would remember that in the hospital she was Angel. It was easier at the Farmers where she was always referred to as Grace.

Sarah was sitting at Angel's bedside reading The Philosopher's Stone to her. He smiled as he thought of his wife's enthusiasm for the Harry Potter books and then sombrely reflected that the little girl in the bed would have known nothing of the wizard's popularity. She had so much catching up to do and that probably involved learning to read above all else.

He moved closer.

'Angel. Sarah,' he greeted them but only Sarah smiled. Angel merely stared.

'Angel, I need to borrow Sarah for a minute. Is that ok?'

She nodded and turned her head sideways into the pillow.

Sarah followed him outside the room.

'Has she said anything?'

'Snippets and she only speaks to me. It seems to me that it was fear, pain and adrenaline that made her speak to the Wainwrights. In here, she simply doesn't find it necessary. She has said that Daddy never spoke to her except when she was in the bath in his room. He just said she was beautiful and she was not to speak. And really that sums up all she has said.'

'How do you think she will react when we break the news that she has parents, that Daddy isn't Daddy?'

Sarah felt angry. 'I think you need to forget her parents for the moment. They're not important. This little girl is seriously damaged and I don't know which is worse, the physical or the mental. Either way, I think you are weeks rather than days away from disclosing anything to her. Let her be a child in a safe environment for a while before you start introducing her to the world. You haven't found him yet, have you? And he's obviously still targeting the family. I understand that beautiful little cottage is now burnt to the ground. She can't be put back into that danger, not yet, not ever.'

Dunbar stared at his WPC in shock. To have spoken to such a senior officer in such a strong manner was totally against the rules, and yet he found himself apologising to her.

'Hey, I'm sorry. And of course, she will never be in any danger again. Treverick will slip up. His anger towards the family will cause him to become careless. He's already out of control. He burnt that cottage down expecting Mr and Mrs Buckingham to be in it, when in actual fact there was absolutely nothing in it, not even so much as a tea towel. It had been cleared earlier that day. Look, go back to Harry Potter with her and let's look forward to the day when she can read it for herself.'

They both re-entered the room and Angel smiled at Sarah. She completely ignored Dunbar but he spoke to her anyway.

'Angel, I'm going to go now. I do need to ask you something though. Did you ever live in another house with Daddy? Or did you always live in the one you ran away from?'

She turned away from him once again and he sighed. 'Okay, sweetheart, I'll leave you two on your own. Enjoy the book, Angel.' He raised a hand in salute to Sarah and left the room.

There was silence for a moment while Sarah picked up the book and found the last page she had read. She settled herself comfortably into the armchair again with the book open on her knee at page 39. Harry was about to be rescued by Hagrid and Angel needed to know about such important matters.

'Tin house,' said Angel. 'Like a tin can.'

Chapter 11

Dawn had volunteered to stay at Hillside for the afternoon and help Lauren organise a suite of rooms for Ken and Brenda.

Josh, along with Freda, Pat and David had driven back to Moorgate Manor to prepare a room for Freda, still loudly insisting Treverick wasn't going to change *her* life, and that she was definitely only staying *two weeks* with the Farmers. *The police had better bloody find the obnoxious little runt damn quickly* were the last words they heard from her as David's Lexus disappeared down the drive at Hillside.

Dawn, Lauren and Pilot moved the big desk so loved by John into a utility room at the back of the house. All three of them stood and looked at it.

'It really is a lovely piece of furniture,' Lauren said. 'At least with it out of the way in here we won't get any more wax crayon marks on it.'

'Maybe we could see about sending it to auction, or something,' Pilot mused. 'I really can't see any of us using it and if someone needs something as special as this, then maybe we should think about letting it go.'

Lauren nodded. 'I know what you're saying. We don't appreciate it, and someone else will.'

'I would,' Dawn said quietly. 'I would appreciate it. And love it. And keep it safe from wax crayons.'

Lauren turned to look at her. 'It's yours. No idea how you'll get it in your hand luggage though.'

Dawn's smile lit up the room. 'Don't you worry about that. I'll sort shipment out before we go home. Thank you so much. We'll have it valued and I'll pay whatever it's valued at.'

Both Pilot and Lauren laughed.

'Yeah, right. As if we'd take it. It's yours, Dawn. You loved him, you made him happy and you gave him Josh. The desk is yours.'

Three hours later, things looked different at Hillside. Ken and Brenda now had a sitting room with an adjoining ensuite bedroom and a room designated as the kitchen area.

Brenda looked inside it and smiled.

'There's no cooker, no sink unit, no cupboards, no washer, no dryer, no fridge – but it's a lovely kitchen.'

Lauren frowned.

'Don't be facetious, Nan Brenda. It *will* be a kitchen, but in the meantime, we all eat together. I'm organising the kitchen tomorrow.'

'Bit slow, aren't you?' Brenda asked with a twinkle in her eye. 'What on earth have you been doing all day?'

Lauren gave her a loud kiss on the cheek, hugged Ken and disappeared to prepare their meal. As she walked down the hallway she shouted, 'And it's Yorkshire puddings tonight, Granddad, just for you!'

Lauren couldn't sleep. She was putting on a brave face with all the joviality and banter during the evening meal, but she was scared. And she was finding it very difficult being patient with regard to her first-born daughter. She needed to see Grace, to hold her at last and to let her know that nothing would hurt her now. She would be safe for the rest of her life.

Dunbar had phoned to say there was very little progress, she still wasn't talking and there was the possibility of yet another operation in the pipeline.

Lauren's thoughts returned to her daughter. She wondered what she looked like. Did she have blonde hair like hers or dark hair like Pilot's, and what colour eyes did she have? It was hard waiting to see her but just to know she was alive would have to be enough for the moment.

Dunbar was with Sarah. She had sent a text to say she had a tiny piece of information and she would return to the station when her night shift operative took over.

'Her exact words were *tin house, like a tin can,*' she said. 'I asked what she meant and she said it was cold, small and tinny with two small beds that they sat on during the day with the curtains closed. That was all I could get out of her. I recognise the signs when she wants to shut out the world now; she sits and shakes her head from side to side. She didn't want any more questions.'

'It sounds as though he kept her in a caravan at first then and it must have been for two or three years if she can remember it. So, does he still have that caravan? Is that where he's run to? For fucks sake, we're in Cornwall. There are more caravans than houses here.'

Sarah had never heard him swear before but understood his frustration. Where do you start looking for one caravan in a county full of them?

'Thank goodness, it's not my problem,' she said. 'I'm back with Angel tomorrow so I'll see if I can get anything else out of her, but I won't push her. She's really so fragile, so insecure. I almost think she would welcome Treverick with open arms now the pain of what he did to her has subsided, purely because she knows him and she doesn't know anybody else she is meeting now. It must be so scary for her.'

Dunbar looked at her. 'We can't wait much longer, Sarah. We need to talk to her, or at least the professionals who know what they're doing need to talk to her. She has to know that Daddy isn't her real father but she does have a birth Mummy and Daddy. And she needs to know the truth about her abduction. When they talk to her, I want you there. She trusts you.'

When Sarah arrived to take over from Alison Grainger at eight o'clock, it was to hear the news that Angel had experienced a very disturbed night. She had slept very lightly, and had talked constantly in her sleep. She had mentioned Sarah's name several times and had even cried aloud for her.

Sarah quickly entered the room, taking off her coat and smiling at her young charge as she did so.

'Morning, sweetheart. Slept well?' and watched in consternation as the young girl burst into tears.

'I dreamed, Sarah. I dreamed about Daddy. He hurts me; don't make me go back to him, Sarah.'

Sarah pulled Angel into her arms and held her tightly. 'I promise you that you will never go back to him, my little love. I promise you. He will never hurt you again and he will be punished one day for what he did to you. We do need to find him but I don't think you know where he is, do you?'

Angel shook her head. 'I don't know anything. I don't know places. I can't read like you can.'

'Listen to me. There are people who can talk to you who have been trained in getting words out of people when they think they don't know anything. If I brought someone to see you and promised to stay with you, would you talk to them?'

'A lady?'

'Yes, I will make sure it is a lady if that is what you want.'

Angel nodded. 'Maybe that is okay,' she said.

And it was as simple as that, or as complicated. Karen Eaves was chosen to talk to Grace and beforehand, closeted with Dunbar, spent two days discussing the case. She met Lauren and Pilot, along with Olivia and the tiny Noah and was then introduced to Ken and Brenda. This would be the home that Angel would be returning to, and she had to understand everything about it.

Dunbar then took her to Moorgate and introduced her to the other set of grandparents, David and Pat, along with Freda, Dawn and Josh. When she came away, she thought of how much Angel had missed. What had come out of her visits was just how much love the little girl was going to experience, a love that had been there from the day of her birth.

Karen went home at the end of the second day and wrote. She made so many notes that her head was buzzing. The next few days would be so important to everyone and it had to be defined.

That night, Sarah went to bed feeling sick. She knew what was to happen the following day and knew it was the right time. Angel had started to open up a little bit more and an expert would be able to make more of that.

Of one thing she was sure. Sarah wasn't leaving Angel's side whilst they were talking to her. She had a promise to fulfil.

Chapter 12

Sarah introduced Karen to Angel, only to see Angel turn her head into her pillow. She prayed that all the softening of attitude from Angel over the past few days wasn't going to take a backwards step and leaned over to stroke her head.

'It's okay, sweetheart. Karen isn't here to hurt you, just to talk to you.'

Angel didn't move and Karen sat down at the opposite side of the bed so that Angel would have to physically move to see her. She somehow had the feeling that when Angel did that, the ice would have been broken.

Sarah held Angel's right hand, and gently squeezed it. 'I'm not leaving you,' she said. 'Will you listen to what Karen has to say?'

There was no movement from the bed.

'Angel?'

Still no movement.

Karen spoke softly. 'Angel, I have something for you. This is yours and it's to keep always.' She reached into her bag and handed Angel a pure white unicorn with a pink horn. 'Do you like unicorns?'

Angel's eyes moved and lifted towards Sarah. 'Angel,' she said, 'a unicorn is like a horse but with a horn on its head. A magical horn. This is lovely. Doesn't Karen deserve a thank you?'

She was referring to discussions she had had with Angel about please and thank you, something she had never learnt from Treverick and which she seemed to have grasped very quickly.

There was a muffled *thank you* from the pillow and she reached out an arm to touch the toy. She pulled it closely to her and slid it under the sheet.

Sarah heard her say something but didn't quite catch what it was. She leaned closer to the little girl and heard her say,

'Is it mine?'

'It is, sweetheart. All yours.'

Angel moved her head and looked at Karen who hardly dared breathe. She watched as Angel put the unicorn against her face obviously enjoying the feel of the soft fabric against her skin.

'Unicorn?' Sarah nodded. 'Can I call her Hermione?'

Sarah laughed aloud. 'I'm sure J K Rowling wouldn't mind. You can call her whatever you want.'

'Hermione,' she said and kissed the unicorn on its nose.

And still Karen waited. So much depended on gaining Angel's trust. The little girl slowly turned her head towards the woman she didn't know and stared at her for what seemed like hours but was actually about a minute. She was clearly weighing up the pros and cons of Karen being there, and Karen still waited.

'Sarah?'

'Yes, Angel. You okay?'

'Yes. What does she want?'

'To talk to you.'

'Okay.'

And it was as simple as that.

She turned her body so that she was facing Karen and said 'I am Angel.'

Karen smiled; what she actually wanted to do was laugh, dance, and sing around the room.

'I know,' she responded. "You're a very special little girl. I need to talk to you because you've been away for some time, and we'd like to know where you've been.'

'With Daddy.'

'And does Daddy have another name?'

'Just Daddy.'

Karen noticed the simplistic style of answer coming from Angel and hoped that it would be enough to get the answers she needed in order to help her. It was obvious she had had no communication with anyone other than Treverick and had been given no education at all.

'Thank you, Angel. I am not going to stay very long today but I will be back tomorrow. Is there anything you would like me to bring you?'

She looked alarmed. 'Don't bring Daddy!'

'Angel, I promise you that you will never have to be in the same room as him again, ever. It will be just Sarah and I talking to you. Would you like some sweets?'

Angel looked puzzled. 'Maybe.'

'Do you know what sweets are?'

'Maybe.'

Sarah looked at Karen and shrugged her shoulders. Treverick must have used the word 'maybe' because it wasn't the first time Angel had used it and yet it was quite a strange word to hear from a young child's mouth.

'Okay, I'll check with your doctor and if they say you can have sweets, I'll bring you some in. I'm going to go now; I don't want to make you tired. Look after Hermione and I'll see you tomorrow.'

She picked up her bag feeling satisfied that at least Angel had talked to her; the general consensus had been that she wouldn't, not on this first visit. Sarah followed her outside the room and they spoke briefly before Sarah went back to sit by her charge.

Angel nodded towards the door. 'She's nice.'

'Yes, she is, and we have lots of things to tell you, Angel, so when she does it will mean a lot of surprises for you. I want you to know that I will always be here for you. I am your friend. And now you have Hermione. She's your friend too. Unicorns are magical and you can tell them your special secrets and they won't tell anyone.'

There was a brief smile on Angel's face and then she closed her eyes. 'Can I sleep now?'

'Of course. I'll go and get a sandwich for my lunch while you're napping and then we'll read a bit more when you've had your rest. Harry will be waiting for you when you wake up.'

She left the room and went down to the hospital restaurant. Standing in the queue waiting to pay for her purchases, she allowed her thoughts to wander. What sort of person never allowed a child to have sweets, or a book or a soft toy? Treverick had so much to answer for and she wanted the day to come swiftly when he would be standing in that dock, being sent to prison for the rest of his life.

The man in the queue behind her reached across her to get some cutlery and she apologised for being deep in thought. He merely said, *don't let it worry you* and she paid and went back to the side ward.

She sat down by the side of the bed, opened her bag to take out her sandwich and found the note.

I will get her back

She froze.

Stumbling, she reached the door of the room and almost fell on to Andy Johnson, patiently guarding the room as he did most days.

'Ring Dunbar. And nobody, unless we have a medical emergency, is to come into this room. Nobody, Andy. No doctors, no nurses. Tell DI Dunbar I need him here now.'

She went back to the sleeping child's bedside and looked down at her, a tear forming in her eye. She carried her own chair to the door effectively blocking entry into the room and sat down to wait for Jake Dunbar to arrive. She knew he wouldn't be long.

It took him fifteen minutes. He had been over at Stonebrook with the Fire Service Investigator being told that the accelerant was petrol and a lot had been used on the cottage, not so much on the outbuildings. It had been poured through the letterbox on the front door, presumably followed by a blazing rag. Evidence suggested that he had then gone round the back of the cottage and had broken a kitchen window. He had poured petrol through that and ignited it. He was probably running out of fuel and used up the rest on the outbuildings, most of which had been spared the conflagration that had happened in the cottage.

His phone showed Andy Johnson was ringing him and his stomach churned. Johnson would not ring him unless something was wrong.

'Johnson?'

'Sir, you need to come to the hospital. I don't have any details yet but WPC Miller has barricaded herself in Angel's room and given me instructions to let nobody enter, not even the medical staff.'

'Tell her fifteen minutes.'

He drove fast. He swore. He screamed inside.

Because he knew Miller wouldn't over react. Her calmness was legendary and she had been his obvious choice to be the carer for Angel. And now she had put Angel's room into lockdown.

He ran through the hospital and held his warrant card up to the small window of the door. Sarah moved her chair and allowed him in, then moved the chair back into place.

She handed him the note, now enclosed in a clear evidence bag and watched his face blanch.

'How did you get this?'

'I think I know how but I'm not sure. We can be sure if there is CCTV in the hospital canteen but if there isn't...'

'So what do you think has happened?'

'Angel, as you can see, is sleeping. I decided to nip down for my sandwich so we could have lunch together. We do that every day. Andy was on duty outside so I knew she was safe.'

Dunbar touched her hand. 'Stop it. You aren't tied to her bed leg! I expect you to leave her occasionally.'

There was the sound of a strangled sob but she carried on. 'I was in the queue waiting to pay for my lunch and a man was behind me. He reached across me to get some cutlery but my thoughts were on what had happened with Karen and Angel this morning. I apologised to him for being miles away and he said *don't let it worry you.* I thought no more about it, came back up here and went into my bag to take out my sandwich. I found that note and immediately made everything as safe as I could and asked Andy to ring you.'

Dunbar stared at the note, unsure for a couple of seconds what to do and then he took out his phone.

'I want additional protection at the hospital,' he said. 'There must be two PCs at all times outside this side ward.' He paused as he listened to the response. 'How long? For as long as I say,' he thundered. 'And I want someone to partner Andy Johnson here within the next ten minutes.'

'Okay, Sarah, he obviously knows who you are. I'll understand if you want to come off this case...'

'Sir, just forget what you're about to say. I'm here and I'm staying, and you don't want to see me when I'm angry. I'm staying with Angel, I'm helping Angel recover and if these two PCs outside the door aren't enough to protect us, I'll bring a damn gun in.'

He looked at her with amusement. She had a reputation at the station for being cool, patient and reliable. He could add fiery to that list. 'You got one then?'

'What?'

'A gun.'

'Not yet but I can have one within ten minutes if that's what it's going to take.'

'Sarah...'

They both turned at the small voice coming from the bed.

'Hello, sweetheart. Have you had a good sleep?'

'Yes, thank you.' She noticed the use of the words thank you and chalked one up to the good guys. 'But why do you need a gun? Is it for me?'

Sarah flinched. Angel must have been awake for at least part of the conversation.

'It was just a joke, Angel. Look, Jake has come to visit you.' She was uncomfortable calling him Jake but it was necessary.

She eyed him with caution and he said, 'hi.'

'Hi.'

'Just thought I would pop in and check you don't need anything. Who's this?' and he picked up the unicorn.

'Hermione. Karen brought it for me. Sarah reads me a book about Harry Potter and Hermione is his friend. This Hermione is my friend.'

'That's wonderful, Angel. Look, I've got to go now. Sarah is staying with you until Alison gets here so have a good afternoon and enjoy your lunch. If you do need anything just tell one of them and they can get it.'

She looked at him solemnly, thoughtfully. 'Okay. Don't get me or Sarah a gun, get us a wand.'

Chapter 13

The CCTV targeted the double doors of the dining area but not the payment queue. It showed everyone who had gone in and come out but Sarah really had no idea what he looked like. She was half aware of maybe a dark blue jacket sleeve, as he had reached across her and her open bag but other than that, she knew nothing. She stared at the screen but they had no idea what time he went in and he could have left at any time. It was a busy hospital canteen open twenty-four hours a day for staff, patients and visitors.

She went home feeling frustrated and angry. They had no idea what he looked like, how he spoke; but Angel did. She felt as though they were in a cleft stick. If they asked Angel questions, such as what does he look like, would this traumatise the little girl even more? She had gone through so much and now should be her healing time, not a stressful period.

Karen spoke to her outside the room the next morning. She explained that she would be starting to introduce the idea of a life after the hospitalisation but if Sarah felt it was going too fast, she was to raise a hand. They would have a further talk before continuing.

Angel seemed pleased to see Karen. 'Hermione's been very good,' she said to the pretty psychiatrist. 'She slept in my bed all night.'

'And I had a chat with your doctor and he said you could have some sweets. I've brought you a few little ones to see which you like.'

She upended a paper bag and small packets of jellies, mints, chocolate buttons and other such sweetness fell on to the bed.

Angel stared at them. 'What are they?'

'Try one.' Karen opened some buttons and offered one to Angel.

She inspected it then smelt at it before placing it on her tongue. She sucked on it and showed no emotion at all initially, then said 'Ooooh.'

'That is chocolate, Angel,' Sarah laughed. 'Have you never had it before?

Angel shook her head.

Karen handed her the packet. 'Here. But just have a couple more for now. We don't want to make you ill.'

Sarah was just about to say *and what do you say to Karen* when she heard a small, quiet *thank you* from Angel.

Karen had decided to play everything by ear; the situation was something new to her and no amount of training was going to help.

'Angel, I need to talk to you. Did you ever see anybody else except Daddy?'

Angel shook her head.

'Not one other person? Did Daddy ever bring another man or a lady to see you?'

Again, she shook her head.

'Angel, do you know what a daddy is?'

'Somebody who cleans me.'

Karen exchanged a look with Sarah.

'No, Angel, that's not what a real daddy is. You're going to have to be a very big girl and listen carefully to what I am going to tell you. Every child starts out life as a tiny baby. You used to be a tiny baby. And every tiny baby starts out life with their own mummy and daddy.' She offered up a silent prayer to an invisible God for forgiveness for the simplification of birth.

Angel stared at her. 'Should I have had a mummy and daddy and not just Daddy?'

Karen nodded. 'Angel, there are some really big things we will be telling you over the next few days. It is important that you understand that the terrible man who made you call him Daddy isn't your real daddy. And that is why you will never have to see him again and why he can never hurt you again. You are a very brave little girl; you left him. We now have to help you start learning all the things you should have learnt and we have to teach you about ... well, about everything.'

Angel seemed to be deep in thought. The side ward was too quiet and Sarah didn't know whether to break the silence or not. And then Angel began to cry; soft little sobs that cut into Sarah's soul like a knife.

She pulled her into her arms and tried to soothe her. Karen watched the interaction between the two of them and decided the session was over for the day.

'I'm going to go. Angel, I'll see you tomorrow and we'll talk more. There is so much still to tell you but it can wait.'

Sarah disentangled herself from Angel's arms and laid her gently back on to the pillow. 'I just have to have a quick word with Karen, I won't be long.'

Angel gave a tearful smile.

Sarah accompanied Karen a little way down the corridor and they spoke in hushed tones.

'This is so difficult. She knows nothing of the outside world. How can I tell her she's got a mummy, a daddy, a sister and a brother when she has no concept of what those words mean? It's not just about filling her in on what is to happen to her, it's about educating her on the first seven years of a child's life.'

'I'm making a start now this session is over. I've bought her a couple of books. They are proper beginner's books in reading and although I don't know what the hell I'm doing, she obviously wants to learn. When I was reading Harry Potter to her yesterday, she asked me when she would be able to read books on her own. I'll pick up a couple of little books on family life later and we can have a look at them before I show them to her. If you don't think they're any good just tell me. I don't want to go over your head but all the time you were trying to explain things to her, I knew she didn't understand the idea of family.'

'Thank you, Sarah. I'll see you tomorrow. We will sort this but it's not going to happen in a rush.'

Sarah went back into the side ward and Angel was talking to the unicorn. She caught the last of what she was saying; *are you a mummy, Hermione?*

Later that day, Dunbar and Karen returned to the hospital and rejoined Sarah, summoned by the medical team. All three of them went to the room used by the consultant as an office. All of them would have admitted to feeling nauseous. They needed no more bad news about Angel.

'The brute who raped this wee girl has infected her.' Callum Donaldson looked at the three people in front of him. 'We are starting to get blood results back now and I'm sorry to have to say this but she has a sexually transmitted disease just to add to all the other problems she has.'

Sarah drew in her breath and once again thought about putting in a request for a gun. It would be used.

'She is now on the necessary medication but it's just one more thing to add to her catalogue of issues. The good news is that it's treatable and there won't be any long-term effects. Everything else is healing nicely. She needs to be built up, she is very much underweight for her age and I suspect he fed her on very little. Her weight is starting to climb but when she leaves here, we'd like to monitor her until she reaches the correct percentile for her age. We will be explaining all of this to her parents when they are allowed to meet her. I just felt you three should know.'

'Thank you, sir,' Dunbar responded. I will leave it to you to tell them, in case they have any questions they need to ask that I can't answer.'

They left the consultant's office and walked back to Angel. The nurse was in with her and giving her some medicine.

'Sarah,' she said, 'I've got some new medicine! It tastes nice and it's to make me feel much better. That's good, isn't it?'

'Yes, sweetheart,' Sarah said with a heavy heart. 'It's very good.'

Chapter 14

She would have seen the note by now, that policewoman, that Sarah. They'd all be running round like headless chickens and upping the security on everybody.

How stupid were they? He knew they didn't know what he looked like, who he was, what his name was. They knew he was good at arson now and they certainly knew he was good at murder.

It had been good to practice on Amy but there were one or two more to have a go at still. He didn't know how much longer he'd got so he was going to make it count.

And he wanted Angel back.

He would get Angel back. She was his.

They had sent teams out around the locality of Treverick's now abandoned house, visiting caravan parks, asking questions of year-round residents and early visitors to Cornwall. So far, they had drawn a blank.

Angel's physical recovery was progressing well despite the minor setback of a small operation and they were ready to give her information about her true family. Dunbar had talked to Karen and they had agreed that he would be there; she had to start to accept that men made up a large part of the population and she couldn't have any sort of a life without men in it.

Sarah would also be there. The little girl trusted her completely and was learning so much from the ever-patient WPC.

Dunbar entered the room to find Sarah and Angel deep in conversation with a book in front of them. Sarah flashed him a smile.

'She's doing so well! We need more books now. I'm going to pick some up later. She's my little letter expert.'

Angel nodded. 'C A T, cat. D O G, dog. A N G E L, Angel. S A R A H, Sarah.'

He applauded.

'That's brilliant young lady.'

He took out his wallet and handed Sarah two £20 notes. 'Get the books she needs.'

They heard Karen speaking outside the door to Andy Johnson and then she came in. They were all aware what a massive day this would be and each of the adults assembled in the room felt shaky with nervous exhilaration.

Karen had brought three coffees for the adults and a soft drink for Angel in with her, along with some doughnuts. They needed to keep the session as light as they could and all four of them took a doughnut. Angel eyed it with suspicion at first but then very clearly enjoyed it.

'Okay, Angel,' Karen began. 'Today you need to be the brave girl that we already know you are. Your life is going to change and it will be a wonderful life. You have to trust us, trust what we are going to say. Remember Harry had to trust Hagrid when he felt a little bit scared?' Angel nodded. 'It's the same thing.'

'Okay,' Angel said, looking puzzled. 'Sarah?' and she turned to hold Sarah's hand.

'I'm here for you.'

Karen began to speak. It didn't matter how many times she had thought about it, practised what she was going to say, imagined Angel's response, she was still groping blindly in the dark.

'Remember Sarah and me telling you about families and how every baby starts out with a mummy and daddy?'

There was a look of panic on the little girl's face. 'Daddy?'

'No sweetheart, not that nasty man who made you call him Daddy. He wasn't your daddy. He was just a wicked man who will one day be punished.'

Angel still looked troubled but a squeeze of Sarah's hand told them she was prepared to listen.

'When you were born, you had your own mummy and daddy. They had you in hospital and they loved you very much. You are their first child. First children are always very special to parents.'

'Parents?'

'That's the name for mummies and daddies.'

'So I've got another daddy who's not Daddy?'

Karen nodded. 'And a mummy.'

There was silence for some time while Angel digested this. Sarah was aware of the young child's limited knowledge, her lack of expectation of the world she had never known and she grieved for what Angel had missed.

'Who is Mummy?'

The question was abrupt and unexpected. Karen flashed a quick look at Sarah and Sarah nodded.

'Her name is Lauren and she has never stopped loving you from the day she had you.'

'And my real Daddy?'

'His name is Richard but everybody calls him Pilot. He is lovely and can't wait to see you again.'

Angel looked around the room at Jake Dunbar, Karen and Sarah and turned her face into the pillow. 'Okay,' she said.

And so Angel controlled the amount of knowledge they had to give her. When she felt she had heard enough she blanked everyone, including Sarah, from her mind. They recognised when this was going to happen but slowly and surely, they told her more of her family.

'Will I have to see them?'

'Eventually.'

'What if I don't like them? What if they are like Daddy.' She looked up guiltily. 'Ronald.' They had told her to stop calling him Daddy because he wasn't her daddy. His name was Ronald Treverick and one day he would be punished for what he had done to her. Her real daddy, they said, was a very gentle man. When she met him, she could call him Daddy.

'The children? They are nice?'

'Olivia is your little sister and she is very nice indeed. Noah is your very tiny brother. He does nothing but sleep all the time. He is only eight weeks old. Angel, you have nothing to worry about at all. When you leave here it will be to have a wonderful life.'

She looked uncomfortable, unsure whether to believe them or not.

'There are more people that your Mummy and Daddy will help you to meet. You have lovely grandparents. Grandparents are the people who had your Mummy and Daddy. There is just one other thing we haven't told you yet.'

She flinched.

Sarah laughed. 'It's not bad news, Angel. Please believe us when we say your worries are over. That awful life you had is gone forever.'

'Is that it?'

'No.' Sarah cast a glance at Karen and Karen waved her hand towards her. 'Go ahead,' she said.

'When you were born, Angel, your Mummy and Daddy named you. Your real name isn't Angel, it is Grace Elizabeth Farmer.'

There was silence in the room, a silence that stretched and stretched.

The three adults stared at each other. They had expected some reaction but not the negativity that had happened. Jake Dunbar spoke first.

'Angel? Honey? Do you like your name?'

Sarah reached out and took her tiny hand. 'Angel?' She felt sick. The child's reaction hadn't been what they had expected.

Karen too felt uncomfortable but they could not have progressed with getting the little girl back to her parents without imparting the knowledge of her true name to her. Her name was who she was, who she would eventually become. A very personal part of her.

It was clear that Angel had been overwhelmed by the information she had been given and it was just as clear that the three adults had grossly underestimated what her reaction would be. It seemed that Angel had never thought for one minute that her name would be something different to the one that they had continued to call her all the time she had been in hospital. As she buried her head into the pillow she felt, without knowing what the word meant, betrayed.

Sarah rummaged through her bag and took out a small notebook. She had, at various times, made notes in it for things that Angel had needed bringing in to the hospital to make life a little brighter. Now she used it for something else.

Grace Elizabeth Farmer

She tapped Angel on the shoulder and the little girl stared at her. Bewilderment was written across her face.

'Look,' Sarah said. 'Tell me these letters.'

Angel shook her head. 'No.'

'I'm asking you to do this for me. You know I love you very much and now I'm asking you something. Please tell me these letters.' She very carefully avoided using her name, unsure what the reaction would be.

A moment of rebellion flitted across Angel's face and then she sighed. 'You're bullying me.'

'I am not bullying you, cheeky madam,' Sarah laughed with relief. Angel had struggled with the letter j and Sarah had jokingly said she would bully her into recognition of it.

Angel took the piece of paper from Sarah and stared at it. 'Is this me?'

All three adults nodded.

Angel spoke in phonetics. 'G...R...A...C...E...E...L...I...' and she paused. 'What's that?'

Sarah quietly said 'Zed,' and Angel nodded in agreement.

'Z...A...B...E...T...H...F...A...R...M...E...R. How did I do?'

'Perfect,' Sarah responded with a huge smile, and Karen clapped.

'That's awesome! You're doing so well. Sarah's been a really good teacher. You'll not be long before you're tackling Harry on your own!'

'It's long, isn't it? My name, I mean.'

'When you go home to your Mummy and Daddy, they will just call you Grace. When you go to school, you will be called Grace Farmer. Be proud of your name, Grace. It belongs only to you.' Karen smiled at the young girl who was in need of so much care. 'They can't wait to meet you. Do you think you are ready to see them?'

Chapter 15

Lauren hadn't slept. Several times during the night she had got up and gone into the pretty room they had prepared for Grace's return. It was pink, just as any little girl's bedroom should be. Olivia approved of it without really understanding that the little girl moving into the room was there forever. She wanted her own lemon coloured bedroom to be changed to pink, just like Grace's room. Noah merely gurgled.

But Lauren was scared. What if Grace didn't like them? What if she couldn't settle? Couldn't understand the restrictions of living family life?

By nine o'clock they were ready to go. They had decided to leave Olivia and Noah with Pat and David; there was no way of knowing how Grace would react and they considered their current priority was Grace's wellbeing. Dunbar had phoned the previous night to say the consultant would like to meet with them before they saw Grace, as he wanted to explain medical issues to them.

Lauren, more than Pilot, had thought about Grace's physical problems that were going to haunt her for the rest of her life. She would welcome hearing about what they had to face.

Tears flowed unchecked down her face. Pilot didn't know what to do, what to say. The damage inflicted to Grace's little body meant that she wouldn't have children of her own and in that moment Pilot knew exactly how Jack and Brenda Andrews must have felt when confronted with exactly the same issues. He sat by Lauren's side and pulled her to him.

'Come on, sweetheart. We're strong enough to get through this. Yes, she is damaged but she will learn to live with that when she is older. We can control everything else with medication, which she is already having, and you heard what he said. A sexually transmitted disease is quickly cleared up these days. We have our daughter back; let's help her start living a proper life now. She must never see our tears. Agreed?'

Lauren nodded, not having any words.

They sat for five minutes and then Lauren excused herself to go and wash her face in preparation for meeting the one person she had ached to hold for over seven years. She did not want her daughter to see a red face made blotchy by tears.

She came back to Pilot looking a different person.

'Come on,' she said. 'Let's meet Grace.'

Dunbar was sitting on a chair outside the waiting room. He stood as they came out of the door and pulled Lauren to him. He kissed the top of her head and said 'Okay?'

She nodded.

'We're fine. We'll deal with it. I'm assuming you know?'

'Apart from Grace's immediate carers the only people who know are myself, Karen, her psychiatrist and Sarah Miller. Grace herself believes her medication is to help make her better after Treverick hurt her. She will have to be told the truth about her injuries one day, of course, but that day is some way off. And the STI will be a dim and distant memory by then anyway. Now come on, I'm taking you to meet your daughter. She couldn't eat breakfast this morning, so I'm guessing she's nervous, excited, unsure...'

'Like us, you mean?' Pilot laughed. 'We can't wait. I think we've been patient enough.'

Dunbar led them down two long corridors and then Lauren spotted Andy Johnson and another PC she didn't recognise, sitting on chairs outside a room. She gasped and pulled Pilot along.

'She's in there, isn't she?'

'Whoa,' Dunbar laughed. 'Don't go barging in. You'll frighten her half to death. Let me go in first. Sarah and Karen are already with her – Sarah has been teaching her to read. She will have been working on her letters with her to take her mind off what is to happen.'

Both policemen stood and together saluted the couple facing the huge challenge. Dunbar turned to Pilot and said 'Those salutes aren't for me.'

He looked through the small window set into the door. He knocked and opened it slightly.

'Anyone in?' he asked.

'No!' came a chorus of three voices. And then a smaller voice said,

'Maybe. Or maybe we've gone to Hogwarts.'

He pushed the door a little wider and they went into the room.

Lauren's first sight of her daughter after all those years astounded her. She was like a dainty little flower fairy, beautifully formed, tiny. So tiny. Her blonde hair hung around her shoulders and she had dazzlingly clear blue eyes.

She walked to the side of the bed and touched the little girl's hand. 'Can I hold you?'

There was a short hiatus while Angel thought about it.

Sarah was still holding on to her other hand waiting to let go as soon as the child decided to welcome her mother.

The silence in the room was overwhelming; nobody dared to breathe, aware of just how important the next couple of minutes would prove to be.

'Yes.'

Sarah let go and Lauren pulled Angel to her. 'I've waited so long...'

Pilot moved to the other side of the bed and Sarah stood, relinquishing her charge to Angel's parents. She glanced across to Karen and saw tears that matched her own. Neither of them had been sure how Angel would react when she saw her parents who were strangers as far as she was concerned.

'Welcome home, sweetheart.' Pilot spoke for the first time. 'I'm your Daddy. It's so good to see you again.'

His smile was proof of what he was saying. Angel looked at him but there was no answering smile. It was clear she was wary of him but everyone had expected that.

Lauren began to speak. 'So you're coming home today! You'll get to meet your brother and sister although your brother is a little baby and won't know who you are. Olivia, your sister, can't wait to meet her big sister.' She felt as though she was babbling. She was babbling.

'I've packed a bag. Hermione is coming with me.'

'Hermione?'

'My unicorn. Look,' and from the top of the bag she pulled the soft toy.

'She's beautiful,' Lauren said. 'And her horn is the same colour as your bedroom. I also have something for you.' She delved into her bag and pulled out a small pink teddy bear. 'The day we had you was Christmas Day and Father Christmas visited you in the morning and left this for you. I've saved it all these years because it was the only thing I had that belonged to you. Now it's yours again,' and she handed it over to her first-born.

Dunbar intervened.

'I think it's time we made a move. Let's get you out of here and home where you belong. Come on, gorgeous girl, you have some goodbyes to say.'

Outside the door stood what appeared to be an army of medical staff, their smiling faces lighting up the corridor. As she left the security of the side ward, everyone broke out into spontaneous applause. They all seemed to speak at once, everyone happy to see the little girl ready for going home. She had touched them all when she arrived in such a dreadful state and now she was leaving for such a dramatically better life. The two policemen escorted the family back to the car park where Pilot's car had been parked for the last couple of hours. He had followed instructions to the letter regarding where he should leave it – they wanted no problems as Angel left the hospital.

She turned at the last minute and waved to the staff, who had accompanied them to the doors.

As one, they chorused 'Bye, Angel.'

She waved again and shouted back to them.

'I'm Grace now. Grace Elizabeth Farmer.'

There was a huge cheer and she climbed into the car. Lauren reached across to strap her in with the seat belt and felt Grace's hands creep around her neck. 'You're my Mummy,' she whispered.

'Yes, I am,' Lauren replied. 'And don't ever forget that. I'm your Mummy.'

Treverick was furious. He watched them leaving the car park and stormed back into the building. He abandoned the white doctor's coat in the room where he had stashed his own jacket and left the hospital via the basement.

When he got her back, she could drop the Grace nonsense. He wanted his Angel back.

Angel, his Angel.

He'd been without her for far too long and she was his child. He'd raised her, helped her when she started to walk, to talk. He'd waited for her to reach seven years.

He wasn't young anymore and he couldn't start over with someone else. No, she had to come home to him, to share his life in the caravan until he could sort out a more permanent home for the two of them. He knew the police had no idea he'd got the little hidey hole so when he did get her back it would be like the good old times in the house; safe, secure.

BOOK TWO
2003

GRACE

Chapter 16

Ken and Brenda Buckingham felt blessed. They had become settled with what Ken called 'the young 'uns' and the rebuild of Stonebrook was underway at last. The Barkers had decided to go ahead with the purchase anyway. As they said, it had really been the business they wanted, not the cottage; that could be rebuilt and they had had total input into the new build. It had been a complicated situation but everything now appeared to be running smoothly.

After discussing the situation with Pilot and Lauren, who had told the Buckinghams in no uncertain terms that they did not want them going anywhere, they had agreed to build onto the side of Hillside to give them an extra room. They would live out their lives with the Farmers.

Grace had proved to be a quiet little girl, nothing like her younger sister. They had all bonded remarkably quickly and life was moving on.

Except, it wasn't.

Treverick had once again disappeared and the police had no idea where his new hiding place was. Every caravan site within a twenty-five mile radius of the detached house had been visited, and every caravan checked. Most of them were occupied and the ones where they had received no response had been put on a list for a later visit. The list had some thirty caravans still on it but Dunbar was confident that a week of following up would have everyone checked.

All doctors and clinics in the area had dealt with requests for male STI patients but there had been remarkably few and all had checked out after production of warrants by the police. Dunbar had expected nothing from the STI lead – online pharmaceuticals around the world had a lot to answer for.

With no child to guard now, Andy Johnson had returned to his duties on the investigative team. He was the one who visited the small caravan site at Polzeath. Indeed, he had jumped at the chance. Polzeath beach was a particular favourite of his for the surfing that he enjoyed so much.

The beach was crowded when he pulled the police car on to the beach car park. He walked down the lane that led to the caravan park and poked his head round the door of the small reception building.

There was a buxom lady behind the desk and two customers, a stocky man who appeared to be about forty years old and a teenager with a small white dog on a lead. The dog barked as he entered and the girl pulled him to her side.

'Max,' she said, 'stop it or I'll roast you on the barbecue.'

Johnson grinned at her and saw the frustration on her face. The dog obviously barked at everyone. The older man moved to the girl's side, tilted his baseball cap slightly and bent down to fondle the dog's ears.

'Hello,' he said to the dark haired woman. 'DC Johnson,' and he showed her his warrant card. 'I have two caravans that I need to check out with you. We couldn't get any answer when we called last week.'

'Right,' she said, 'what numbers are they?'

'Sixteen and eleven.'

She pulled a book towards her and ran her finger down the list of names.

'Number 11 is coming down tomorrow so you'll have to come back then. He rang this morning to ask me to get some milk in and to check his gas containers.'

'And number 16 is mine,' the man said from his kneeling position. He looked up. 'I wasn't here last week, only came down this weekend.' He stood and shook Johnson's hand. 'How can I help?'

'We're checking all occupants of all caravans, sir. Can you tell me your name?'

'Liam Ryland. My wife is Jean but you can't see her at the moment. She's taken the car into Wadebridge to get some groceries in. I have some ID somewhere if you need it. I have a driving licence. Sorry, I don't have a passport, we've never been abroad so don't need one.' He opened his wallet and showed the driving licence to the DC.

'That's fine,' said Andy. 'I just need to make a note of your permanent address.' He copied it into his book and then thanked him. 'That's fine, sir. I will need to see your wife. I take it she will be back later?'

Ryland shrugged his shoulders as if to say *who knows.*

'Maybe,' he smiled and put his wallet back into his pocket.

By the time they realised Liam Ryland didn't exist, he had evaporated into thin air. They sealed off the caravan and sent the forensics team in; DC Johnson had the debriefing of a lifetime but Dunbar knew that whatever he could remember about how Treverick looked now, it would all have become irrelevant. He would have completely changed his appearance and vanished off the face of the earth.

They took Grace to the caravan. Dunbar felt that they needed to check every minute detail with regard to Treverick. He didn't want to assume that this was the only caravan. It was possible that he had another one.

She began to scream as soon as she went through the door. They had their answer that this indeed was where he had kept Grace in the initial days of the abduction and had probably kept her there until she was around three years of age.

Sally Newsam, the lady in reception, confirmed that he had always spoken of his wife, Jean, and she had often made a point of asking him about her. He had always said she was good and he had always had a genuine reason for her not being with him. She would be shopping, or even at home in Stockport and she didn't seem to be there that much when they had their baby. He had said he was the househusband as Jean had a career.

Dunbar had taken Karen with him to the caravan and she was left to deal with the distraught little girl.

'You said... you said I would never have to see him again!' Her face was red; she was absolutely furious with these people who said they would protect her.

'He's not here, Grace. We just needed to know if you recognised the caravan. We can go home now. I'm sure you want to be back with Mummy and Daddy as soon as possible.'

They had asked Lauren and Pilot to stay away from Polzeath and let them do their job. Pilot had reluctantly agreed. Lauren had no desire to see where the monster had kept her daughter locked away from the world.

Karen took her to the car and got into the back seat with her.

'Shall we talk about it, Grace?'

'Talk about what?' The look on Grace's face was mutinous.

'Talk about how you're feeling now. I'm sorry we had to do this but we had no one else who could do it.'

'Well, I've done it. Yes, it was the place he kept me, yes, he did used to hit me a lot when I was naughty and he took me from here in the dark one night to another place, the place I ran away from. I can't tell you anything else,' she sobbed.

Karen put an arm around her shoulders and once more, was struck by how frail she was. 'Okay, that's enough. There'll be no more questions, honey.'

Grace was silent all the way to Hillside and was met by Lauren as she got out of the car. One look at her daughter's tear-stained face told her mother all she needed to know and she gathered Grace to her. Karen made a move to follow them into the house and Lauren stared at her.

'Go to hell,' she said and closed the door.

Chapter 17

He hadn't thought Angel would remember the caravan.

She was only just turned three when they had left it, so how the hell could she tell them about that? He had thought he was safe there. So now, he was wondering what other stuff they'd managed to get out of her. And where could he go? He couldn't go too far, he needed to be close. He was sixty-nine with maybe not so many years left and he had to finish his project.

So, the list: He was going to need to rejig it a bit.

He reckoned Ken and Brenda, like him, hadn't got much time left anyway, so he would move them to the bottom. If he'd time, he would finish them off.

Number one would be David Farmer. He was part of it. He should have died when John did. Amy killed John. She as good as said she had but she'd no reason to kill David. He had. He just didn't like the bastard, always sticking up for the whole bloody family.

Number two would be Pat. Just because he'd always felt she had been a bit strange on the wedding day, as if she hadn't quite approved. And Amy had always listened to her, taken her advice. Amy had been his, not Pat's.

Number three was going to be Freda. She knew. He was sure she knew. She never really trusted him and she knew somebody was coming back for Amy. She was a wily old bird, so she would be the third to go.

These people had made his life a fucking misery. And now they'd got Angel.

He needed somewhere to live. He couldn't stay in a tent for too much longer, it would be too cold. He would sort out another identity; perhaps get a different caravan a bit further afield where they wouldn't think to look. Everything had gone wrong.

It was all Angel's fault. She shouldn't have left him!

Oh – number four. Lauren. But he'd leave her alive.

He hadn't thought Angel would remember the caravan...

Freda had felt a big sadness at the departure of Dawn and Josh. She had grown particularly fond of John's son and their late night chats had kept her entertained despite the repeated worries about security and the whereabouts of Treverick.

They had had to return to St.Louis but had promised to be back by the beginning of December. Lauren had felt it important that they have a big family affair for Grace's very first Christmas.

The shipment of John's desk had been organised and completed and Dawn's smile had lit up the room on the day it had been packaged and despatched.

With their departure, Freda had felt it was time for her to return home.

'No,' Pat had said.

'No,' from David.

'Yes,' Freda had responded.

'You can't,' David had come back in. 'It's not safe and you know it. Don't give us the added worry, please Freda.'

'But I miss my independence,' she had moaned. 'Please let me go home.'

Pat had shaken her head. 'Honestly, we can't. Wasn't Stonebrook a big enough warning? And as for what he's done to Grace...'

David had interrupted. 'Look, let's have a bit of compromise here. Why can't we do for you what Lauren and Pilot have done for Brenda and Ken? We can make one side of this place just for you; give you your own suite of rooms. You can have your independence but still have the protection of being here under Mark's security. I promise that when this thing with Treverick is resolved, you can go back home and be as independent as you like but for now, I need you here. Please don't argue, Freda. Not this time.'

Freda had looked at David's face - no longer the young eighteen-year-old man she had first known - and she had seen the seriousness there ... and the fear.

The wait for her answer had stretched. She had nodded.

'Okay. You're right, of course you are. I'm just a silly old woman who thinks she can fight off a younger man and win. I can't. I'll stay here as long as necessary. And thank you.'

Pat had been pleased. She had grown to love Freda over the years, the bluntness, the wisdom, everything about her. 'Come on,' she'd said, 'let's go sort your residence out.'

It was a warm August day when Freda headed down the road towards Hillside pausing momentarily to speak to a cow with its head hanging over the hedge. It seemed most of her life had been dominated by Treverick and now that she was reaching the end of it, it was making her so damned angry. Pissed off. Murderous.

What he had done to that little girl ... an image of Grace's pretty little face flashed into her mind and she ached for her whenever she saw those beautiful blue eyes cloud over. They were all learning to recognise when Grace went into memory mode and became withdrawn from everyone, but all credit to Lauren, Freda thought, she was handling the situation with considerable skill.

Grace was proving to be a very bright child and a quick learner. She had arrived at Hillside far too near the end of term for the Farmers to consider sending her to school so they had hired a tutor for her.

Lauren wouldn't have allowed her to go anywhere anyway; while Treverick was still on the loose, she was taking no chances. They just had to hope that he would be in custody by the time September came around because in September both Olivia and Lauren would be due to go to school.

The tutor was a young woman, Jessica Cantrell. They had interviewed four people for the position and Jess had proved utterly capable and clearly cared about her young charge. Once she had accepted the job, they had filled her in on all the details surrounding Grace's return.

Freda saw Jess and Grace walking towards her and she waved. They were followed closely by one of Mark Carter's security men.

'Where are you two escaping to?'

'We're taking Sam for a walk,' Jess grinned. The man in the suit grinned and said nothing. His eyes never stopped moving as he watched everything around him.

Grace smiled. She liked Aunt Freda.

'We're going down to the stream to draw. We've done lots of sums and letters and spelling this morning so Jess said we could go for a walk in the sunshine.'

Sam intervened.

'Sorry, ma'am, I need to know exactly what you propose doing so I can tell your chap.' Freda had forgotten all about the poor fellow who had been given the job of staying close to her whenever she went out; she knew she led him a merry dance at times. She looked round and waved at him standing some ten yards behind their little group.

'Sorry. I'm going to draw at the stream and then I'm going to Hillside.'

Sam spoke into his radio and then relayed information to Freda. 'You're to inform him when you wish to return home, ma'am, and he will either walk up to Hillside to accompany you on the walk home or he will bring a car to get you. Either way he wants reassurance that you won't do what you did last week and walk home on your own.'

Duly chastised, Freda said, 'Tell him I promise to ring.'

The three of them, with Sam following closely behind them, headed across the field and dropped down the sloping bank to the small stream.

Jess laid out the picnic blanket and handed out pencils and paper.

'Okay, I want you to think about what we were talking about yesterday, Grace, about the different seasons, and I want you to draw a tree. Any of these around here,' she said and waved her arm expansively. 'Then when you've drawn it, we're going to draw it three more times and we will see how different it looks in different seasons.'

Both Grace and Freda began to draw, giggling their way through the lesson. When Jess had first met Grace, the little girl hadn't smiled much, let alone giggled. Jess thought it a wonderful sound. Out of the corner of her eye, she saw Sam move and her head swung around to see what he was looking at. She could see nothing and yet felt a chill run down her spine. He had noticed something. He then spoke into the radio on his shoulder and the returning crackle told her there had been a response. Within a minute, a car was at the edge of the field, followed closely by a police car.

Neither Grace nor Freda had noticed until Jess stood.

'Jess?' Freda spoke softly.

'I don't know...' She moved towards Grace and knelt down by her side. 'Grace, get behind me and don't move.' They watched a man in a suit and two police officers begin to walk towards the hedgerow that separated the field from the road. Sam moved closer to them.

'Okay, ladies, here's what we're going to do. We are going to stay very still and quiet and let the others deal with this. I thought I saw movement, a figure. It may all be perfectly innocent but we don't take chances. And if we have to move, you leave everything here and follow my instructions to the letter.'

They waited patiently for something approaching thirty minutes; Grace didn't say one word during that time. The police officers and the suited man approached them from the far corner of the field and shook their heads as they reached Sam.

'Nothing now. If it was anyone, they're long gone. I suggest you all go home but please get into the cars. We'll get you safely inside Hillside and then we'll come back here for another look around once you're all out of any dangerous situations. Thank you, ladies.'

They gathered everything together and set off back towards the road. The drive to Hillside was uneventful although a little quiet. Freda breathed a sigh of relief when they arrived home, followed by an overwhelming feeling of anger towards Treverick. He was still ruling their lives after all these years.

He smiled. He was learning the level of security surrounding all of them. They would need a greater show than that to stop him. His Angel looked well, very well.

Chapter 18

Grace felt frightened. She had tried not to show it when they were waiting in the field but she knew there was something very wrong. They thought 'Daddy' was in the area.

She ran through the front door before anyone could stop her and moved swiftly through the house looking for Lauren.

Lauren was feeding Noah and looked up in surprise. She hadn't expected them back quite so soon.

'What's wrong, sweetheart?'

Jess reached the door and answered for her.

'There's been an issue. Dealt with and there proved to be no danger but it's shaken Grace a little.'

'Issue?' She looked at her daughter and pulled her close. 'Okay, Grace. We can deal with anything. And you're safe. Nobody can get to you. Olivia is in her room, do you want to go play with her for a bit?'

Grace looked uncertain but Jess led her away down the landing to her younger sister's room. She then returned to Lauren and filled her in on the day's activities.

'So Freda is here?'

Jess nodded. 'Such a rock, that lady. She never left Grace's side while they were checking the perimeter of the field and held her hand very tight as we walked back to the car.'

'We need Dunbar here.'

She picked up her mobile phone and spoke to Pilot who said he was on his way. Her next call was to Dunbar's mobile phone but he confirmed he was already driving up their driveway.

She went downstairs to let him in and immediately felt comforted by the big man's presence.

Pilot arrived a few minutes later accompanied by Pat and David; they all moved into the lounge feeling unsettled and nervous. Sam began the discussion by telling them that he had definitely seen a figure moving in a crouch behind the hedgerow. Whoever it was would not have been seen normally because the hedge had its summer greenery covering it but there was a gap. That was where he had seen him.

'You're sure it was a man?' At least three voices raised the same query.

He nodded.

'I am. Dark clothes and just looked like a man. Short hair. I know women can look like that but his movements were masculine. And his movements were furtive. It was that really, above everything else. He was moving bent over.'

'We currently have half a dozen men going round that field with a fine tooth comb.' Dunbar's face was set. 'And well done, young man. You did everything right. Stay close to the family, step up the awareness level and we'll provide the foot soldiers.'

There was a tap at the window and Lauren waved.

'It's Mark,' she said and went to open the door.

He walked into the room and greeted everyone by name.

'I've come to review everything,' he said.' Do you need extra men, Pilot?'

Pilot shook his head.

'I don't think so but one thing I am going to insist on is that we stop with this fantasy that we can continue to live our lives as normal people and we won't let Treverick win by acting like scared rabbits. We are scared rabbits. We know things about him; he is a master of disguise, he is evil, he wants Grace back and he will stop at nothing to get what he wants.'

He looked around at his family.

'There will be no more trips away from the house, nobody will move without one of Mark's associates being glued to their side and these instructions are gospel and not to be argued or talked about. Freda?'

Freda looked up, with a guilty expression.

'Okay, I hear you. Anyway, I am at David's for the foreseeable future. I'm sorry if I'm causing you stress, Pilot, I don't mean to, it's just so bloody annoying that after all these years we're still fighting that monster.'

'I'll tell Jess.' Lauren stood and moved out of the room, heading towards where she could hear Olivia giggling. Such a lovely sound; she hoped the day's actions hadn't put Grace back into the quiet state she had arrived in.

Dunbar left saying he would report back if anything had come to light in the field. Mark, Pilot and David went into the kitchen to discuss any changes needed to the protection detail.

Freda joined them, wanting to hear of any further changes. The protection at Moorgate was unobtrusive but welcome although she wasn't sure it would be so welcome if it had to be increased. Pat and David felt they weren't really targets while Freda wasn't so sure. In Treverick's eyes, David was on a par with John. Both of them had looked after Amy when they were at school together and Freda knew that, before she had married him, Amy had told Treverick about her childhood.

Lauren stood in the doorway of the bedroom and watched her two daughters sitting at the table with Jess.

Although Jess had been employed solely to teach Grace, she had always included Olivia in any fun things. Today, both girls were reading and she was astonished to hear Olivia spelling out words correctly.

'How long has she been doing that?'

Jess lifted her head and smiled.

'Just a couple of days. She's doing really well. But listen to this.' She handed a Winnie the Pooh book to Grace and the little girl began to read aloud. Lauren listened in awe. This child had had no formal education at all and yet she was fluently reading the words in the strange Cornish accent she had picked up from Treverick.

Lauren's heart sang. She was coming back to them. Her daughter was home.

The police team scoured the area where Treverick had been seen and found an empty box of tablets, prescribed for patients with sexually transmitted diseases and originating from America. It bore his fingerprints and they knew it had been deliberately placed on tree roots for them to find.

Dunbar now ordered immediate lockdown at both Hillside and Moorgate Manor.

Chapter 19

David drove slowly into Padstow; he very rarely went into the office now, his semi retirement had become almost full retirement but Pilot had asked for his help.

David's father, Alistair, had started the business many years ago and it had always been successful; John Thornton, under Alistair Farmer initially and then handed to David to nurture had added to that success like no other of their stable of authors. His books were still widely read and sought after and they had recently acquired a new author who seemed to be heading along the same path as John. David had always enjoyed his role at the office and looked forward to the odd day or two when he was needed for management or board meetings. Other than that, Pilot had successfully continued the high standards of the Farmer Publishing House.

He parked his car in the small rear car park and, as instructed, waited for the accompanying car to reverse into the spot at the side of him. Alan Shimwell was his guard for the day and David opened his car door at the same time as Alan opened his.

He realised that wasn't such a good idea when he saw Alan's face. He grinned at the bodyguard and waved an apology.

'Sorry,' he called, 'I forgot to wait.'

Alan shook his head at him. 'You're paying for our protection, Mr. Farmer. Use it properly, please.'

David had been chastised. He walked into the building followed closely by Alan. They travelled in the lift together and as the doors opened at the top floor Alan placed an arm across David's chest.

'I go out first,' he said.

David waited without speaking and then moved as soon as Alan indicated it was safe to do so.

'Do you really think he will come here?' he asked.

'We have absolutely no idea but after the sighting in the field we take no chances. He was definitely there, Mr. Farmer. He could be anywhere now.'

David nodded. 'And please can you call me David? If there's a bullet coming for me, it's quicker to shout *get down, David*. I could be dead by the time you've said *Mr. Farmer!'*

Finally, Alan smiled. 'David it is.'

They went into the room and David went to the coffee pot. He held up a cup and waved it at Alan.

'I'll have a very quick one until your fellow attendees arrive. Then I'll be outside the door until your meeting is finished. Have they all worked here for a long time?'

'All of them. Normally Pilot would be here taking the chair but after yesterday...'

Alan nodded. 'His family comes first.'

The meeting was uneventful. There was much discussion about Sally Hardstaff, the new author who was climbing various charts at the speed of light and about two new authors who had submitted first novels that looked promising with a little editorial work on their part.

It was agreed that Pilot would continue to mentor Sally and two of the younger editors would take one each of the new authors. After the business was formally closed, there was quietness in the room that was unusual for a meeting at Farmers. Usually there would be a babble of sound, a palpable excitement at new responsibilities handed out, future commitments made; today the room was almost silent.

David looked around at the young staff and waited.

'Mr. Farmer...'

The tone was hesitant.

'Yes, Lynne?'

'Can we help in any way?' Her words came out in a rush.

'Thank you, thank you...' His words were hesitant. 'But no, you can't. This man is after our family, our extended family, and until he's caught, we are in considerable danger. So above all else, you must not attempt to help us. Don't put yourselves in dangerous areas, stay safe. But thank you...' and he began to clear his notes from in front of him. He felt overwhelmed.

Slowly the room cleared and he walked across to the window to look down of the car park. It was starting to feel as if they would never be safe again and not for the first time he thought about leaving Cornwall for good, going travelling where Treverick would never find them. And then he thought of his grandchildren; the ones produced by Pilot and the ones still to be produced by his other offspring. He sighed. No travelling then.

Alan was waiting outside the door for him and lifted his eyebrow in query. 'All done, Alan,' David confirmed. 'Let's go home.'

Alan moved towards the lift and they stood quietly waiting for it to travel up to their level. When it arrived they both entered and Alan pressed for the ground floor. David bent down and picked up a small piece of paper, which he slipped into his jacket pocket.

On the ground floor, he crossed to the reception area and threw the piece of paper on to the desk.

'Put that in your waste-basket, will you, Claire? Thanks.'

He walked out of the door and round towards the car park, Alan never more than two feet away from him.

Claire picked up the piece of paper to throw it away and then smoothed it out first to check it wasn't something important. She froze momentarily.

Farmer, you're next

She stumbled as she left her chair and negotiated the large teak desk. David had disappeared and she ran to the main car park before realising he wasn't there. She came back across the front of the building and round to the rear car park.

Alan's car was already moving and David was locking his seat belt into place. She waved frantically but only Alan saw her.

He started to get out of his car just as David's arm came up to turn on the ignition. The explosion and the flames lit up the sky; the barrage of noise, the intense heat was horrific and Alan dropped to the floor, unconscious. He had been only a few feet away from the Lexus and his body had shut down.

Claire screamed and more and more people came from Farmers and other local buildings to stare in horror. Several of them were on mobile phones summoning emergency services and many were in tears. Farmers Publishing had always been a family based company and now they had lost one of their own.

It was obvious that David's car couldn't be approached and Alan's car was too close for comfort to the flames. Two of the men who had arrived at a run reached

Alan and pulled him by his feet, screening their faces with one hand and holding on to a foot each with the other. They managed to get him into a safer area and one of them knelt down. He felt for a pulse both on Alan's neck and his wrist. He looked at the other man and shook his head.

It seemed hours before emergency sirens were heard in the distance. It was about five minutes in reality. The police were first on the scene and they moved everybody away from the danger zone.

The man in the white overalls that were emblazoned on the back with Transit Lifts picked up his toolkit, pulled his baseball cap a little lower over his eyes and walked away.

Claire confirmed a lift service man had been earlier to service the lift that took visitors up to the board-room. CCTV pictures showed a fleeting glimpse of him but Dunbar knew exactly who he was.

Chapter 20

Dunbar looked around the room at his team and began to speak.

'I know we have been over strategies and protocols so many times but we're going to go over everything again. There must be something we're missing at this point in time. I don't want another death to happen and for us to ask why didn't we think about that possibility. We have to understand Treverick. There will be more deaths if we don't.

He once more cast a sweeping glance over everybody. Nobody spoke. They were waiting for him to continue.

'We believe he spent the entire time he was banged up making plans to get back at the entire family of Amelia Andrews. He blamed them for his imprisonment and he hatched a complicated plot involving a complete change of identity in order to get close to John and Amy Thornton. He succeeded to the extent that he married Amy Thornton on the day that he killed her. He became known as Brian Lazenby at that time. Then he disappeared.

'He then began to plot and plan again, this time targeting Amy's adopted daughter Lauren. Christmas Day 1995 Lauren and Pilot had a baby daughter. He stole her from under their noses.

'This man is capable of anything. We must never underestimate him. He is clever, he is very good at disguise and he is plausible. Ask PC Johnson,' he said grimly.

Johnson flushed. He knew he would never live it down that he had been a couple of feet away from Treverick and hadn't known it.

'So, we don't know where his plans will lead us next. David Farmer's death, along with Alan Shimwell's, is a tragedy. More will follow if we don't catch this man very soon. As I said, he has considerable brain-power. Not everybody can make a bomb that will stick magnetically to the underside of a car and be remotely detonated. He did it.'

There was a shuffling of feet and a small murmur of voices as they thought about what they were hearing.

'Any questions?'

'Yes. Excuse me, sir, but are we involving the press enough? Surely somebody out there knows something, probably without realising that they know it.'

'I'm doing a press conference later. Having no idea what Treverick looks like now hampers us somewhat but we do have a couple of names he has used at various points in his life, so we can issue those. It may not throw anything up but we won't know if we don't try.'

'And the family?'

Dunbar paused. 'As you can imagine, they're devastated. They're trying to keep it away from Grace and Olivia but Grace is a particularly bright young lady and she knows something is very wrong. Don't forget it's her grandfather who has been killed and eventually she's going to connect all the dots and blame herself.'

Sarah Miller stared at Dunbar and ached for the little girl she had grown to care for in hospital.

'So, I'm going to give out the list of names that we know Treverick has used before and see if that throws anything up.' He ran a hand through his hair. 'We have to find him. He can't take out anyone else. We thought we had the family covered but we are now looking at moving all of them to a safe house. But I'm telling everyone in here, that even that will not stop this man. I think he is possibly the most evil criminal I have ever come across and his ability to disappear is the most worrying aspect. He is one step in front all the time. But one day it will be us one step in front of him.'

There were murmurs of agreement all around the room.

'Okay, I'm going out to Hillside after the broadcast. Sarah, come with me, please. I understand Mrs. Farmer is with them at the moment and I may need your calmness. Right,' he said to the rest of the team, 'on with whatever your assignments are, and find me this fucking bastard.'

The room fell silent and he looked round sheepishly. 'Sorry,' he said. 'Sorry, ladies.'

The press conference was short and to the point. They had very few leads, were baffled as to where the perpetrator was even though they knew who he was and they needed the public's help.

Dunbar handed out a printed sheet of names to the reporters and then went outside to do a television interview.

'We are looking for an individual named Ronald Treverick. He knows the locality very well and is dangerous. We are looking for information from the public, but please do not approach him.'

He read out the dedicated telephone number and added what he hoped would be the one thing that might produce results.

'His birth name is Ronald Treverick. He has also used the aliases Brian Lazenby and Liam Ryland. Did you employ somebody in the late sixties who then disappeared? Did you have a friend around that time who you are no longer in touch with?'

He paused briefly. 'We are now going to show you six pictures. The first one was taken while Treverick was in prison. The second is when he was known as Brian Lazenby. You will notice they in no way resemble each other. The other four pictures are mock ups by our police artist as we attempt to show how he could possibly look now.'

Again, he paused while he gathered his thoughts.

'Search your memories and I repeat, whatever you do, do not approach this man.'

His own face disappeared and the six pictures of Treverick began to cycle across the screen.

Dunbar walked back into the police station and headed for his office. He had no idea whether the appeal would work or not but they were getting desperate. The sight of the burning car was etched into his brain; this man had to be caught, and soon.

Chapter 21

Hillside was shrouded in silence. Dunbar had phoned ahead to say they were calling round and had been answered by a simple 'ok' from Pilot.

It was a haggard-looking Lauren who opened the door to them. Noah was sitting astride her hip-bone and Olivia was holding on to her skirt.

'Come in, Jake, Sarah,' she said quietly. 'We're all in the lounge.'

Grace was playing with the doll's house with Jess sitting by her side.

Dunbar was lost for words. He looked around at all the faces; Lauren moved to sit by Pilot and Pat was ensconced between Ken and Brenda. Freda was rocking slightly in the old rocking chair by the fire.

The grief was palpable.

'Thank you for gathering together for this. Did you all see the news broadcast?'

Only Pilot spoke.

'Yes and what good will it do? Is he going to pick us off one by one? Is that his plan?'

Dunbar looked at him. 'Probably.'

Grace gave a small cry and Jess pulled her close.

'Sssh,' she said soothingly.

Lauren looked towards her daughter.

'Jess, would you mind taking Grace to her room, please? Maybe do a little reading with her?'

'Of course. Come on, Honeybun, let's go see what Harry's up to today.'

They left the room and Lauren explained. 'We've employed Jess as a live-in nanny to all three of our children now, instead of her just being here to tutor Grace. She's brilliant with all three of them and it just makes sense. She's fully aware of the situation so you can feel free to say anything when she is here.'

Dunbar nodded.

'Thank you for clarifying that. I have very little to tell you about the investigation itself. We know the perpetrator and that's not what this investigation is about. We have to find him and he's excellent at covering his tracks. What I can tell you is that the bomb was attached to the underside of the car at some point during the meeting that David attended. That conference room overlooks the rear car park and is actually the only room in the building where you can see that car park. Of course, during that meeting, everyone was sitting around the large table and it is unlikely anybody would have been looking out of the window. Treverick not only had skill on his side, he had luck. It would have only taken him seconds to place the bomb because it was magnetised and then all he had to do was wait out of sight until he saw David and Alan get into their cars. I actually think he panicked slightly when he saw Alan getting out of his car and the young girl trying to attract their attention because he didn't hang about. He remotely detonated it.'

Dunbar turned to Pat. 'I'm so sorry you have to hear all of this, Pat. It's hard enough losing David without having to hear the details but I have to make you all aware of the danger you're in.'

Pat briefly waved a hand in acknowledgement of his words and then wiped away her tears.

'Just get on with it, Jake. Tell us what you have to tell us and leave us to grieve.'

He nodded. 'We would like to move all of you to a safe house...'

Pilot interrupted angrily.

'No!'

'Listen to me, Pilot...'

'Jake, I said no. We have full protection here round the clock and now we have Jess who sleeps in the room at the side of Grace's room. We have four of Mark's men allocated just to this house now; they work shifts of two operatives at a time and everyone in the family is in one place.'

Dunbar opened his mouth to speak and Pilot continued. 'We also have two police cars parked permanently here, one at the bottom of the drive who check out our cars and us every time we move, and one at the top of the drive. We are protected, Jake. We are not moving out. And to be honest, have you got a castle that's a safe house? Because that's what you would need to make us secure, and to accommodate all of us. Plus Dawn and Josh.'

Inwardly, Jake Dunbar groaned. So Dawn and Josh would now be added to the mix.

'When are they coming?'

'Tomorrow. They fly over tonight.'

'We're running out of rooms,' Pilot smiled. 'Dawn, I've had to put you in with Freda, so behave yourselves, you two. Josh, you're in a tiny little box room on a camping bed near the children's rooms. You'll be comfortable enough, if a little cramped.'

'No worries,' Josh said. 'We're here to help, not to be cosseted. What can we do?'

'Absolutely bloody nothing,' Pilot said grim-faced. 'Both of you come with me into my office and I'll fill you in on everything that's happened. You need to be aware.'

The police received many calls following the television broadcast. All were logged and as each member of the team checked them out, they were either discounted or placed in a file for further investigation.

Dunbar activated his screen and went into the file. He glanced down to see who was doing what and saw that there were still quite a few for follow-ups. He looked down the list once more and his eye fell on one where the caller had rung in from Bude. His name was Anthony Taggart and he used to have a photography studio in Bude. He said that he thought he recognised the man but wasn't sure as he had left around March 1966. He wasn't called Ronald Treverick, he had been Carl Jameson.

Logging out the link in his name so that nobody else would duplicate the call, Dunbar dialled Taggart's number.

'Mr. Taggart? My name is DI Jake Dunbar and I'm leading the investigation into the Ronald Treverick case. I understand you've called us?'

'Yes, Detective Inspector. I'm not sure, of course, but there's just something... I've looked at your photograph and mine several times...'

Dunbar cut him short. 'You have a photograph?'

'Yes. It was my business,' Taggart said.

'Would you be available to speak to me soon, Mr Taggart? I can leave Padstow now and be with you in about an hour.'

'Yes, of course. I'll get the stuff out ready for you.'

Dunbar thanked him, put his address in his pocket and went downstairs to his car. He reached forward to start it and it hit him. Stuff, the man had said. Stuff.

He drove down a tree-lined road and slowed down looking for number 103. It was a bungalow, well maintained from the outside and with an immaculate front garden.

He followed instructions and went round to the back where he saw an old man sitting inside the conservatory that looked to be a fairly new addition to the property.

The man waved and Jake opened the door.

'Mr Taggart?'

'Yes, sir. Come in.'

Dunbar went in and a much younger woman popped her head round to ask if he would like a drink.

'I'd love one, thank you. Tea, milk, no sugar,' he smiled.

'My daughter. She pops in most days to make sure I'm still alive.'

'Well the sooner you're gone, the sooner I'll inherit!'

Dunbar heard the laughter in the woman's voice and saw the grin on her father's face. Clearly a good relationship.

He waited without touching on the subject of Treverick until she had brought in the tea and biscuits and then was somewhat surprised when she joined them. She looked at him.

'My name is Elaine Wright and if this man is who you are looking for, then I knew him too. I'll just sit and listen to what you two have to say.'

'Mr. Taggart...'

'Tony. Call me Tony. Let me tell you what I know and then you can make your mind up. Until my retirement four years ago, I had a very busy, very large photography studio in Bude. I inherited it from my father so it's been there for some time and the business still continues with my son to this day. When I handed everything over to Stewart, he closed down the premises for about two months and did a complete refurbishment job. I have a garage here, so we moved everything into it, many years of proofs, paperwork from pre-computer days, old cameras, screens ... everything, so he had a blank canvas to work with. Of course, it's now too posh to move it all back,' he finished with a twinkle in his eye.

Dunbar grinned. 'Of course. So you're lumbered with it all.'

'Yep. Now, to go back to the time you're interested in. In 1965, January, I think, a young man turned up and asked for a job. He had brought a portfolio with him of his photography work and a diploma from some college he had attended. I honestly can't remember any details of that diploma. However, his photographs were outstanding. We had a chat and he said he would work for free for a month and if I wasn't happy, he would walk away. Well, I was happy and we had a really good relationship. He was particularly good with the children; they responded to his instructions and we achieved some cracking pictures that were down to him. I trusted him and left him many times in the studio on his own when I had outside work. He was also very good at weddings, came back with some truly artistic shots before artistic shots became the norm.'

He paused for a moment and then reached behind him. Elaine immediately stood up and handed him the cardboard box he was trying to reach. He took off the lid and reached inside for a photograph. It was paper clipped to a newspaper cutting of one of the pictures released by the police.

'Look,' he said. 'This is the man I knew as Carl Jameson. He was with me for just over a year and then suddenly, unexpectedly, he said he had to go up north to look after his sick mother. I told him to keep in touch and he would always have a job with me whenever he wanted and hoped he would return to Bude one day. I gave him a cracker of a reference and off he went. I pushed him for a telephone number and he gave me one and I tried to call him a few times but it never worked. I never heard from him again.'

Dunbar placed the pictures side by side on the coffee table and knew he was looking at Treverick.

The shape of the head was the same, the eyes were the same, the nose was the same – the hair was a different colour but this was Treverick.

'Did he know you had this picture?'

Taggart shook his head.

'No, I was taking random shots of the studio to make a new advertising brochure for us. I intended putting Carl's name on it as an associate photographer, so I took a couple of shots of him at work. He left before the brochure reached production.'

'Did you take anymore?'

'Yes, several. I just think that one shows his full face better than the others. You can compare face shape with that one. Here, you might need all of this,' and he handed Dunbar the box.

Dunbar lifted the photographs out of the box to look at them more closely. At the bottom of the box was a comb, a toothbrush and a part used tube of toothpaste.

He looked at Tony Taggart without speaking, and Tony nodded. 'His. He left them in our little washroom area when he left in 1966 and because I thought he would return, I put all this little lot into a box to save for him.'

Dunbar looked at Elaine. 'Obviously I need to take all of this. We are going to have to release this new name to the press in the hope that it will trigger further memories in people. We have no idea where he is now or what he is calling himself so we're basically trying to track his life. Is there anything else you can remember about him to add to your father's excellent memories?'

She nodded. 'I was born in 1959. In 1966, I was seven. If I am reading between the lines of this horrific case – yes, I went on the internet – then you will know he likes seven year old little girls.'

Dunbar saw Tony stiffen and knew that whatever Elaine was about to reveal, it was news to him.

'He touched me. That day Dad had an outside event to go to. Mum was in hospital because she'd just had my brother, Stewart, and I was off school with tonsillitis. I had to go to work with Dad because there was nobody else to look after me. Dad asked Carl to keep an eye on me while he went to the shoot and I remember him saying she'll probably sleep anyway. I got on to the couch in the studio and fell asleep. He woke me up by taking off my clothes. He was touching me all over and his camera was at the side of him. I am assuming he had taken pictures of me. I really couldn't think of anything beyond not being able to swallow and my temperature was raging. I said don't do this but he said he was just cooling me down. Because he was an adult, I believed him. And then he used his fingers to rape me. I cried and after he had finished with me, he gave me some tablets to take which I remember him crushing in a spoon so I could swallow them. I fell back to sleep and by the time I woke up he had gone.'

Tony Taggart looked sick. He had not known of this.

'I didn't say anything to Dad because I didn't know what to say. You don't talk to your Dad about such things. By the time Mum came home from the hospital a week later the bleeding had stopped, so I threw away all my pants and just put it out of my mind.' She gave a wry smile. 'She never understood what had happened to my pants. So, Inspector, Do you need any more proof that it's him?'

Chapter 22

Dunbar pointed to all the photographs on the board and said,

'Carl Jameson. We are just waiting for confirmation with any DNA we can get from the comb or the toothbrush but we have clear fingerprints on the toothpaste tube anyway. Carl Jameson was his name in 1966. I believe he stopped being Carl Jameson when he became Brian Lazenby in October 1970. That's when he joined the BBC. So, we have a bit of a timeline going now. He was released from prison in February 1960 and he spent the next four years or so building a new identity so that by the time he joined Taggarts in January 1965 he was Carl Jameson.

'I actually think he might have stayed in Bude longer but he molested the seven-year-old daughter of Mr. Taggart so must have decided it was time to move on. He left the same day that the attack occurred which is why he slipped up and left his toiletries at the studio. He disappears in March 1966. He then surfaces again in October 1970 when he joins the BBC as Brian Lazenby. He builds a considerable reputation at the BBC over the next four years and meets John Thornton and his family in February 1974. This has been his aim since he was sent to prison.

'Amy Thornton was always his target and so he hunkered down for the long wait. He had nothing to rush for, nobody suspected he was anything other than a BBC producer called Brian Lazenby and he waited.

'As you all know he married Amy in July 1992 then killed her on the same day. That's when he stopped being Brian Lazenby. He then worked on the new identity of Liam

Ryland. And that's where we are at the moment. He must have changed his name by now because Liam Ryland is all over the news.'

They were all writing notes and he realised they now all had the somewhat complicated timeline committed to a listing, just in case they needed it.

Tony Taggart and Elaine Wright had completed the picture for them and they now had to get this new name out in the wider arena. He felt guilty at what Tony was now going through but had nothing but admiration for his daughter. It couldn't have been easy for her talking about it in front of her father.

The second television interview felt easier for him and he delivered the news that information received had led them to believe that Treverick had also used the name Carl Jameson between 1960 and 1970. They would now like to speak to anyone who had known him under this different name. He once more listed all the names they had and finished off the broadcast with a repeat viewing of the pictures, plus two from the box given to him by Tony Taggart.

Five days later, it came as something of a surprise to receive a telephone call from a young woman who said her name was Marcia Ann Shaw and that she believed she knew Liam Ryland. She said on her voice mail message that she had just returned from a holiday in France and had only just seen the television broadcast.

Dunbar tried three times to reach her before finally getting a response. She explained she had been at work and he was very welcome to call and see her. Yes, she would be in that night, and yes, he could set off straight away. If he wanted milk in his tea he would have to bring his own. She didn't take milk.

Dunbar liked the sound of this young woman.

Her home was in Wadebridge and he drove there thinking about nothing but the case. They were getting information now but nothing was leading them towards where Treverick was at the present time.

He pulled up outside a small terraced house and as he lifted his hand to knock on the door, it opened. Marcia Ann Shaw was a beautiful woman of about thirty years, possibly a little older, with skin that gleamed like ebony. Her brown eyes smiled along with her lips as she said,

'DI Dunbar?'

He showed his ID and followed her into her home. She led him into the lounge and he smiled at the decor. Pure Africa. Leopard print wallpaper, bright oranges and greens and a beautiful dark brown leather settee afforded warmth that he welcomed. He sat down and she offered him a drink, albeit without milk.

'No, you're ok,' he laughed. 'I don't need one. So, you think you know Liam Ryland?'

She nodded. 'Pretty sure it's the same person. It was ten years ago but...'

'Ten years?'

'Uh-huh. I met him in a pub in Padstow. I went there for a job interview. I didn't get the job, by the way.' She grinned and sat on the curved part of the angled settee.

'How long did you know him for?'

'Well, technically, one night. He was a real charmer, knew the right words to say, told me his name was Neil.'

'So...?'

'So how did I know he wasn't Neil? He dropped his wallet. I found it under my bed the day after. It had a five-pound note in it and a driving licence. I kept it for a couple of weeks and then posted it off to him. I thought he might call back for it but he didn't. That's why I waited two weeks. Anyway, I never heard from him after this and I actually tried to find a telephone number for him a few months later but he didn't exist at the address on the driving licence.'

'You wanted to get in touch with him a few months later?'

She nodded and stood up. 'Yes. I had good reason.' She walked across to the mantelpiece and picked up a photograph frame.

Dunbar took it from her and looked at the smiling child in the picture. He was clearly mixed race and looked to be about seven or eight years old.

. 'That's Matthew. He's ten now and there's just the two of us. He's a bit of a rogue, but also a bit of a charmer. It's awful to say this but he reminds me in so many ways of the man I slept with that night and never saw again. It's the smile, the laugh...'

'We need a DNA sample from your son. That way you will know for definite...'

She interrupted him. 'I'm not sure I want to know, if this man is who you say he is.'

'And you want to spend the rest of your life worrying if your son is the son of a rapist and a murderer? It's better that you know the facts so that you can deal with them.'

'I know you're right. Matt knows the circumstances of his birth. I've always been honest with him about it, but this is another matter altogether. He's not old enough to know the real facts about his genetic father.'

'I'm inclined to agree with you on that but when he becomes an adult you may want to talk him through it. Don't let him find out by accident.'

He stood to leave and confirmed he would be in touch about the DNA sample.

'You don't want the wallet then?'

'What?'

'The wallet. I posted it to him but the address was false. I had put my address on the package so it came back to me when Royal Mail couldn't deliver it.'

'You've kept it? For ten years?

'Yes. I put it away in a cupboard still wrapped in the brown paper and forgot about it until this cropped up. I couldn't bring myself to just get rid of it. Fished it out when I saw the news.'

She moved to the sideboard and took a package out of the drawer. 'Hope it helps,' she said as she handed it to him.

The wallet contained very little. The five-pound note was still there, as was the driving licence in the name of Liam Ryland. There was a small newspaper cutting about the opening of Amy Thornton's business, Optimum, and a larger newspaper article about John Thornton. It detailed all his books and was promoting a book signing in one of the big department stores in the West End of London. Dunbar passed it on to forensics but didn't imagine they would get anything from it.

He felt strangely at odds with himself now he knew of the existence of a child of Treverick's. How would that child cope when he found out what his father was? How does anyone live with the knowledge that his or her father has killed and ruined lives? Matthew hadn't been there so he hadn't met him, but he acknowledged to himself that he wanted to. He would arrange to take the forensic colleague down to Wadebridge to get the DNA; it was a loose end he needed to tie up.

Chapter 23

The funeral cortege left Moorgate Manor amidst such heavy-duty security that everywhere that Pilot looked seemed to be thronged by policemen and Mark's associates. He held tightly to Pat who seemed on the point of collapse. Looking ashen, the quietest of the Farmer children, thirty-two year old Bryony was with Tilly, her partner of three years.

Bryony couldn't imagine a world without her Dad. He had been the first one she had told when she had asked Tilly to move in with her and his support had been total. Any problems she had encountered he had been her first port of call and she was quite simply bereft. Tilly was doing her best but David hadn't been her dad. He was Bryony's and she was going to miss him so much.

What she really couldn't cope with was that her Mum and Dad had kept quiet about the problems with this man. Pat had explained that because they lived in Aberdeen, they figured they were about as safe as they could be, as was Rhys in Australia. Treverick wanted the people who had been there when he was sent to prison and who had been close to Amy Thornton.

It had been a long and uncomfortable evening when they had sat around the fire in the large sitting room at Moorgate with the Farmers, Buckinghams and everyone on the periphery. Pilot had taken the lead and the discussion that ensued had left nobody in any doubt about the depths that Treverick would plumb. Bryony had sobbed through most of it. Her parents had coped with so much and along with his bodyguard, her father had paid the price.

Mark Carter had been at the family meeting and had relayed details of Alan Shimwell's funeral. Alan's family had asked that it be kept private. His wife had said that Alan would not have wanted anyone to face the possibility of attack at his graveside, so she had requested a quiet affair. It had been close family only but the presence of police officers had been obvious. The funeral had passed without incident and now his wife and baby daughter were staying with her parents for a few days.

David's funeral was huge. Many people had to stand outside the church for the commendation. The burial in the cemetery grounds was overwhelming. Pat needed to get home; she would come the following day to say her goodbyes. Her red rose landed on the coffin with a thud followed by dozens of others coming from all directions. The wreaths were piled high on the mounds of soil at the side of the newly-dug grave and she gave them just a brief glance as she moved away at the end of the graveside committal. She would read all the cards tomorrow. Today she wanted to go home and weep until she passed out from exhaustion. In fact, today she wanted to die.

Daniel put his arm around his mother and escorted her to the lead car while his long-time partner, Erin, stayed at the graveside for a few moments longer. She needed time to say goodbye to this man who had been so welcoming towards her and who had supported their venture into property refurbishment in both a financial way and as an advisor. They had asked for a loan to buy their first property and he had given them the stake they needed with no repayment strings. David had been the person she could see Daniel becoming and she offered her thanks to the man now inside a coffin, who had treated her so well.

Slowly, they all drifted away and when there was no one left, the soil at the side of the grave was placed back into the hole, sealing David away forever. The cemetery staff placed the many wreaths on top of the mound and cleared everything away before walking back down to the gatehouse to clock off for the day.

Dunbar walked across to the grave and solemnly moved around it looking at the names on the wreaths. There were so many he didn't recognise, so many people who had been friends with this man. The wreaths from the family said everything that needed to be said and he wiped away a small tear. Policemen don't cry he told himself.

He said his own prayer, used his own words and thoughts, albeit awkwardly. He didn't pray; didn't even know if he believed with any conviction but he gave it his best shot and hoped somebody was listening.

Somebody was.

Treverick had stayed behind the wall until he had seen Dunbar walk away. He had thought everyone would have been gone by now but Dunbar and his guilt must have decided to stay a little longer.

He had guessed Dunbar was blaming himself. He was supposed to protect them all and hadn't been able to do it. He had watched him wipe away a tear and it had given him joy. And then the little prayer had built on that feeling, although Treverick wasn't sure God would want to hear the word bastard in any prayer.

He had stayed behind the wall for nearly an hour before deciding to risk going to the flowery mound, flowers that were covering all the little bits and pieces that had once been David Farmer. It amused him that they hadn't been able to go and view him at the Chapel of Rest.

And so, it was another one ticked off the list. Either Freda or Pat would be next.

He had hoped they would bring his Angel but there hadn't been any children at the service so he assumed they were all under lock and key and mega protection back at Hillside or Moorgate.

Getting her back was going to take some careful planning but maybe the plan would work better if Pilot were out of the equation. That would leave them more vulnerable. Maybe. But he needed Lauren and Angel as a pair and he needed them soon.

He straightened up and pulled down the legs of his council overalls. He looked exactly like the cemetery workers once again, just as he had done that Christmas Eve when he had watched a very pregnant Lauren and the considerate Pilot navigate the headstones and pathways as they headed home to have their baby. His baby.

If there had been any police to stop him, he would just have said he was bringing a late wreath up. It already had a false card on it that said simply 'Rest in Peace, David, from the Mountjoys' and he would have quietly placed it on the grave and walked away.

But there was no one to challenge him so he laid down the wreath in a prominent position and carefully swapped over the card. He would have given anything to see Dunbar's face when he read the card but he knew that wouldn't happen. He couldn't risk being here again.

The replacement card said:

'Gotcha! Love Ron and Angel'.

Chapter 24

Pat rose next morning and told Will and Martyn, the two men shadowing her that she was going to the cemetery. She needed to be there, without family, just her and David. She was accompanied to the cemetery by both of the men and so was well protected but nothing could have cushioned her from the sight of the red carnation wreath and the card.

Both men stayed a respectful few feet away from the grave leaving Pat to begin to look at the cards in peace. The first two made her cry and she removed the cards to take home with her. She intended getting in touch with everyone who had taken the trouble to send flowers or donations to Childline and she dropped the cards into an envelope she had brought with her.

She looked at the beautiful red and white wreath and then screamed. She staggered to the side of the mound of flowers and vomited. Both men were at her side in seconds, supporting her. She pointed at the wreath and they lifted it away from all the others.

'Sir, it's Martyn Pearson, Carter Security. We have an issue. There is a wreath on the grave from Treverick.'

Dunbar arrived in minutes and took the wreath away with him. He had spoken briefly with Pat, now sitting in the back of the car, and had told Martyn to take her straight home.

'She needs a doctor. She needs something to take the edge off. Talk to her family and tell them what's happened, they'll know what to do.'

When she got home Pat collapsed on a sofa and, helped by medication from a caring doctor and an arm placed lovingly around her by Bryony, she eventually succumbed to exhaustion and slept.

Josh pulled Lauren to him. She looked ill, almost as bad as she had looked when Grace had been taken. He couldn't begin to estimate the depth of worry the family must be going through and he thought about the conversation he had shared with Dawn the previous night.

They had discussed returning to England. Permanently.

He kissed the top of Lauren's head and she shuddered.

'I don't know what to do,' she said quietly.

'About something in particular or just generally?'

'Everything.'

'Come on,' he said and took her hand. 'Let's talk.' He pulled her over to the kitchen table, poured out two coffees and sat down facing her.

'Talk.'

'The first thing is the education of our children. Until he is caught, I daren't let them out of my sight. They both need to be in school now, Grace more than Olivia. We've done such a lot with Grace and she's proving to be a clever little girl, but there's a limit to how much we can teach her. She needs to be with children of her own age for a start and she needs teachers who have been trained for the job. Jess has been brilliant with all three of them and I know she does so much research on how to teach and what comes next but she can't provide peer support.'

Josh looked at his half sister and smiled. 'Okay, let's think about this logically. If we are still having this discussion in a year's time, then we will need to be worried. At the moment, Grace is still very much in recovery. She needs to get to know you, all of us in fact, and surely that's part of what she has to learn? She saw nobody for the first seven years of her life. Well, apart from him.' He paused while he tried to keep the anger out of his voice.

'I know what you're saying, Josh, and maybe I'm wrong. But I'm her Mummy and I ache every time I look at her. She's like a little girl lost when she thinks nobody is watching her and then she switches on the act when she is brought back into our world. And I actually think she feels guilty about David.'

'What?'

'She knows Treverick killed him. That's where the guilt is. She feels that she brought that monster into our lives and yet I don't think she is old enough for us to tell her just how wrong she is.'

Her mobile phone began to play God Only Knows and when she saw it was Dunbar, she answered.

'Jake, I hope you're ringing to tell me you've got him.'

'I wish, Lauren. No, but I am ringing to tell you he is still in the area. It's almost as though he wants to be caught. A wreath was left on David's grave and I'm going on television tonight with details of it to try and find out where he bought it. Lauren, the card said it was from him and Angel.'

She gave a small cry, partly in anger and partly in grief.

'For God's sake, are we ever going to be rid of him? We'll watch the news and thank you for keeping us informed.'

The broadcast was over in a couple of minutes. He showed the wreath, showed the card with the words blanked out and said they were looking for the florist who had made up the wreath. He then followed up with the pictures of Treverick – he needed these faces out in the community.

Very quickly they had a response. It wasn't from a florist's shop, it was from a woman who owned a roadside stand selling flowers. She was very apologetic as she began to speak and Dunbar had to reassure her that they took very seriously any information that came in.

'But it might not be who you're looking for.'

'It might be.'

'Well...'

'Did he buy a wreath from you that looked anything like the one on the television?'

'No, I don't sell wreaths.'

'Okay.' He waited.

'He bought two dozen red and two dozen white carnations. And he bought that card that you showed. I know a lot of people sell that card but he bought one exactly like it at the same time as he bought the flowers.'

'What made you remember him?' Dunbar was curious. Lots of men bought flowers.

'He bought red and white flowers. We don't normally sell red and white flowers. They're bad luck.'

'What?'

'Bad luck. They represent blood and tears, so I've always understood anyway, and I always tell people that if they're buying flowers to take to hospital or something. I told him.'

'You had a conversation with him?'

'Of sorts. It makes me feel sick now I know who he is.'

'It might not be him.'

'Oh it was. It was the way he smirked when I told him about the superstition. As though it didn't matter what the colours meant.'

'Okay, Jeanette, I need to come and see you. I'm going to bring a police artist with me and I need you to think about anything that could help us identify him now. What he looked like, his eyes, his clothes, what he was driving, anything at all.'

She gave him her address and he promised to ring her back when he had managed to organise everything.

Within three hours he was in Jeanette's kitchen enjoying a cup of coffee. She was concentrating on working with the police artist, trying to get him to square the chin up more. In the end, she stood up.

'You're not getting it right.' She reached on to the top of the bread bin and picked up a piece of paper.

'That's him.'

Both men looked at each other and then at the woman. She grinned. 'Sorry, I came home after spending a few hours trying to hold him in my brain and sat down and drew him. I can draw,' she said almost apologetically.

'And this is accurate?'

She moved into the other room and came back with a framed pencil sketch of herself.

'It's as accurate as this one,' she said.

Dunbar looked at it, put the pencil drawing in his folder and said, 'It's very accurate.'

'So, thank you Jeanette, for that. At last, we know what he looks like now. Or at least what he looked like a couple of days ago. Can you remember how he talked?'

'He's from Devon unless he's a good actor. His voice is a bit gravelly, as though he's got a sore throat. And his front teeth are a bit crooked. I would say his nose has been broken at some point, because it's still bent.'

Dunbar thanked his lucky stars for an artist's eye.

'He was wearing overalls. Dark grey ones with a logo on the breast pocket. I'm sorry I can't help you with the logo because he carried the flowers across it so I couldn't really see what it was other than it was there but as he walked away from me I saw the overalls had Parks and Cemeteries on the back.'

Dunbar was stunned. It made sense. Nobody took any notice of cemetery workers, not even other cemetery workers because he could just say he'd been drafted in for the day or week to give additional help. He was an invisible employee.

He shook her hand and both men moved towards the door, expressing their thanks. But she hadn't finished.

'Oh, and he's got a tattoo on his right arm. It's just a word.' She handed Dunbar another smaller piece of paper. 'I can't guarantee the accuracy of this because it was a very brief glimpse but I think this is how it was written.'

He stared at the paper, at the single word.

Beautiful.

Thousands of copies of Jeanette's drawings were handed out over the next few days; Cornwall and Devon were awash with them. On the other side of the leaflet was a picture of the tattoo along with an explanation that this was only the result of a swift glance. The word was correct; it was the font that was an uncertainty although the intricate capital B was a definite.

Dunbar had needed no further proof that it was Treverick. No mention was made of the wreath or the flowers – he hoped the man wouldn't connect his purchase with the sighting of him. Treverick had no reason to know that Jeanette was a skilled artist with an eye for detail.

Six calls in total came in and all six proved to be innocent men. There were no calls referencing the tattoo.

Dunbar felt frustrated. What had seemed to be a good lead had fizzled away.

He visited the man in charge of the cemetery that had been the scene of so much activity and showed him the picture of Treverick. He looked at it for long moments.

'Sure. I know him. His name's Liam. He works at that big cemetery in Wadebridge but occasionally turns up here to help out. Nice bloke, doesn't say much, just gets on with his work. His supervisor over at Wadebridge knows he lives near here so if they don't need him he asks him if he wants to come here to help out. That's what he says anyway. Wadebridge pay his wages, I just find stuff for him to do. As I said, he's a nice bloke and he'll turn his hand to anything. Is he in trouble?'

Dunbar gave a wry smile. 'A bit. His real name is Ronald Treverick.' He saw the shock flash across the man's face.

'I don't think he'll be volunteering to help you out any more, somehow. However, if you know anything, any tiny little thing that he might have said, I need to know it.' He handed him a card. 'That's my direct line. Anything at all, call me.'

He drove across to Wadebridge and went into the lodge at the cemetery gates. The supervisor there confirmed that he had never seen the man, had no idea who he was and he most certainly wouldn't send any of his workers to another cemetery unless on the strict orders of the council.

'My workers are *my* workers,' he said.

'Have you heard the name Ronald Treverick recently?'

'Sure. He's...' and then it hit him who the pencil sketch represented. 'Shit – it's him, isn't it?'

Dunbar nodded. 'It is. I don't think you're likely to see him, but just in case...' and he handed out another of his cards.

Another loose end tied up.

Chapter 25

Grace watched as Pilot stacked wood into a triangle shape. Jess had told her about bonfire night, about Guy Fawkes; they had made a big stuffed man with a pair of Mummy's trousers and an old jumper and he was sitting on a chair.

She now took the added presence of the security men who spoke very little as normal. She had heard her Father refer to this one as Guy and it had made her giggle. Two Guys but one was going to be burnt on a fire.

She was looking forward to the evening festivities because it meant she didn't have to be in bed by eight o'clock. She didn't have to stay motionless and rigid pretending to be asleep until tiredness finally overwhelmed her sometime before midnight. It was hard to get rid of the feelings that Daddy – oops, Ronald – had implanted in her. She had taught herself to feign sleep during the three months of abuse before her escape but sometimes he had made her wake up anyway and the memories would not go away.

Nan Brenda had told her about fireworks, about the loud bangs and the pretty showers of lights. She had never seen a bonfire. Jess had found a book for her that she had read on her own and it explained a lot about it. She had tried explaining it to Olivia but the little girl didn't seem to understand. She thought they were going to light the fire in the ingle nook in the lounge.

The house was beginning to recover from its sudden influx of visitors. Brenda and Ken now had a suite of rooms just for them – their lounge was John's old office with its stunning garden views, linked to the lounge by new double doors, their kitchen was the room that had been used for storage. The bedroom with its ensuite facilities was a separate room next door to the kitchen. It worked very well and the elderly couple were happily settled there. They had used their own furniture and had made the decision to see the rest of their lives out there.

Lauren and Pilot had been over the moon. It was what Lauren had wanted. Ken and Brenda had virtually brought her up and she had felt it was now time to repay that love; it was her time to look after them.

They had also put considerable effort into making Jess a room where she could have down time away from the children. They blessed the day she had arrived on their doorstep. Grace had blossomed under her tutelage and Olivia clearly adored her.

Pilot had returned to work on a part time basis. After taking Mark's advice, he decided to work three days a week but never the same three days.

Thinking about work all the time, Pilot was building the bonfire. The business would ultimately be Grace's; or he could sell up and move them all to the States away from all this horror, this stress. Dawn and Josh had made the move and it had been a successful one.

There was a little light bulb moment when he thought about the impossibility of leaving his mother, Ken, Brenda and Freda and he smiled to himself. He would just have to battle on and trust in Jake Dunbar and Mark Carter. He piled on another log and thought again about Dawn and Josh. They would be there tonight but in two days time flying back to the States. Dawn had been such a huge support for his mother following his dad's death and he knew the American branch would be missed terribly.

Freda seemed to have accepted that staying with Pat was a non-negotiable issue now; she had stopped insisting she would return to her own place. David's death had rattled them all; prior to that it had been a *what-if* situation. Now, it was more of a *when*. As a result of the forced move into Moorgate, Freda and Pat had grown very close. Pat hoped Freda would make it her permanent home.

They all arrived at Hillside in one car, closely followed by a second car containing their security detail. These men had given up bonfire night with their own children to watch over this threatened family; not one of them regretted it. They would have next year's bonfire night to look forward to.

Pilot was manning a barbecue set up just outside the double doors leading from the lounge; inside Lauren had prepared a spread of food that she hoped was enough. Everybody laughed at her and asked if she'd invited everyone in the neighbourhood. The stuffed Guy Fawkes sat on his chair surveying the scene with drawn-on eyes.

Once everyone had arrived, Pilot lit the bonfire and heard two of his children squeal with delight. The third one was fast asleep in his cot, oblivious to the celebrations. The flames grew quickly and he knew he had been right to bring everyone together. They needed some release from the terror that constantly surrounded them. He glanced quickly around the men guarding them and nodded at the placement. They knew what they were doing.

'Okay, you lot! Beef burgers? Sausages? Who wants what?'

Grace and Olivia were first to his side, and Grace tugged on his apron.

'Papa,' she said. 'I'd like a beef burger please.'

He felt tears prick his eyes. Since her return, Grace hadn't actually called him anything. She had had no problems with calling Lauren Mummy, but he simply hadn't been allocated a name. He knew the connotations of *Daddy* in her mind and although he and Lauren had spoken about it, they had taken the decision to simply leave it and wait for Grace to provide the answer. And she had: Papa.

Lauren had heard. He turned to look at her and saw tears slide down her cheeks. He blew her a soft kiss and bent down to kiss his daughter's head.

'A beef burger it is, my lovely. Ketchup?' She nodded and he handed her the plate.

'Me too, Daddy,' said Olivia. Pilot's love for his daughters felt momentarily overwhelming.

He served the other guests and then said,

'Right, the fire's dying down a little. Shall we burn Guy?'

Grace felt an excitement like she'd never known before.

'Please!' she called.

But before Pilot had chance to follow up on this, Dawn spoke.

'Can we just have a couple of minutes, folks?'

Everyone turned towards her and she grinned.

'As you know Josh and I are going back to St. Louis on the 7th November. We are going back to sell our home there and get everything packed up to come home. In view of the relationship I had with your Dad, Lauren, I know it's strange, but we feel part of all of you and that we need to be here. Pat, we will need to impose for a short while. We will need somewhere to stay when we come back, just until we find the house we want. Will that be possible?'

Pat gave a broad smile.

'You are always welcome. After everything we have shared over the years, how could it be any other way?'

Grace started to clap and everyone laughed and followed suit. She knew very little about her family but she sure liked Josh.

Pilot and Josh went to get the Guy Fawkes and hoisted him on to the flames between them. The flames went higher with a terrific whoosh and everyone watching from inside and out cheered.

'Fireworks on the side patio' Josh shouted above the noise. 'Give me ten minutes to set up.'

Josh moved to the metal bin where he had stored the fireworks and began to nail two Catherine Wheels to a post he had already installed. He had bought far too many but felt it was important that Grace had a night that would stay in her memory forever. He hoped it might erase some of her bad ones.

He thought it might be nice to finish the evening with the sky-rockets, so he put them on the bottom and the other fireworks on the top. He placed the packets of sparklers on the windowsill, ready for the girls coming round.

Lauren, Grace and Olivia were the first to walk around the corner and Lauren apologised.

'I couldn't make them wait any longer. Grace has only seen pictures in books of fireworks so she's flying high at the moment.'

He laughed.

'Okay, Grace, two more minutes until everyone else walks round and then we'll see some Catherine Wheels.'

The little girl nodded and moved to his side. She slipped her hand into his and said,

'Show me.'

He swallowed, fighting the emotion. Grace was changing. Was starting to absorb the love of this family. Finally.

He picked her up so that she could see the round firework at the top of the pole and she nodded.

'Is it pretty?'

'Nearly as pretty as you,' he laughed. 'Now go stand with your Mummy and don't leave her side when the fireworks start. We don't want anybody getting burnt.'

She watched the Catherine Wheel sitting on Pilot's shoulders. He was aware of the significance of everything on the magical evening, a lessening of tension in Grace. If bonfire night could do this for her, how much more could Christmas do?

Once the Catherine Wheels had finished, Josh moved to the paving slab he had placed on the lawn for the standing fireworks. He took with him a Fairy Shower and lit it. He could hear the squeals of delight – and not just from the two little girls – and he grinned. A good night indeed.

They watched a few fireworks and then moved back towards the fire that was starting to die down. Pilot built it up again and they stood and watched as the flames began to climb higher once more. Guy Fawkes had disappeared completely.

At first, they thought it was the bang of a firework. And then Freda crumpled to the floor.

Four of the security men ran, leaving Guy to deal with Freda. 'Inside the house,' he ordered. 'Leave the fire, leave everything.'

Pat dropped to her knees by the side of Freda.

'I'm staying here,' she said to the stern faced young man. 'Get the others safe.'

He ushered them all in and locked the door. He went back to the two women.

'Mrs Farmer, we don't know where he is. It's dark out there and there's no guarantee we'll get him. Please...'

'I'm staying,' she said. 'Ambulance?'

'On its way.' He knelt down by Freda's side and checked her neck for a pulse. It was there, but faint. Freda moaned but didn't move. Pat took hold of her hand and spoke softly to her friend telling her the ambulance was coming, just to hold on.

Police cars arrived within minutes, one bringing Jake Dunbar. Paramedics worked on Freda on the patio for fifteen minutes before lifting her onto a trolley and into the ambulance. Pat went with her and finally the group inside the house began to get information.

Jess had taken the two girls up to bed and the adults waited in the lounge. Dunbar tapped on the patio doors and Pilot went to let him in.

'Jake,' Pilot said, tiredness in his voice. 'He's picking us off one by one.'

'We are moving you all to a safe house...'

'No! If you think he won't find us, then you're being particularly stupid! We're going nowhere, because there is nowhere we can go. And I promise you this, DI Dunbar, if he harms my Grace in any way, I'm coming for you.'

They found no trace of the man they were seeking but they did find a sky-rocket standing in a bottle ready to be ignited. There was a message attached that said:

And there goes another one!

Chapter 26

But Treverick was wrong. In intensive care for two weeks, Freda was still alive. The bullet had entered her back causing a lung to collapse and breaking ribs. Her room was guarded just as Grace's had been and although she was in a wheel chair when she went home ten days later, she did go home to Moorgate.

Dawn and Josh had delayed their departure until they knew she would make it and had then gone home to the States to tie everything up as quickly as possible. They had arrived back in England on 1st December and gone straight to Moorgate.

Pat folded her arms around Dawn and said,

'Welcome home.'

Tears appeared in Dawn's eyes.

'Damn,' she said, 'I was determined not to cry. Well, we're back for good. It looks as though the house is sold, barring any last minute hitches, and my lawyer says we can do everything now by fax. Our belongings are in a container somewhere between St. Louis and here, so we have what's in our suitcases at the moment.'

'We can all help if you need anything,' she said with a smile. 'Freda is coming home in a couple of days and I've moved her to a downstairs room You two are now upstairs and I hope you'll stay as long as you need to. What I'm trying to say is, don't go out and buy the first house you see, take your time and make sure it's right for you. And besides all that, let's not stretch Mark any further with security. Hillside and Moorgate are enough to have him scratching his head already.'

'And they still have no idea where he is?'

Pat shook her head. 'Not a clue. I don't think Dunbar is too welcome over at Hillside these days and I quite understand Pilot's stance on it, but they're dealing with a truly devious man.'

Dawn and Josh unpacked and rejoined Pat downstairs. Dawn looked puzzled.

'Is nobody here protecting you?'

She sighed. 'Oh, yes. There are a couple of extremely fit young men patrolling the perimeter and there's one inside. It's Sam. He doesn't say much apart from "*You okay, Mrs. F?*" It's a comfort to know he's here. They're totally organised. Stagger meal breaks, pass information on to incoming agents – Mark has so impressed me with his company. Utter professionals.'

'So, we'd like to pop up to Hillside. Do we notify Sam?'

'Doesn't work like that. He is quite amenable to us being able to go where we want but he works out how many people go with us and what size car we need. I'll go find him. Josh, you know where the kitchen is – a cuppa before we go? The boys outside like tea with milk, no sugar. Sam has coffee, black.'

Josh grinned at her.

'Slave duties then. Mom, we have to find a new house PDQ.'

'Why? Do you think you won't be on slave duties in our new home?' Dawn grinned.

He shook his head and moved into the kitchen. He had no idea what the next few weeks would bring but he was happy to be back in England. He had left good friends behind in St.Louis but in an ever-shrinking world, he would see them soon. And meanwhile he had some precious people to protect, alongside Pilot.

Sam organised them into one vehicle and they all drove to Hillside. Lauren was feeding Noah and the little boy grinned as he spotted Nanny Pat.

'Oh well, that's done it,' a disgruntled Lauren said. 'There's no chance of getting this broccoli down him now.'

Josh laughed. 'And quite right too. Nobody should ever be force-fed broccoli, it's probably against the law. Come here, youngster, come join the men of the house,' and he swung the baby up from his high chair.

Noah giggled and pulled his uncle's hair. Josh carried him towards the double doors and before he had chance to open them one of Mark's associates was standing there.

'Oh – sorry Noah, maybe we'll go play in the playroom then.' He guessed it might take him a little while to get used to the stringent rules governing living arrangements now.

He carried the little boy upstairs to the room filled with toys of various shapes and sizes; Jess was there with Grace and Olivia.

Looking flustered, she stood up.

'Sorry, did you want the room?'

'No, no...' he said. 'It's me that should be sorry; I thought it was your day off.'

She laughed. 'It is. But I live here. And these two monkeys are my world now.'

'You've no family then?'

'Sort of. I have a mum but she's remarried and they're always off on holiday. She's cruising round the Caribbean at the moment, so there's just me. And these.' She hugged the girls.

'So, no boyfriend?'

'You're holding him. Noah is my love, aren't you, sweetheart? He's the only man I want in my life.'

Josh placed the baby on the floor and pulled a red and yellow toy laptop towards him. 'Come on, Noah; let me teach you to type. We need you to be an author just like your Granddad John. He was a cool guy, buddy. You would have liked him.'

Jess smiled and turned her attention back to Grace and Olivia who were both working on separate jigsaws.

She heard Grace mumble something but hoped she had misheard. 'What did you say, Grace?'

'Fucking bastard, John,' the little girl repeated.

Jess looked at Josh in horror. 'I'm so sorry...'

'Hey,' he laughed, 'I've heard much worse than that.'

'Grace,' she turned to her young charge. 'We definitely do not use words like that. I think you need to apologise to Olivia, Noah, Uncle Josh and me. Now.'

Grace looked around and a tear left her eye.

'I'm sorry. I'm sorry, Uncle Josh.' She jumped up from the table and ran to the door. She slammed it behind her as she ran to her bedroom.

Josh stood. 'I'll go. Can you keep an eye on these two?'

She nodded and he followed Grace to her bedroom. She was face down on the duvet, sobbing. He sat by her side and pulled her to him.

'Come on, you didn't hurt anyone. It just wasn't nice to hear words like that coming from such a dainty little thing like you.'

She looked at him. 'He said them. He said them a lot.'

Josh felt out of his depth.

'Ronald Treverick?'

She nodded. Her bottom lip dropped. 'Please don't send me back to him. I promise not to say it again.'

He felt numb. 'Sweetheart, you will never see him again. You're with your real Mummy and Daddy now and you will never go back to Treverick. I promise you.'

She looked at him; weighed him up, nodded.

'You coming back to play with the others?'

'No. I'll stay here and read. And I'm sorry.'

He kissed the top of her head and stood. He could feel the tension in her and hoped half an hour in a book would help, albeit temporarily; this little girl needed some reassurance.

Jess looked up at his return.

'Thank you,' she said. 'Is she okay?'

'Reading. She's calmed down now but that's one mixed up young lady. It's like she doesn't trust us to keep her safe.'

'I know. She needs constant praise, constant encouragement around everything she does. I don't have a problem with being like that with her but at some point, she has to take responsibility for herself and begin to trust in herself. Maybe that will happen when she eventually starts school but until he's either caught or dead she won't be going to school. Lauren and Pilot won't take the risk.'

'Then it's simple. We'll kill him.'

'It's not as simple as you seem to think. They have absolutely no idea where he is. They knew what he looked like last week but he'll not look like that this week. And this isn't the States you know,' added Jess with a laugh. 'We don't have guns for sale on every corner.'

'He got one.'

'And that's exactly my point about him. He knows what he's doing. I'd lay odds on him having bought that gun twenty years ago ready for possibly – probably - needing it one day. Just look at the number of names he's used since he got out of prison. He must have had everything set up ready for him to take on a different identity at the drop of a hat. And he must have money, lots of it.'

'You've clearly given this some thought.'

'When Lauren told me the full story, it took her a long time. Brenda was there as well, so between them they left nothing out. They felt it was safer for the children and me if I knew everything and really, I think they expected me to throw in the towel at that point. I didn't. Initially I got angry but as time has gone on, I've applied a bit more logic to the situation. The anger has not died but now it's a more thoughtful phase I'm going through. I try to outthink him but I'm not sure I ever could.'

'Have you come up with anything?'

'Not really. I've tried putting myself in his place with regard to where he is. He's lost the house he hid Grace in for all those years but then he went back to their first place, the caravan. I imagine he thought he was safe there but our plucky little one remembered she lived in something like a tin can, which led the police to that caravan site at Polzeath. He lost that refuge and his face is now familiar all over Devon and Cornwall so his options are narrowing. Winter's here now so he's definitely not camping out. He'd stand out like a sore thumb. He needs to be under the radar, so I suspect a squat somewhere.'

'Round here?'

Jess nodded. 'I may be being a bit thick here, but driving a car seems a bit risky. It would only take an accident on the roads for the game to be up for him. And he must know the net is closing, which puts pressure on him. No, I think he's got to be local. He got away from here pretty fast after shooting Aunt Freda so he's clearly got good local knowledge. Neither the police nor the Carter men could find any trace of him, just that rocket left for them to find. He knows exactly what he's doing, everything is planned to the tiniest detail and that's the scariest part.'

Josh looked at her with something akin to adoration.

'My God, you're awesome!'

She laughed and picked up her bag. 'Here. Have a look through this. Every time I think of something, I write it in here. There are bits of maps and all sorts in it; make of it what you will but let me have it back when you've been through it. Feel free to pick holes in my theories, but don't underestimate Treverick.'

'Is it okay for me to show it to Pilot?'

'Show it to whoever you want. Just remember they're just my thoughts and there's no proof I'm anywhere near on the right track.'

He flicked through the handwritten book and looked at her. 'Wow! I'll have to take you for a drink to say thank you.'

She grinned and winked at him. 'Yes, please. Anytime. After he's been caught. I don't want to go for a drink with you accompanied by a bodyguard!'

And Josh, for the first time, was lost for words.

Chapter 27

Grace felt frightened. Insecure. She had said those bad words about the man who was her Granddad, a man she had never known and she remembered the dreadful *naughty smacks* that Daddy had inflicted on her. No, not Daddy. She mustn't call him Daddy. He was Treverick. Everybody in her new house called him Treverick. She didn't want anybody in this new home to give her *naughty smacks* because they hurt so much.

Her mind drifted back to the day she had stumbled and accidentally toppled the bucket she had just used. The wee went everywhere and when he came home from work, he had beaten her on her bare bottom with a slipper and it had hurt so much. He didn't feed her for a long time after that and she thought about the bitter taste of her own wee she had drunk because she was so thirsty.

She didn't want them to hurt her like that in this house. The door to her bedroom opened and she screamed.

Jess looked shocked.

'What's wrong, sweetheart? Tell me what's wrong?'

'Please don't do naughty smacks,' she sobbed. 'It hurts so much.'

Olivia peeked around the door, her eyes wide.

'Olivia,' Jess said quietly. 'Can you tell Mummy I want her in Grace's room?'

Olivia didn't need to tell her. Lauren, closely followed by Pilot, was at the door, a look of terror etched on her face.

'It's okay, Lauren,' Jess said calmly. 'I think you and I and our beautiful Grace need to have a little talk. She's a little bit scared and we need to put things right.'

Pilot took in the scene and turned to head back downstairs.

'Call me if you three ladies need me. Olivia, you come with me. Is Noah asleep?'

Jess nodded. 'He's fine.'

Relief flowed palpably through Lauren. She turned a questioning face towards Jess and Jess began to tell her about the problematic afternoon. She included Grace in the telling and Grace once more apologised, this time to her mother. Lauren felt sick that her child should be so distraught about something she hadn't realised was wrong.

Lauren listened through to the end and said quietly

'Thank you, Jess.'

She pulled Grace towards her and held her tightly. 'Grace, my love, I promise you that no child in this house will ever be smacked for anything. There will be no *naughty smacks* and if you make mistakes, as you did with the bad words you used, then we will just tell you. We won't shout, won't tell you off; we will just explain why it is wrong. We love you so much, little girl, and we need you to know that. Now, I want you to go downstairs, find Papa and tell him everything is okay. I'll be down in a minute.'

Grace climbed off the bed and headed for the door. She closed it behind her and Lauren turned to Jess.

'Naughty smacks? Naughty smacks? I need to find this man and I'll bloody show him what naughty smacks are like. God, Jess, it's going to take years to guide her through this, and it's such a minefield. Thank you for your input today. What we've found out from her clearly needed to come out and you've been a massive help. And for goodness sake, take your day off!'

Jess laughed. 'I will. I've got a good book planned for after our meal and an early night to follow.'

When Lauren went back into the lounge, all eyes turned towards her.

'She's absolutely fine,' she said and looked towards Josh. 'Absolutely fine.'

Christmas was becoming problematical. Pilot and Lauren needed to go Christmas shopping but this involved leaving the children at home. In the end, and after discussions with Mark's men and the police officers who still guarded their property, they decided to take all three to Pat's for the day where they would be under the protection designated for Moorgate. Pilot and Lauren would take the full day to do everything that was required for Christmas but they had to be accompanied at all times by one of the Carter associates. They decided to head for Truro and hope for the best.

And so it happened. It was a shopping expedition like no other with every available space in the car they had borrowed from Ken and Brenda filled with goodies. They knew they wouldn't be able to organise another day like this and so they had to make the most of it.

They did quite a bit of the shopping in the big department store, particularly in the toy department. Pilot was looking at a flashing ball for Noah and Lauren nudged him.

'Look,' she said and pointed to Father Christmas' grotto. 'There's one in Padstow in one of the shops on the quayside. Do you think...?'

Pilot grinned.

'I promise you we'll take all three of them but answer me honestly. Is this for you or them? Do you just want to sit on his knee and tickle his beard?'

'You've seen through my cunning plan.'

Pilot looked thoughtful. 'Grace won't really know what's going on, will she? She's never had a Christmas. We have to give her the full experience this year, so we'll sort it out with the security and take them down. Now come on, let's go and decide on the books for the girls.'

Sam helped them back to the car with the last of their purchases and then checked underneath the car before he allowed them to get in it.

'Right,' he said, 'You're okay. Stick to speed limits all the way, make sure I am always behind you and don't do anything stupid. We're going straight home, Mr. Farmer, we aren't stopping anywhere for anything. Guy is escorting the children and Jess back home as soon as you ring Moorgate. You'll need some time to put this lot away.'

His own car was full to bursting and he grinned to himself as he followed the borrowed Range Rover. The Farmer kids were going to have a hell of a Christmas. Pilot drove carefully and they arrived back at Hillside without incident. Everyone breathed a sigh of relief and they hid everything in a wardrobe that had been left in the garage. The wrapping would come later.

Grace and Olivia burst into the house chattering away excitedly. Nan Pat had told them all about Christmas, about the magic of Father Christmas and Olivia had tried her best to explain to her big sister about all the presents that appeared under the tree. At first, Grace hadn't understood; Nan Pat brought out photographs from the previous year and then watched in amazement as Grace's face lit up. It was going to be a good Christmas.

At the weekend, they took the children into Padstow and parked on the quay. Sam and Guy came with them and parked their car next to the Range Rover, once again borrowed because of the size of it. This time they needed it to transport a Christmas tree.

Grace's eyes were like shining stars; she saw the Father Christmas grotto in one of the craft shops that closed for the winter and squeaked with excitement.

'Is he in there?' she asked.

'He certainly is, my love, do you want to meet him? And he might have a little gift for you.'

She nodded, now unable to speak.

They bought three tickets and went to stand in the queue. They didn't have long to wait and they wheeled a sleeping Noah in the pushchair up to the red suited man. He smiled at the baby, stroked his head and handed over a present from the shelf that was designated boys 0 – 2 years.

'I'll not wake him,' he whispered quietly.

Olivia went next and he asked her how old she was.

'I'm four and a half, Father Christmas,' she said and smiled. He turned to the shelf marked girls 3 – 5 and handed her a gift that was rectangular; impossible to guess the contents.

'And what do you want me to bring you on Christmas Eve,' he whispered, obviously still aware of the sleeping Noah.

She shrugged.

'Nothing really,' she said, 'but will you bring Grace lots of good things because she should have them.'

Tears pricked Lauren's eyes. It was clear that Olivia, even at such a young age, had picked up on adult discussions.

'Well, little one, I'm sure we can still manage to get the elves to make something special for you,' he whispered once again. 'And is this Grace?'

Olivia nodded. 'Yes, she's my sister.'

Grace stepped forward, her head down. She was finding it hard to reign in her excitement.

'Hello.'

'Hello, Father Christmas, I'm nearly eight.' She hiccoughed. The anticipation was threatening to overwhelm her.

'Then we need to find a special present for you.' She had to lean forward to hear what he was saying; he pressed her gift into her hand. And then she did squeal.

'I've got a Christmas present!' She turned to face her parents and they were overcome themselves at the sight of her face. She was glowing.

She swung round to Father Christmas and lifted his hand. 'Thank you,' she said. 'Can I open it now?'

'Best wait until you're home and your Mummy can help.' He continued to whisper, watching baby Noah. 'And don't wake your little brother. Have a lovely Christmas and I'll see you all on Christmas Eve.'

They left the grotto with Grace and Olivia chatting excitedly. Sam and Guy moved forward and escorted them to their car. Once again, it was checked for explosives but Guy had remained outside the grotto all the time they were inside; he was sure no one had approached the car.

The two cars pulled into a massive yard that was filled with Christmas trees of all shapes and sizes and they spent the next half hour choosing just the right one. It was loaded onto the Range Rover roof rack with some difficulty and fastened securely. Grace and Olivia were bursting with excitement; Mummy had promised them they could spend the next day sorting out tree ornaments and putting up the tree in the lounge.

The girls hugged their gifts all the way home and tumbled out of the car as soon as their seatbelts were released. They couldn't wait to get in the house to see what Father Christmas had bought them.

Olivia climbed on to the rocking chair and began very carefully to remove the wrapping paper. Grace waited patiently; almost afraid to do something she had never done before. Inside the parcel were two books, one about dinosaurs and one about fairies. Underneath the reading books was a sticker book that she immediately began to flick through.

'Look, Grace, look what I got. It's stickers.' The excitement in her voice was infectious and Grace began to laugh at her younger sister. 'You are crazy, Olivia Farmer. Let me open mine and then I'll come and sticker with you.'

Pilot lifted his camera to get the best position for a picture. This was their daughter's first Christmas present ever and he wanted a picture of the moment she opened it.

She slowly took off the paper, clearly savouring every moment. Like her sister's package, there were two books suitable for her age. Underneath was a photo frame. She looked up at her father as she registered the flash of the camera, a puzzled expression crossing her face.

The picture in the frame was the one being distributed around Devon and Cornwall of Treverick.

Chapter 28

By the time the police reached the grotto it had been abandoned and the small crowd outside were only too happy to tell the police about Father Christmas disappearing round the back of the shops that lined the quayside. They wanted their money back for tickets already purchased and Dunbar had to deal with angry parents and crying children. The elf that had taken the money and handed out tickets was looking quite distressed and scared. Having only met Santa the day before and been offered the job she thought it would give her a little spending money towards Christmas presents; no, she said, I didn't know him.

The area was cleared, names and addresses were taken for follow up interviews and Dunbar left uniformed officers to deal with searching the locality. He knew Treverick was long gone and he guessed that the man had tried this tactic more in hope than certainty that the Farmers would visit Santa.

The detective needed to speak with Grace to see if she had recognised anything at all but deep down he knew she couldn't have. She would have completely freaked out if she had thought Treverick was sitting down next to her.

Dunbar arrived at Hillside where calm had been restored. Pilot and Lauren had managed to convince Grace that the photo frame had been put into the parcel by mistake and the two books were her real present. She had departed for her bedroom where she was currently reading the books.

Lauren was scathing.

'How the bloody hell could this have happened, Jake? How did he get permission for a grotto without a police check being involved? This is contact with children and he's a fucking paedophile!' Her voice rose as anger and panic threatened to overwhelm her.

'I have no idea yet,' he replied, 'no idea at all. He would have needed council permission for a start, never mind a police check. But by tomorrow, I will have some answers.'

Pilot cradled Lauren in his arms as she sobbed. He normally had anger to deal with but this was something else. It was almost as though she was admitting defeat; he didn't know how to handle her except by holding and soothing her. Sleep wasn't going to be easy.

He had no words. No words that would help. He was rapidly coming to the conclusion that the police were never going to catch him and they would be living in fear until the day Treverick died. Lauren's sobs began to quieten and after half an hour, he felt comfortable that she had lapsed into sleep. He carefully pulled back the duvet and got out of bed. She stirred and he paused, waiting until she had settled once more.

He went downstairs and into the kitchen. Their overnight protection was a new addition to the team, Iain Dunne, a bear of a man with a height of 6' 7" that would intimidate anyone who came across him on a dark night; a man who had knelt on the floor to play in a dolls house at Olivia's insistence with an apologetic glance at the adults who had all laughed at his plight.

'Iain,' Pilot said, with a nod in the big man's direction.

'Everything okay, sir?'

Pilot shook his head. 'I wish.'

'The police will get him eventually, you know.'

'Will that be before or after he kills us all?' was Pilot's dry response.

'Trust Dunbar. He's a good man.'

'We've been trusting Dunbar for almost eight years and it's not helped.'

'Does he keep you fully informed?'

'No idea. I certainly don't feel fully informed. How the hell did Treverick manage to get that shop? Who granted him a licence to open it as a grotto?'

Iain moved across to the window and looked outside. Pilot had been careful not to turn on the kitchen light so that the backlit kitchen would not compromise Iain's view into the outside darkness. The anxious young father moved across to look outside with him.

Soon there would be Christmas tree lights on the tree they grew just outside Ken and Brenda's new lounge, but he felt a sense of dread about the whole idea of Christmas now.

He remembered Treverick's last words to them – *see you all on Christmas Eve* – and he was scared. Their protection would peak on that night.

He spoke haltingly to Iain, telling him of the visit to Father Christmas and the threat inherent in Treverick's words.

Iain Dunne looked at him.

'Mr. Farmer, I will be on duty Christmas Eve here, I'll make sure of it. And there will be at least three others here. Nobody, and I mean nobody, is going to get anywhere near your precious babies. You need have no worries about that. And I'm pretty sure we're putting extra on at Moorgate as well. But,' he hesitated, 'let's hope he comes, yes?'

'Oh yes.' Pilot's tone was icy. 'You can bet your life I'll be staying up to catch Father Christmas making his deliveries this year.'

'Me too.'

Both men turned to see Josh standing in the doorway.

'Josh, you can't get involved...'

'I am.' There was finality in the words.

Pilot hesitated marginally before speaking.

'Okay. Then we need to talk.'

He wished Iain goodnight and they left him to continue his surveillance. They moved into the lounge and switched on the lamps. Josh spoke first.

'We need a gun.'

Pilot grinned at him. 'Spoken like a true American. Guns aren't in every store here, you know.'

'I know, but we need one.'

'I have one.'

Josh stared at his brother in law. 'You have one?'

He nodded. 'My children are my priority, Josh. Treverick doesn't care whom he kills but he's not taking out my children while I am still breathing. So, I acquired a gun.'

'How?'

'Does it matter?'

'Can you shoot?'

Pilot shrugged. 'Sort of. But if it's aimed at Treverick then the answer is simple: too right I can bloody shoot!'

'Where do you keep it?'

'Out of the children's way but available if I need it. On Christmas Eve, it will be in my hands.'

'You really think he'll come here?'

'He said so, didn't he? He's coming for Grace. I have no doubt of that. Josh, if I end up locked away for the rest of my life, that man will not survive if he comes for her.'

'And we can't even come up with a plan! We can't second guess him, can't begin to imagine how he intends getting her.'

'I have a plan of sorts.' Pilot spoke quietly. 'I intend waiting until Grace is asleep and then spending the night in her room. The gun will be loaded and in my hand.'

'Then I'll join you. At least if you feel as though you're nodding off – and that's the biggest danger really – I'll be there to either cover for you while you nap or I can keep you awake. But it does need two of us, Pilot.'

'Thank you. I thought of asking Iain but that's not fair. The only stipulation I make is that if he comes and if I kill him, you must get out of that room. I'm going to need you to be with Lauren and to help her bring our children up. You can't do that from a prison cell. You can be first on the scene because you heard the shot but you can't tell anyone you were in the room. You have to leave immediately before Grace wakes and realises you're there. Okay?'

They climbed the stairs to their rooms, both deep in thought. It was a plan based on what-ifs and perhapses, but it was all they had.

Dunbar had some answers.

He arrived at Hillside after their evening meal the following day. Over-excited, the two girls were by the Christmas tree in the lounge; they had helped Mummy put on the decorations and Grace had climbed a stepladder to install the fairy on the top.

'Isn't it beautiful, Jake?' she said, her eyes wide.

Lauren opened her mouth to say “It’s Mr. Dunbar”, but the detective held up a finger and mouthed a no. Grace had called him Jake during her hospitalisation and he didn’t want her to stop now.

‘It certainly is,’ he said. ‘And did my two favourite girls do all of this?’ he waved his hand around the room encompassing all the decorations. It was clear the Farmers had pulled out all the stops, this year.

Grace nodded. ‘Yes, and we’ve got another tree outside that’s got lights all over it.’

‘I saw. Father Christmas will certainly know where to find all of you this year.’

Grace and Olivia giggled and Lauren looked towards Jess.

‘Hey girls,’ Jess said. ‘Let’s go upstairs and get these Christmas cards coloured. We’ve a lot to do.’

They waited until the children had left and then Dunbar spoke.

‘I have some news. I’m holding nothing back, what I know you will know in about five minutes.’

They waited.

‘The shop Treverick turned into the grotto is owned by a chap called Ralph Burgin. He sells crafts and other tourist stuff all summer in the premises, then shuts up shop and overwinters in Spain. He met Liam Ryland at the beginning of summer, in May he thinks. They became really friendly and when it came time to leave for Spain, Ryland asked him if he could stay in the flat over the shop until Burgin returned in March, saying that it was much better than the flat he was living in. Burgin agreed and asked him to keep an eye on the shop instead of paying rent. He needed some repairs doing and Ryland said they would all be done by the time he came home.

'Once Burgin had departed for foreign shores, it seems that Treverick began to put his plan into operation. The shop had full frontage shutters so nobody had any idea what was going on behind them. He set up the grotto, figuring – hoping, I reckon – that you would take your three children to see Santa, especially Grace. He made a damn good job of it and cleverly didn't advertise it until a couple of days before it opened.

'Then he really got lucky because you turned up on the opening day. His biggest problem was always going to be that someone in authority might realise he didn't have a licence, a police check, or anything that would make his grotto legal.'

'But why?' Lauren looked bewildered. 'What did he gain from that?'

'He needs Grace. He needed to see her and I think it's as simple as that. Plus, he needs you scared. He's punishing you for taking Grace away from him. Don't forget that this all started because he punished your mother for being what he perceived as the cause of his imprisonment. He is very clever at disguise, planning his life and the incessant stalking he seems to crave and is by far the most dangerous man I have ever come across during my time with the police force.'

'So he disappeared as soon as we came away from the grotto?'

'Immediately. The ones who followed you in to see him said he simply wasn't there. They hung about a bit thinking maybe he'd gone to the toilet. Even Santa needs to pee. But it seems he ducked under the sparkly fabric drape at the back of his chair and disappeared. We found the Santa outfit in the back room so I suspect he had all his normal clothes on underneath the outfit to make him look a bit fatter. He couldn't hang about just in case you let Grace open her present immediately. He just wanted you to know he's still here, still following and controlling you and making you aware that you need to be on your guard at all times.'

Pilot growled.

'It makes me sick to my stomach that he actually touched our kids. And of course, he was lucky because Noah was asleep. He dropped his voice to a whisper using the old excuse of not waking the baby but really, it all helped with the disguise. Grace would only know his normal voice. And to be honest I think he'd disguised his accent anyway. He sounded like a posh Geordie rather than a Devonian.'

'The biggest plus side to all of this,' Dunbar continued, 'is that he is starting to take chances. This was a very risky thing to do just to have a two-minute contact with Grace and to let you know just how unsafe you all are. If you hadn't turned up on the first day he could very well have had a council visit after about three days and then he would have had to disappear because a second council visit would have had police back up. I think he is getting desperate to have Grace back with him.'

'And Christmas Eve? Do we have extra protection?'

Dunbar nodded. 'Yes. There will be two armed officers and there will also be dogs. He might be able to escape humans but he'll not get away from dogs.'

Pilot didn't comment and didn't look at Dunbar, afraid his face would reveal too much.

'There is one other thing. I'm not sure whether it's relevant because Treverick doesn't know this and it doesn't help with the investigation as it stands at the moment, but Treverick has a son. I wouldn't normally tell you but I said you would know as much as I know, so there it is.'

'A son? Did he marry?'

'No, a one-night-stand with a lovely girl who fell for his charms. She never saw him again – tried to contact him but he'd done his disappearing act once again. I've met the little lad who is ten now. He's a bright intelligent kid who's going to have to be told one day just who his father is. So, we have lots of information about what brought Treverick to this point but nothing that tells us where he is, or what he's going to do next...'

Chapter 29

His beautiful Angel would be eight on Christmas Day. He was looking forward to spending it with her. Her holiday break was over now, she had to come home.

On Christmas Eve, it rained. It was more or less torrential all day and Grace and Olivia spent time baking with Lauren. Grace enjoyed her first mince pie ever and everyone else the first mince pies of the season.

They had all come over from Moorgate to help with preparations for the following day. Josh was constantly at Freda's side. She was very frail. The bullet from Treverick's gun hadn't killed her but it had taken so much else away from her. She now spent her days in a wheel chair; she never complained outwardly but inwardly she raged.

While her family saw her as a much-loved family member who needed their help, Freda saw herself as a burden. Josh passed her a small knife and she sat listening to the chatter while on sprout preparation duties.

There was an undercurrent to their chatter that she recognised as fear. What hadn't they told her? Did they know something they had deliberately shielded her from? It didn't take much guesswork to know the subject of the fear.

And Pat was too quiet. Freda looked across at her as she sat on the floor playing with Olivia and smiled. The answering smile was bleak. Her first Christmas without her beloved David was clearly going to be hard.

'Freda?'

She looked up at the sound of Josh's voice who mimed drinking a glass of wine from the open doorway leading into the kitchen.

'Please,' said Freda, 'Merlot if we have it.'

He laughed. 'It's like they bought the entire stock of Sainsbury's wine department. Trust me, they have it. Merlot, it is,' and he disappeared into the kitchen.

It was like having John back. His smile, the way he held his head when he was joking with her, even the way he stood. His son was almost a mirror image.

Dawn moved behind her and kissed the top of her head and whispered, 'I know. It almost breaks my heart, too.'

They had a makeshift lunch and then everyone went to the cemetery except Freda, Jess and Noah, They took the wreaths for the two graves as they did every year, along with a third one for David's grave. But it was different this year, for they were accompanied by two policemen and two of Mark's men. They didn't stay long, just said their own private messages to these people they had loved so much and headed back towards the cars, slipping and sliding in the mud. Grace and Olivia were a little bit bewildered. They knew nothing of John and Amy other than they were grandparents they had never met. But David, they had both known. They hadn't been to the cemetery before and neither of them looked particularly impressed by this strange trip out on what had, so far, been such a lovely day.

Noah was having his afternoon nap and Jess was in her own room. She was looking forward to Christmas this year. Last year she had spent it alone in a tiny flat while her mother enjoyed the sunshine of Fuerteventura. This year, people she had grown to love and admire surrounded her. Their lives were lived under such difficult circumstances and yet only Lauren occasionally allowed the mask to slip. Only she showed the utter frustration of living like a prisoner and knowing she could do nothing about it.

Jess heard a knock on her door and called that it was open. Josh popped his head around it.

'Can I come in?'

'Of course.'

He laughed at the tiny Christmas tree on her desk. She had a few cards scattered around and had put some decorations up around the window area.

'Is this it? Is this Christmas?'

'Don't be cheeky. I have to do this with a baby on my hip, you know.'

'Sorry.' He looked contrite.

'Does Lauren want me?'

'No.' He hesitated. 'I do.'

She looked puzzled.

'I'm not doing this very well, am I? I'd like to take you out, maybe for a meal, or cinema or something?'

She looked a little shocked. 'Me?'

'Of course you.' He laughed.

'When?'

'Boxing Day?'

'Can I let you know once I've checked that Lauren doesn't need me?'

'She doesn't. I've checked.'

'Oh.' She looked stunned. 'Then thank you, I'd like that.'

'Good. I wouldn't have accepted a no, anyway.' He grinned as he quietly closed her door.

She put her book down. There was no chance of carrying on reading now. Standing, she moved to her wardrobe. She took out the grey silk dress she had bought to wear for Christmas Day and smiled. No way would that be worn at that time, it would be saved for Boxing Day.

And so, Christmas Eve drew to a close. Pat, Freda, Dawn and Josh returned to Moorgate. They had delivered all their gifts for the Hillside branch of the family, mostly wrapped in festive wrapping paper but a few wrapped in birthday paper for the child they had thought they would never see again. Pilot and Lauren had been quite emphatic that the birthday celebrations had to be kept separate to Christmas so the plan was a huge Christmas lunch and then a birthday tea party later in the day when Grace would open her birthday presents.

Freda was in bed by eight o'clock, exhausted after her day trip out; Josh, Dawn and Pat stayed up talking. They shared memories of David, of Christmases in past years until finally Dawn and Pat took themselves off to bed just after ten o'clock.

As Dawn began to climb the stairs, Josh touched her arm. She stopped.

'Something wrong?'

'I'm taking the car.'

'What? But...'

'I'm going back. To Hillside.'

'Oh, Josh, be careful. They've got enough protection, you know. Do the security men know you're going?'

'Don't worry. Pilot's told them to expect me at eleven o'clock. I'm going to sit in Grace's room. Hopefully, it's just a precaution. See you in the morning,' and he kissed her. 'Love you.'

'And I love you. Take care.'

'I will.'

He climbed into the Mondeo, the rental car they had hired until they bought a new one, and drove to Hillside. He was followed by one of the Moorgate protection group until he reached the police car parked at the bottom of the Hillside drive. He waved to them and one of the officers got out of the squad car to check the Mondeo. He saw the Moorgate car turn around and drive off and then wound down his window to speak to the policeman.

'Josh Thornton. I'm going up to Hillside for the night.'

'Pop your boot please, sir.'

He looked a little nonplussed but did as they requested. He heard the boot close with a bang and the officer returned to his window.

'Thank you, sir. We're taking no chances. Have a good night.'

Josh thanked him and drove up to the house feeling impressed. They quite rightly didn't trust anybody. He heard the growl of the dog as he put a foot outside the driver door. He stopped, not sure what to do.

Another policeman came up to him, this one holding tightly on to a dog leash attached to a massive German Shepherd.

'Luther, stay.'

The dog dropped down and the policeman opened the driver door. 'You're okay now, sir, but please don't walk about outside tonight. The other adults in the house have been advised.'

Josh nodded. He had nothing to say. He kept an eye on the dog all the way up to the front door. Once inside, he found himself wishing Treverick would actually turn up...

The tree looked magnificent. The children's presents were piled underneath the tree and spilling out across the carpet. To one side was a folding table with a large pile of birthday presents and cards and Lauren had left on the tree lights. It was a magical display to greet the children when they came downstairs the next morning.

It was at that point that Josh changed his mind about wanting Treverick to turn up. He realised it would completely spoil Christmas for the children and that above all the others, Grace needed to see the festive season in all its glory. She didn't need to be woken by the sound of dogs barking, or the report from a gun; she needed normality.

Pilot entered the room and stood by him.

'Looks lovely, doesn't it?'

Josh nodded.

'She'll love it.' Both men knew who 'she' was.

'Okay,' said Pilot, 'there's an armed officer positioned at the top of the stairs and we'll actually be in Grace's room. I've had about three hours sleep while Lauren was doing all of this so I'll be okay all night. If you feel the need to nap, come out on to the landing. There's a comfy chair there. And it's just outside Grace's room, so if I need you I can easily get to you.'

'Where are Mark's men?'

'At various points inside and out. Iain is covering this room and the patio area and I think Sam has drawn the short straw with the top of the drive area. He's in for a cold night.'

'Is that all we have?'

'No. We have two police officers with dogs, two armed police officers and four of Mark's men. And us.'

'If he comes.'

Pilot looked at him. 'You don't think he will?'

'Well, let's think about this logically. He deliberately said *See you Christmas Eve* in that grotto. When has he ever given us advance warning before? There was definitely no indication of the bomb under David's car and no warning at all of the bullet that came within a hairsbreadth of taking out Freda. He is one of the most devious men out there and he'll know what is waiting here tonight. So, no, I don't think he'll come tonight. I think he said that just to wind us up. He knows we cannot have this level of protection all the time. He'll turn up when we've dropped our guard. I don't know what we can do, Pilot.'

'For tonight, we stick to the plan. I'm not leaving my daughter at all. When she wakes up, I'll be there.'

Josh nodded. 'Of course. I wasn't suggesting anything different. Let's go get comfortable.'

They climbed the stairs and walked along the long landing to the end. Grace's door faced the room now used by Jess and she must have been listening for them. She opened her door and whispered,

'Good luck, you two. And take care.' Pilot handed her two gifts, one to be placed in Noah's cot and the other to be placed on the end of Olivia's bed.

'For the ends of their beds,' he explained.

Lauren and Pilot had decided to leave just one gift on the bed, and put the rest around the tree. Jess took them and Pilot said he would place Grace's on her bed.

Pilot had already placed two chairs in Grace's room and put two bottles of water on the bookcase that was rapidly filling up with books. They moved as quietly as they could and settled down for the long night ahead of them. Both had brought a book with them knowing they would be able to see by the light of the lamp that Grace liked to have on at all times. Pilot's right hand rested on a gun placed on the small table between the two chairs.

She was laid on her left side, her back to them. Pilot felt an overwhelming upsurge of love for the little girl. He hoped Josh hadn't noticed the moisture in his eyes. Josh had done, but said nothing.

Grace lay very still with her eyes tightly closed, controlling her breathing so they didn't know she hadn't yet given in to sleep. Mummy had told her to go straight to sleep so that Father Christmas could call with her presents and she had simply nodded.

She had learnt not to show any sign of life when a man came into her room in the dead of night.

Chapter 30

To Josh it felt anticlimactic. For Pilot it was relief. Josh had clearly read the situation correctly and Pilot put it down to being one step removed from the issue. As Grace's Papa, he was too close. As Grace's uncle, Josh had used logic. And had been right.

Grace had finally succumbed to sleep by about one o'clock and had woken just after seven o'clock. At around five o'clock, Josh had moved out of her room and on to the chair on the landing. Pilot had put Grace's gift on her bed at the same time, his Father Christmas duties now complete.

By 7.15 am, all three children were downstairs and staring in awe at the massive pile of gifts. Lauren was giddy with relief. Josh kissed everyone and disappeared back to Moorgate, to join the others for bacon sandwiches and champagne for breakfast. A good start to what they prayed would be a good day.

During the opening of the presents, Grace spoke very little. Olivia chatted constantly and had to immediately take each gift out of its packaging before going on to the next one but Grace seemed overwhelmed.

Lauren put her arms round the little girl and held her tightly.

'You have nothing to fear, sweetheart,' she whispered. 'You're safe here and we love you very much. Would you like some help opening your gifts?'

Grace shook her head.

'No, thank you. But can I leave them for a bit? There are too many. I...' She looked around the room and burst into tears.

'What's wrong, Grace?' Pilot moved across to her.

'He came.'

'What?'

'Father Christmas. He came during the night and I fell asleep. I tried not to fall asleep, Papa, but I had to because I couldn't keep my eyes open any longer. Did he touch me, Papa, did he touch me?'

Her parents stared at each other in horror.

'No, my love, Father Christmas doesn't touch anyone except his reindeer. He just delivers gifts to all the children in the world.'

'He's never delivered to me before.'

Jess rescued them.

'Ah, but did you ever send him a letter asking for anything?'

They had spent the best part of an afternoon composing letters for posting to Father Christmas; Grace had done two, one for her and one for Noah. Jess had helped Olivia with hers.

Grace shook her head.

'Then he wouldn't have known where to deliver to, would he? But now he does.'

'But he does touch children. He touched me in the grotto!' Grace was getting increasingly distraught.

'He's just one of Santa's helpers. He's not the real Father Christmas.' Lauren tried to soothe her anxious daughter.

'I know.' Grace was almost screaming. 'I know he wasn't real. It was him … It was Ronald! And he touched me. Did he come in the night?'

Olivia was looking at her sister, bewilderment etched into her features. She had never seen Grace so much as raise her voice before and now everything seemed to be going wrong.

'Why didn't you say something, Grace?' Pilot asked. 'Why didn't you scream inside that grotto?'

'Because I didn't realise until I got outside. He smells strange. I smelt that when he pulled me to him. And then when I opened my present I knew I was right. I didn't need to say anything after that because you rang Jake and we had lots of visitors, so I didn't bother. I knew Jake would know what to do.' Grace was becoming quieter.

Lauren pulled her on to the settee.

'Okay, here's everything you need to know. That man in the grotto was Ronald but because we had taken you, you had nothing to fear. We, your Papa and I, didn't know it was him. He ran away as soon as we left with you. The Father Christmas who came here last night is the real Father Christmas and he brought all these gifts for you, Olivia and Noah. He is a good man, Grace, and would never hurt a child. He loves all children.'

She was now very much calmer and looked up at her mother. 'Okay. So Ronald didn't leave that present on my bed, it was the real Father Christmas?'

'That's right.'

She now turned to her father. 'So did you see him? You stayed in my room all night, didn't you?'

Pilot realised his daughter must have still been awake when he and Josh had started their guard duties.

'Yes, I did but I had to go for a wee and when I came back the present was there.'

Grace thought that one through, then nodded. 'Okay. I think I understand. I don't want to open anymore just now. Can I just watch Olivia and Noah open theirs?'

Lauren breathed a sigh of relief. Who would have thought that a man in a red suit could cause so much trouble?

'Of course. You can open them anytime you want.'

The rest of the morning was uneventful; Lauren was grateful. She began the mammoth job of cooking the Christmas meal and at around one o'clock the Moorgate visitors arrived. The security people had now been significantly reduced; the dog handlers had disappeared, the armed officers also. The two patrol car officers were ever present and there was just one of Mark's men on duty at Moorgate and one at Hillside.

Lauren had set the table for twelve and hoped that nine-month-old Noah wouldn't create too much havoc when his high chair was pushed up to the table. The table itself looked beautiful; a small centrepiece, kept deliberately low so that her guests wouldn't have to strain to see over the top at the opposite person, small candles the length of the large table, gleaming white table linen, and place cards made by Jess and Grace. She stepped back and checked that everything was perfect.

Ninety minutes later, the table looked as if a bomb had landed on it. It had been a truly successful meal in which the wine had flowed endlessly. Josh had produced a box of party poppers, which had caused major uproar and that the children had loved. The dining room was covered in streamers, the pristine white tablecloth spattered with red, rose and white wine and privately Lauren thought it might take her till Easter to clean it all up, not that she minded as, in spite of the sadness caused by David's absence, so far Christmas was going very well and the children were really enjoying themselves.

With the exception of Ken, Brenda and Freda who had declined coffee and mints and within five minutes of their escape into the Buckingham wing, had fallen asleep, the rest went into the lounge.

Lauren served up coffee and Josh and Jess sat on the floor with the children, playing with the toys that were scattered around from the mammoth opening session in the morning. There was a small pile of around half a dozen brightly wrapped gifts still underneath the tree for Grace to open.

She sat close to the tree and pulled one of the presents towards her.

'It's from Nan Brenda and Granddad Ken.' She carefully removed the wrapping paper and revealed a Barbie doll. 'Oh, that's beautiful.'

She placed it carefully to one side and pulled out another package. 'This one's from you, Josh.'

He looked puzzled. 'Well I know I'm the best uncle ever, but I haven't a clue what that is. Maybe it's something I picked up for you while we were still in St. Louis. We brought a couple of things over with us.'

She looked at the label one more time. 'It definitely says Josh.'

'Pilot...' Josh turned to his brother in law.

Pilot understood. Josh would have put Uncle Josh.

'Grace, I think that one's a mistake. Just hand it to me and carry on with the rest.'

She didn't argue, just handed over the package and then turned to pick up another one from under the tree. Pilot and Josh left the room with Pilot handling the parcel carefully. He had no idea what was in it but was taking no chances. They went out of the front door and on to the lawn where Pilot laid it down, carefully.

Iain Dunne walked across to them. He had been on duty for about thirty seconds.

'Hey, you two,' he said, 'what's this? Socks you didn't want?'

Pilot stood and pointed at the package.

'This is a package for Grace. It says on the label *To Grace with love from Josh.* To all of my children he is Uncle Josh, not Josh. And this isn't his writing. He didn't write it, Iain.' Pilot could hear an edge of panic in his own voice and he swallowed.

'Contact Dunbar, will you. He'll know what to do. I don't think it's a bomb, it doesn't feel very heavy, but we all know to our cost that he can make bombs...'

Iain rang Dunbar on his mobile phone and Dunbar immediately called in everyone he considered to be necessary. Pilot and Josh were ushered back into the house by a professional Iain, all first names dispensed with and replaced by sir. The package remained where Pilot had placed it, in the middle of the large lawn so loved by John Thornton.

Lauren was in the lounge trying desperately to lighten the atmosphere and keep the children from guessing there was a problem. Grace had now got to the end of the parcels and Pat was clearing away the paper. 'And now you just have your birthday presents,' she joked to the little girl.

'I'm so tired of parcels, Nan Pat,' she said.

'I know. It wasn't very clever of your Mummy and Daddy to have you on Christmas Day, was it?'

'Papa.' Grace looked angry. 'He's not Daddy, he's Papa. Don't call him Daddy.'

Pat was devastated. This granddaughter was so precious; she would have given everything to take back the words she had used.

'Grace!' Lauren intervened and she heard a muttered *sorry, Nan Pat* before the little girl ran from the room. She stood to follow her but Pat said,

'Let me go.'

Pat and Grace were both full of smiles when they returned five minutes later and Pat just nodded in Lauren's direction. Crisis averted.

Chapter 31

Dunbar stared at the parcel that had been left in the middle of the lawn, despair etched on to his face. *How the fuck had Treverick managed to get this inside the fortress that was Hillside?*

He had called in experts who had stated quite categorically that it wasn't a bomb and he watched as one of the men pulled on gloves before lifting it and carrying it towards the patio area. Once there, he placed it on a garden table. He carefully peeled off the outer wrapping with the gift card still attached to it and put it in an evidence bag. Revealed underneath was a different gift card. This one said,

Happy Christmas my Angel
Love
Daddy
xxx

It had been sellotaped to the top of a maroon box that looked as though it had come from a jeweller. When the top was removed a silver pendant and chain was revealed. Dunbar stepped forward to look at the box but it had no jewellers name on it, no identification marks at all.

The pendant was a tiny angel.

Following the terse phone call from him, DC Johnson had accompanied his boss and now Dunbar turned to the young constable..

'Andy, you can go home to that family of yours. I'm sorry to have called you out but if this had been a bomb...'

'Are you going home, sir?'

'Not yet.'

'Then I'll go when you go. How can this bastard carry on scaring this little lass like this? What do you want me to do?'

'Come in the house with me. We have to talk to them but we need to get the children out of the way. Some Christmas this has been. Take notes, will you, while I try to get to the bottom of how this can have happened?'

Dunbar put the box and the pendant into another evidence bag and handed it to Andy for him to put with the first bag.

They walked towards the patio doors and Dunbar tapped on the window. He saw Grace's face light up and she waved at him. He waved back and waited for Pilot to unlock the doors.

'Okay, we need to talk. Jess, can I ask you...'

She nodded.

'Come on, mes enfants; let's take some of these toys upstairs to play with. There are too many big people down here.'

Grace and Olivia giggled and ran for the stairs. Jess scooped up an almost sleeping Noah and carried him up to join his sisters.

The remaining members of the family turned expectant faces towards Dunbar.

'First of all,' he said, 'well done on the way you acted, Pilot. A bit foolhardy, maybe, but you got it away from the house.'

'Foolhardy?'

'If it had been a bomb at the very least it would have blown off your hand. Or killed you. Foolhardy.'

Pilot looked down at the floor, resting his elbows on his knees. 'And just what else could I have done?' he muttered. 'Let it kill my children?'

Dunbar smiled at him. 'You did exactly what I would have done.'

He held up the evidence bags and read out the card that had been hidden by the outer wrapping paper. He heard a strangled sob from Lauren and turned to her.

'We now have to find out how this appeared under your tree. Is that where Grace got it from?'

'Yes.' Lauren paled. 'Does this mean...?'

'That he's been in here? Well, that's a starting point for us. Have you had anyone in except the close family since you put those gifts there? And where were they before Santa delivered?'

'They were in the utility room in big black bags. Four black bags.' Lauren was picturing the sight that had greeted her when she went into the room at nine o'clock on Christmas Eve. 'I don't think anything had been disturbed; it seemed to be just as I had left it. I had actually sealed all the bags with sellotape just in case Grace wandered in and none of that tape had been removed. So, even if someone had got in the house, they certainly didn't tamper with the bags.'

Dunbar nodded, his brain racing.

'So, you put the presents under the tree around nine o'clock. Tell me exactly what you did, Lauren.'

'The bag with the gifts from us was sorted first. I went through it and put three piles of parcels, one pile per child. It was a bit confusing; there were a lot of presents. I took out three gifts, one for each of the children, so that Pilot could take them up with him when he went to sit in Grace's room for the night. After I had done all that, I placed those three piles underneath the tree. Our gifts were nearest to the central stem. Then I emptied the bag from Brenda and Ken. I would say there were about a dozen gifts in that bag and I added them to ours. The next bag was from Pat and...' she paused and gulped. 'I'm so sorry, Pat, I was going...'

Pat held up her hand.

'Say it, Lauren. Don't leave David out. He was in my head all the time I was shopping for the children. He's here; you won't upset me by talking about him.'

'I know. So, I emptied Pat and David's bag next and their gifts sort of surrounded the ones I had already done.'

She paused for a moment, looked at the tree and carried on. 'Just checking I'm remembering properly,' she said. 'So, next was the last bag, the one from Freda, Josh and Dawn. This one had loads of presents in it; they'd bought lots of little gifts, crayons, colouring books, paints, books, that sort of thing. They had been wrapped in all different papers and it was a glorious jumble when I took them out. It took ages to sort, and that was the last bag. I'm telling you, Jake; none of those bags had had the tape removed.'

Dunbar turned to Dawn.

'When did you start buying all these gifts?'

'As soon as we got here from St.Louis. We brought lots of things with us and then topped it up here.'

'When did you bring the gifts to Hillside?'

'Last weekend. I brought them in a massive shopping bag and I helped Lauren transfer them into a black plastic bag so that I could take the shopping bag back with me. I was with her when she sealed it so I know it was secure. She didn't want inquisitive children spoiling anything about this Christmas.'

'So how did he do it? How did he get into our house and put that damn present under the tree?'

'I'm pretty certain you put it under the tree, Lauren. I think he got into Moorgate. I don't know how yet, but don't forget what we're dealing with here. He's so bloody smart. But he'll slip up one day.'

Pat reached for Dawn's hand and they looked at each other. He'd got into Moorgate? With all the security they had?

'So you think he got in somehow, simply placed the present in with the others and got out again?'

Dunbar nodded. 'That's exactly what I think. Was there ever a point when the house was empty since you got back from the States?'

Again Pat and Dawn looked at each other, thinking. It was Josh who answered.

'We went Christmas shopping. All of us. We took Freda in the wheelchair and went to Truro. We had two of Mark's men with us, and we left one back at the house. We made it easy for him.' His tone was flat. 'But how the hell did he know?'

'He watches. He thinks as if he were you. He knew at some point you would have to go out. It's Christmas. He simply waited. And of course, there's the added bonus being that when you go out the security goes with you. We protect you more than your property. We have no choice in that. He knows that.'

'So all he had to do was put a label on saying it was from Josh. I can't bear thinking about Grace opening it and if he had put Uncle Josh that's exactly what would have happened.'

Dunbar could hear the anger in Lauren's voice.

'I'm taking the paper and the gift itself as evidence. This man is getting a great deal of pleasure out of playing with your minds. Don't let him make you so angry that you slip up. Don't put yourselves in danger. Keep doing what you have been doing. The protection that is in place is keeping you safe.'

He stood and prepared to leave. DC Johnson put away his notebook and they moved towards the patio doors. Mark Carter arrived as they opened the doors and spoke quietly for five minutes or so with the two policemen before slipping inside.

He looked around for Pilot who held up a hand.

'Let's go into my office,' he said and beckoned to Josh to join them.

Mark was sporting a spectacular Christmas silk tie and Pilot pretended to shade his eyes.

'I don't know how John worked with you for all those years without going blind. I've seen lots of your ties, Mark, but that one is something else.'

Mark grinned.

'I'm applying for the job of lead position on the sleigh next year, this will light our way round the rooftops.'

'So, you've heard about our bit of festive excitement?'

'Yes. Iain rang me. Do you want additional operatives?'

'Do we need them?'

Mark paused. He had been thinking about the plan for Hillside and Moorgate all the way from Bude.

'I don't think so. If Dunbar is right, and I think he is, then Treverick got lucky when you all went out together. How often does this happen? I don't think we need to increase cover except for occasional one-off days. If, for example, you were all meeting up for something and it meant empty properties, then we would provide additional cover but I still think you have enough men for normal everyday life. You are still taking all the usual precautions like locking doors when you're inside?'

Pilot nodded. 'Always.'

'Mark...' Josh looked uncomfortable.

Mark turned his head and looked at the young man he had only come to know since John Thornton's death.

'Josh? You have a problem?'

'I don't know,' he said. 'Maybe I just watch too much crime drama on television but he seems to be one step in front of us all the time.'

There was a gentle tap on the door and Ken Buckingham poked his head around.

'Can I join you?' he said quietly and came into the room without waiting for an answer.

Mark stood and pulled a chair towards them.

'Please,' he said, indicating the chair.

Ken sat down and looked around him.

'Stop leaving me out,' was his opening gambit.

'What?' Pilot looked shocked.

'I said, stop leaving me out. I know I'm in my seventies but I'm fit – my God, Pilot, I've only retired from a pretty hardworking life in the last six months, so I'm here to help. Lauren is my granddaughter, Grace my great granddaughter and you're keeping both Brenda and I out of it because you think we're too old.'

Both Pilot and Josh laughed; Mark would have done if he hadn't been there in a professional capacity. He permitted himself a smile.

Pilot was the first to respond.

'For Heaven's sake, Ken. I'm sorry if you feel like that but that's not how it is. Neither Josh nor I actually do anything except have meetings with Mark, and they're very rare. Believe me, if we need you for anything we'll make damn sure we rope you in. Your biggest job is protecting this end of the house by just being aware, making sure alarms are set and basically keeping your eyes open, and looking after Brenda. She's not as mobile as you but I never worry about her because she's got you.'

Ken looked grumpy. 'Us Yorkshire lads get a bit miffed if we're left out t'loop,' he said. 'So what's to do then? Where do we go now?'

And then Mark did laugh.

'God, I've missed that Yorkshire accent, Ken. What's to do is that we remain vigilant. We're keeping the protection at the same level and I might just say I'm glad Christmas and shopping trips are out of the way. Nobody is going out tomorrow are they? No visits to sales or anything? I really wouldn't recommend it.'

'Er...'

Three pairs of eyes turned to Josh and they all waited for him to carry on.

'I am.'

'What? Where?' Pilot looked puzzled.

'Is nothing secret here?' Josh countered. 'If you really have to know, I'm taking Jess out for a meal tomorrow night, down in Padstow.'

There was silence.

'You'll take protection,' Mark said firmly.

Pilot, Ken and Josh doubled up with laughter; Mark's face turned red as he realised what he had said.

'Stop! You know what I mean, you set of dirty minded individuals. Josh, if you go, take Sam with you. He'll be discreet but we know Treverick is in the area and I won't risk any more lives.'

The laughter died at the mention of Treverick's name and Josh agreed to Mark's request. He knew Jess would understand; she had lived with the fear for quite some time now.

'I'll need to know where you're taking Jess, Josh, so that I can brief Sam. And be careful...' The laughter erupted again and he stood up.

'Right, I'm going. I can't say anything and have you take it seriously. Have a good time, Josh … and be vigilant.'

Pilot escorted him to the patio doors and everyone called goodnight. The locks were checked and peace of some sort began to settle over Hillside.

Josh drove the Moorgate residents home around eleven o'clock but not before he had spoken to Jess. She had understood completely and even suggested they postpone.

'I don't want to postpone,' he said. 'It's taken me three weeks to ask you and I'd like us to go tomorrow night. And it's booked.'

'Okay,' she said quietly. 'We'll just have to watch what's going on around us. And we'll have Sam. Thank you, Josh, I'm looking forward to it.'

That had been an interesting Christmas. It seemed they had found his gift to his beautiful Angel before she had chance to open it. They must have thought it was another bomb. But he had decided the next one to die wouldn't be by bomb.

He would never kill his Angel. All he wanted was for her to know he thought of her all the time.

Today was a good day. Boxing Day and he had been given somewhere to stay where he didn't have to pretend. His new identification was in place and his next move was almost worked out. There were many pitfalls to the next one because the police were ever more on the alert, but he knew he would triumph.

Very soon.

Chapter 32

Dawn was sitting in the lounge to the right of the huge bay window at Moorgate. The magnificent Christmas tree took up most of the space in the window area and she thought that this was what she wanted in the house she was seeking; plenty of room, space for the things in life she enjoyed.

She missed John so much and felt an almost permanent ache inside her when she thought of all they could have achieved together. It was criminal that he should have died so young with such an incredible talent that he should have still been sharing with a world eager for more of his books.

She had talked of John so many times with David; he was convinced that Amy had somehow managed to conceal the life-saving pills that John had needed in those final moments. Amy's strange behaviour of visiting Dawn at her house - the mistress as she scathingly called her - had convinced Dawn that Amy had been in some way to blame. Dawn would never know for definite, but...

She sighed and brushed away the tear that leaked from her eye. She had his books. She had photos of a shared life. She had Josh. Her son was almost a mirror image of John and yet in character was totally different. His work in the States had been in accountancy and when they had taken the decision to return to England, he had intimated he might look for a different career move. Treverick had stopped that, temporarily. The security issues around going into a workplace were insurmountable. David had lost his life by simply 'going into work.'

The door opened and Pat walked through with a tray of mince pies and a full coffee pot.

'We need this,' she said and pulled a small table towards Dawn's chair.

'Too right.'

The two women were quiet while they filled their plates and poured the coffee and then Pat looked at her friend. 'You ok?'

Dawn shook her head.

'No. John and David were as close as brothers and now they're both gone. I miss them.'

Pat nodded. 'And both of their deaths are ultimately down to Amy Thornton.'

'You blame her and not Treverick?'

Pat shrugged her shoulders. 'Oh, I don't know. Dawn. I blame everybody. David's death is still too raw. I suppose I blame Amy because she's the one who kept Treverick tied to us even if she didn't know it. And let's face it; she paid the ultimate price, didn't she?'

Dawn sipped at her drink. 'She did. What worries me is how many more he will take out. He may have been slightly off with his aim when he shot Freda, but she's so frail as a result. He took the rest of her life really. She can't walk more than a couple of steps now but more than anything he's made her afraid. Freda afraid! That would have been unthinkable. She was the rock for John. He had so much admiration for her, loved her forthrightness and the way she never pulled punches. Now she says very little.'

'I've left her to sleep in this morning. It was a busy day yesterday and a late night so I'll go and wake her in an hour or so if she's still not up.'

'I haven't called Josh. I'll leave him. He's going out with Jess tonight so that will be another late one, I don't doubt. I like Jess.'

'Me too. Did he leave anyone special in the States?'

'About a hundred, I think,' Dawn laughed. 'But nobody serious. He was in with quite a big crowd of friends and he's in touch with them all the time even now but no, I don't think his heart is over in the States.'

'Good. We need him here, not pining for lost loves.'

Dawn smiled. 'There's enough of that for the two of us.'

They sat in near silence waiting for the rest of their world to come to life and eventually Pat went to refill the coffee pot.

'I'll do this and then I'll take a cup of tea in to Freda. She'll be annoyed if I don't wake her soon and she scares me,' she joked.

Dawn picked up a magazine and began to flick through its pages, not really reading it but looking at pictures. There were quite a few house interiors and, Ronald Treverick or no Ronald Treverick, their search would need to start soon for their own accommodation, She had a few ideas of what she wanted...

'Dawn, oh God, Dawn...quick, come here.'

Dawn dropped the magazine and ran across to the doorway leading into Freda's suite. Pat was white.

'I think she's gone...'

At first Dawn didn't realise what Pat meant. Gone? Packed her bags? And then understanding hit her.

'No.' The single word was long and drawn out.

They approached the bed and it was clear that Freda had died during the night. She still had on her reading glasses; a book had fallen to one side with her hand still touching it and her late night cup of tea was now cold on the bedside table.

Pat knelt by the bed and took hold of Freda's right hand. She kissed the cold fingers and turned to Dawn.

'Freda's doctor is the top number on the pad by the phone. Can you call him? It's his home number so he should answer. If not we need to ring – oh, I don't know. Who, what do we ring?'

'I'll be two minutes.'

She spoke to the doctor, Freda's lifelong friend and employer for many years, and he was there within quarter of an hour. Josh was downstairs still in pyjama bottoms and a t-shirt with St. Louis stamped on it. He supported the two women and took charge of notifying everyone at Hillside. Dunbar arrived shortly after the doctor but was reassured to know that Freda had died of natural causes. He left soon after to leave the family to grieve in their own way but privately he knew it was another death down to Treverick.

Brenda was devastated. She had met Freda on the day she had met Jack – brother and sister had accompanied each other to a dance and then separated. Jack had asked Brenda to dance and until the day of his death, they had never been apart. Brenda had been introduced to Freda at the dance; she had joined them to put Tommy Taylor off pursuing her. She remembered the first words she ever heard from Freda – *get me out of here, Jack, before I hit Tommy Taylor with a bottle.*

Jack had laughed as he did a lot until the day Treverick entered their lives. He had linked arms with his sister on one side and Brenda on the other and they had left the dance hall together. He had walked Freda home first and then taken Brenda back to hers.

Brenda and Freda had shared the destructive assault on Amelia, the trauma of Jack's early death from cancer, the appearance of Ken a few years later, the un-timely deaths of John and Amy and Brenda felt bereft. Freda had been much more than a sister-in-law; she had been the glue in the family.

Freda's body had been taken to the funeral home and everyone except the children and Jess were at Moorgate. Brenda had spent five minutes alone with Freda before they had taken her away and she held the memory close in her heart. She had been comforted by the peaceful look on Freda's face and knew the end had been sudden and on her terms - reading while enjoying the final half hour of the day comfortably resting in bed.

'Ken,' she whispered. 'I want to go home. Take me back to Hillside, please.'

He went to retrieve their coats from the cloakroom and explained to Josh that Brenda wanted to go. He nodded. 'I'll take you.'

They said their goodbyes and within five minutes were back at Hillside. Brenda sat quietly in their own lounge while Ken made her a drink. She was lost in thought and Ken chose the option of not saying anything. He knew she would speak when she was ready.

Josh ran up the stairs to find Jess; he guessed the children would be in the playroom enjoying their gifts from the previous day's haul. She greeted him with a half smile, all too aware of the importance of the woman who had just died.

'Is everyone ok?'

He shook his head.

'Far from it. I've brought Ken and Brenda back here. It's knocked Brenda for six and I think she just needs Ken at the moment. She was very close to Freda, known her forever. I wanted to bring them back because I wanted to see you. I hope you don't mind but I think we have to postpone tonight.'

'Don't be silly. Of course, I don't mind. It wouldn't feel right going out. I'll stay in and watch a film or something.'

'Can I stay in with you?'

She nodded. 'Yes. I'd like that. Now, everything's fine here. Go back to Moorgate, you might be needed there. I'll see you tonight. I'll tell Lauren what's happening when she gets back.' She placed a swift kiss on his cheek and he grinned. Yes!!

Josh went back downstairs, out onto the driveway and climbed into the Mondeo. He was accompanied to Moorgate and then waved at the following car to say he was safe. He felt angry at all the organisation that was required when any of them wanted to move beyond the boundaries of their home; where *was* the man who was causing all this disorder and turmoil? He had to be somewhere close. And how come he seemed to know everything about them, their movements, even their plans?

Inside Moorgate, everyone was quiet, thinking his or her own thoughts about Freda.

'Are the children ok, Josh?' Lauren asked. 'Jess is a real star. She never seems to get her day off.'

'They're fine, Lauren. Jess is coping perfectly well. Noah was asleep and the two girls were making a bit of a mess on the painting table.'

She smiled. 'Thank you. I really don't know what we would have done without her. Are you still going out tonight?'

He shook his head. 'No, she'll tell you herself when you get back to Hillside. We've decided to postpone. It just doesn't seem right. We're going to watch a film at Hillside instead. Either something that's on television or a DVD from her collection.'

There was a tap on the window and Lauren visibly flinched. Mark's tie, a bright orange with emerald green stripes silk affair was the first thing they saw. Pat pointed towards the door and he nodded. He moved away and Pat went to let him in.

'You've heard?' she asked.

'Yes. I knew pretty quickly, but I didn't want to intrude. Is everyone ok?'

'Far from it. Treverick did this, Mark. I know it will be on the death certificate as natural causes but he caused it. There was nothing wrong with her until she took that bullet.'

He pulled her to him and held her tightly. Kissing the top of her head, he simply said,

'I know.'

They moved into the lounge together and everyone turned to him. Greetings taken care of, he said how sorry he was. Freda had been such a joy in his life for quite a long time, he would miss her wit, and her spade is a spade attitude.

He turned to Pilot. 'We need to make extra plans for whenever the funeral is to be but we'll deal with that nearer the date. Treverick will find out about this whether you try to keep it quiet or not so don't deny her the obituary she deserves. Let everyone in this community know one of their leading lights is gone and let's all celebrate her life. The police will put extra men on and so will I. We'll have your backs.'

Pilot nodded. 'You've mirrored my feelings exactly, Mark. Freda wanted cremation so we will be spared the graveside ritual and that should make things a little easier but she will have exactly what she wanted.'

'She's left instructions?' Lauren looked at her husband, her eyebrows raised.

'Yes. I've got an envelope with some bits and bobs in it. Whenever she thought of something, she would write it down and give it to me to put in what she called "the afterlife collection." She's chosen her music, her quotations, everything. Some of it is funny, some very serious. She mentions you, Mark, specifically. She wants you to forget the black tie bit; she wants you in a red and white striped one. And she's actually left you a tie pin to wear with it with her name on.'

Mark laughed uproariously.

'God, I loved that woman! And I'll be honoured to follow her wishes.'

Pilot looked around. 'And I'll be letting the rest of you know what she's requested as soon as I've worked my way through it. This should be a very good funeral.'

Grace was sad. Her Mummy had taken them into the lounge and explained about Aunt Freda not being there anymore and she now felt very sad. She liked Aunt Freda. She didn't like it when she was shot but Aunt Freda kept saying she was getting better. And she hadn't got better, she'd died.

Freda had bought both 'her girls' matching pink jumpers for Christmas and Grace wondered if they should go and put them on.

'Olivia,' she said. 'Come with me.'

The little girl crossed the room and looked expectantly at her older sister. 'Let's go upstairs for a bit.' Olivia nodded, ever compliant, and they disappeared to the playroom where all the Christmas presents had been taken prior to being sorted into relevant places.

Grace rummaged around until both the jumpers came to light. She looked at the labels to make sure she was giving Olivia the smaller size and handed it over.

'Let's put them on.'

There was very little difference in the sizing. Grace was so small for her age and took a size smaller than the recommended size. They put them on and looked in the mirror.

Grace put her arm around her younger sister and said they both looked lovely. Olivia said it was very pink. They went back downstairs and Lauren burst into tears.

Grace was devastated. What had she done? Would she be punished? Olivia looked puzzled by the strange behaviour but wasn't the slightest bit worried. She sensed the panic in Grace and reached out to hold her hand.

'She'll be okay,' she whispered, 'she's just upset about Aunt Freda.'

Pilot pulled his daughters towards him and kissed them both.

'Just bear with your Mummy. She's having a bad day. You both look lovely in your new jumpers. Have you put them on because Aunt Freda bought them?'

Grace nodded miserably.

'I'm sorry, Papa. It wasn't Olivia's fault. I told her to do it.'

He felt sick. It was clear Grace still panicked every time she thought she had done something wrong; it was just as clear she expected to be punished.

'Sweetheart, neither of you has done anything wrong. This is a lovely idea wearing the jumpers for Aunt Freda and I'm sure she's smiling down on the pair of you for doing this for her. Mummy didn't cry because you had done something wrong, she cried because you had done something right. And she already misses Aunt Freda very much, as I'm sure both of you do.'

'Is she with Granddad David?'

It occurred to Pilot that he could very easily be lumbered with awkward questions here and it briefly crossed his mind that maybe he should burst into tears and leave the room but he didn't.

'Yes, I'm sure she is.'

'But he's in the ground. We went to his grave with the ring.'

'The wreath, Grace. It's called a wreath. And it's only Granddad's body that is in the ground. His soul is in Heaven as is Aunt Freda's.'

'Soul?' This was from a wide-eyed Olivia.

'Look girls, I just need to go and make sure Mummy's okay, make sure she's stopped crying. Please keep your jumpers on. Aunt Freda would have loved to see the pair of you in them. Wear them for her. Mummy will explain about soul when she's feeling better. Don't forget to ask her, Grace, will you?'

'I won't, Papa.' Grace was now very serious.

He watched them climb the stairs back up to the playroom then went to find his wife. She was with Ken and

Brenda who were all helping themselves to tissues from an almost empty tissue box.

'Tea, anyone?' he asked, and they all nodded.

'Are my girls all right?' a tearful Lauren asked. 'They looked so lovely in Freda's jumpers and I just felt pole-axed. Have you made sure they know they haven't done anything wrong?'

'Oh yes, my love. Completely. Erm ... just one issue, though. You might want to think about souls and such-like. Mmmm. It sort of cropped up. I'll make the tea, shall I?'

Chapter 33

Dunbar gazed at the whiteboard with its assortment of pictures and words. His own office was quiet but he was all too aware of the cacophony of noise in the outer one where everyone involved with the case was working.

He knew he had to go back to the beginning. He was missing something and whatever it was, everyone else was missing it, too.

He started with Angel's escape. He looked once more over the interview with the Wainwrights but they couldn't have been anything more than totally random. Angel had chosen their red door; they hadn't enticed her in first. They had repeated everything Angel had said as far as their memories held out and he spent some time looking down that part of the interview but it revealed nothing new.

The file was thick; he began turning over pages, reading until his headache began to really surface. He could find nothing.

He stood and went to his coat hanging behind the door. In the inside pocket he hoped to find painkillers. There were none. He went out into the main office and asked if anyone had any and Sarah Miller waved a strip in the air.

'Thank you,' he said taking them from her and popping two tablets out.

'You're welcome; I'd just taken two myself.'

'You working on anything specific?'

'Is there anything specific? You want me to concentrate on something?'

He sighed. 'Not really. I'm reading through everything. We are missing something but whatever it is, it's staying hidden. How the hell did he get into Moorgate with that gift? What's his plan for Freda Andrew's funeral? Because I can't believe he'll let that go by without doing something. It's just so damn frustrating.'

'Then let's try to outthink him. Let's be there first this time.'

He looked at her for a long moment and said 'Come into my office. I'll clear the desk.'

She followed him, grabbing a pen as she left her own work-station. His version of clearing his desk involved stacking everything on it into a big pile and putting it on to the floor. He then handed her a large notepad and sat down facing her.

'Okay. Ideas?'

She opened the pad and wrote the date on the first page while she gathered her thoughts.

'Is Grace going to be there?'

'No, they wouldn't take that risk.'

'Then the main focus of our protection has to be Hillside or Moorgate, wherever she will be. Because the only thing that seems to be a constant throughout all this is that he wants her back with him. God, sir, that doesn't bear thinking about.'

'No it doesn't. So you think he won't be at the funeral?'

'I think he could probably work it out that Grace won't be there and he will have the possibility of getting his Angel back from the house. I think we have to get Grace, Olivia and Noah away from here, get them into a safe house with their Nanny – Jess is she called? – and take that stress away from everyone while this funeral is going on.'

She scribbled down some more notes but made no reference to them.

'You're right. I'll go see them tonight. But I'll just speak to Pilot and Lauren – oh and Jess, of course. I'll have to reassure Jess that it will be a safe house and she will have protection with her at all times. I don't want anyone else in the family to know.'

'Why not?' Sarah stared him in the face almost daring him not to answer her.

'Because...' he hesitated as if deciding whether to say his thoughts aloud.

She showed him the note on her pad that she had just written.

Treverick has to have an accomplice, someone close to the family or in the family. Security men? Police?

The mood at Hillside was sombre. Brenda wasn't taking Freda's death easily and Ken could only stand by helplessly and watch her crumble. He hugged her when she needed a hug, kissed her when she needed a kiss but he felt it wasn't enough.

He was scared. He couldn't imagine a life without Brenda and she had aged overnight. He covered her with a soft throw and kissed her head. She had gone for a rest in their bedroom but had quickly fallen asleep.

He closed the door quietly and then took the unusual step of leaving what they laughingly termed *The Buckingham Wing.* He went through to find Pilot.

Pilot was going through his mail, sitting in front of his computer. Mail and newspapers were now delivered daily by one of the officers who sat in the police car all day. Nobody was allowed up the drive, other than family members.

'Sorry to bother you, Pilot...'

Pilot looked up in surprise. Since Ken and Brenda had moved in, they saw less of them than when they lived at Stonebrook Cottage.

'You need something, Ken?'

He shook his head. 'No. Just a bit of company really. But you're busy, I'll go.'

'I'm not busy. More filling in the time to stop me thinking. Come on. I'll make us some tea.'

They moved into the lounge. The tree was flashing its lights and everything appeared normal. Ken could hear the chatter of children's voices and the hum of a vacuum cleaner; he guessed the rest of the family were upstairs.

Ken sat down and waited for Pilot. He came in from the kitchen carrying a tray with a teapot, cups and plate of biscuits.

'Eat,' Pilot ordered, 'because if you and Brenda are anything like us, food hasn't been much in our thoughts since yesterday.'

Ken smiled. 'You're right. I can't get Brenda to have anything. She's sleeping now and I simply didn't want to sit on my own. When you're on your own, you start to think and then you end up crying and I'm from Yorkshire and Yorkshiremen don't cry. But this one did yesterday.'

Pilot nodded. 'Me too. We're going tomorrow to make the funeral arrangements and I can't tell you how much I'm dreading that. I've been going through her 'afterlife' envelope – that's what caused the tears – and I've got the list of songs she wants and she wants everyone to wear something red. One little piece of paper made me smile. It was inside a sealed white envelope and she gave it me a few weeks ago, certainly before she was shot. It simply said she wanted Treverick in the coffin with her.'

Ken laughed. 'God, she can even make us smile after she's gone.'

They sat without speaking for a while until Ken stood up to leave and go back to check on Brenda.

'I'm worried about her, Pilot.'

'Brenda?'

Ken nodded.

'They were so close; Brenda and Freda and when something like this happens you start to question your own mortality. I think she's doing that. We've never considered death really and Treverick is making us do that.'

'I have no answers, Ken. When he killed Dad it was almost too much to bear but the thought that he might just be smart enough to get to Grace, or indeed any of the kids, would be unthinkable.'

Dunbar replaced the receiver and winced. He had so much respect for Mark Carter, always had done from the first day he met him. Now he had just brought that respect into question by asking him for a complete list of his employees; office staff and field operatives.

Mark had hesitated and then said,

'Yes, of course.' He hadn't needed to ask why, it didn't take a genius to work out that Dunbar suspected somebody of something and this was the information he needed to begin this aspect of the investigation. Mark stared at the phone for quite some time and then pulled the keyboard towards him. He loosened his emerald green tie before beginning to type. He could easily have copied and pasted the information but forcing himself to write the list from memory focussed his mind. He wanted to ensure it was accurate, didn't want Dunbar coming back to him asking for more. He wondered how Dunbar would take to being told he might want to look at his own staff.

He began the list with Linda Chambers, the woman he employed in the office. He had recruited Linda into his business purely because he had been impressed by the organisation of the files and other paperwork he had taken on when he had inherited the post she had held with John Thornton. He had found out at a later date that Amy Thornton had actually forced her out of the secretarial position she had enjoyed for some time and in a way he hoped that employing her would ease his conscience a little.

Although Dunbar had only requested a list, he decided to add all the contact details on a separate sheet. He had nothing to hide and he was damned sure his employees didn't either. The vetting he applied to anyone who worked for him had to be intense; the nature of his business demanded nothing less.

He started to list his field operatives beginning with Alan Shimwell, his most trusted worker who had died along with David Farmer. He wasn't sure why Dunbar wanted the list – he had simply said list everyone who at any time has had connections with the surveillance and protection detail at Hillside and Moorgate. Alan Shimwell had been at the top of his choices for that work.

Linda Chambers (office)

Alan Shimwell (d) Guy Pridmore Sam Marks
Iain Dunne Joe Bachelor
Bob Adams
Luke Stones Dom Stones
Linc Stewart
Will Dawson Martin Acker
Martyn Pearson

Gerry Williams Anthony Harvey Dave Bailey
Dan Gibson Jim Brooks Jay King

On a separate sheet of paper, he copied and pasted all the personnel contact details, printed everything off and put the four sheets into a large brown envelope. He emailed Jake Dunbar to say it was ready for collection, and sat back and waited.

Dunbar's emailed response was almost immediate.

Can you email the file, please?

His response was just as fast.

No, would prefer that you collected the package.

He had no intention of sending such personal information via email and he made sure to put a warm smile of welcome on his face when Dunbar arrived. It would do no good to antagonise the man, he thought. And he hoped Dunbar might open up about the direction of the investigation if they met face to face.

'Thank you for calling, DI Dunbar. I just thought it safer to hand them over to you. Anyone can read emails and there is a lot of data in this file.'

'No problem, Mark. I needed a chat anyway.'

'Oh?'

'Yes – I didn't want you to think we were targeting your business in any way. We're going to be questioning everybody who has had any contact at all with anyone in the Farmer extended family. And this includes our own men and women on the force. And, of course, the family.'

'That's fine,' Mark said. His tie had now resumed its normal knotted position and he was the consummate professional. 'I've given you a list of my people and then on separate sheets I've given you their contact details. I will get in touch with all of them to explain you will need to see them. I don't need to ask them to cooperate fully – they will.'

'I don't doubt for one minute that they will,' Dunbar laughed. This was a totally professional outfit and Mark was king.

'Can I offer you a coffee? Tea?'

'Coffee would be good, thanks.'

He sat down opposite Mark and watched him pour two mugs from the percolator.

'So, am I any nearer getting my men back?'

'What do you think?' Dunbar sighed. 'He's like the bloody Pimpernel, isn't he?'

Dunbar took a sip of his coffee. 'You have biscuits to go with this?'

Mark pulled open his desk drawer and produced chocolate digestives.

'Help yourself,' he said and placed them where they could both reach.

'Ok, now we've got chocolate inside us, let's think. Knowing everything you know about Treverick, where would you hide if you were him? Where's your bolt hole?''

'Close to Grace,' Mark said promptly. 'She's like a drug to him and he needs his fix. He's not going to let her go, you know. Only death will stop him.'

'We can but hope,' was Dunbar's dry response. 'So we're talking Padstow? Rock?'

'Rock's not that big, harder to hide there. My guess would be Padstow, but it is only a guess. He could be in Torquay, Newquay or somewhere like that where it's big enough for him to hide in plain sight. Cornwall's a big place, DI Dunbar.'

They both reached for another biscuit and laughed.

'Will more chocolate help our brains work better?' Mark asked.

'I think mine's stopped. I was having a chat with one of my WPCs and she came up with something, an idea, which I had been tentatively tossing around in my mind and dismissing. When she came up with it, it all made sense. She must eat more chocolate than me,' he added ruefully.

'Hence the lists,' Mark said, nodding thoughtfully.

'Hence the lists … and I will be grateful if you can let all your employees know that we'll be coming to see them over the next couple of days. I know it's not going to be easy because they work days and nights, so I'll be ringing you pretty regularly to find out where each of them are. I don't want to go getting them out of bed when they need sleep. And I have no intention of talking to them when they are at work; they need all their attention to be focussed on what they are doing.'

'Well, when you want to speak to Linda Chambers, she works in the office across the corridor from this one.'

'Linda Chambers? As in Linda Chambers, John's ex secretary?'

'Yes. She works for me now. Very efficient. Only works three days a week so check with me first to make sure she's here.'

'She here today?'

'Yes, all day today. Pop in and see her.'

Dunbar put down his cup and stood. 'Thanks for the coffee, Mark. I'll be in touch shortly. And thanks for this.' He waved the envelope.

'No problem,' Mark said. 'And if you need to chat about the situation at any time, I'm here. You know it will go no further. Might be better than a young WPC showing you up!'

Dunbar laughed. 'Thanks. I might just take you up on that. I'll just say hi to Linda and I'll be off.'

Mark sat back and the smile disappeared from his face. This was really dragging on and Dunbar was bound to be getting flak from his bosses but he was up against a man who could work comfortably outside the law, make complicated plans, build bombs, acquire guns; all for Angel.

Mark closed his eyes. Time for thought.

Dunbar knocked on the door across the corridor and opened it slightly. Linda looked up and smiled.

'DI Dunbar! Good to see you.'

'And you, Linda. How's your mum these days.'

She laughed. 'No different at all. I still live with her; I tell her it's because she needs looking after, but it's not that at all. She washes, irons and cooks for me.'

'I must go, but its been nice to see you again.' He nodded his head at her. 'Take care.' He quietly closed the door.

Chapter 34

It took a lot longer than a couple of days for Dunbar to speak to all of Mark's operatives and to check their credentials. At some time, most of them had worked in the police force and several had lived outside the Devon/Cornwall area before moving to Padstow. The Stones brothers, Luke and Dom, had been a pleasure to deal with, and so funny. He had personally interviewed them, catching them both before they started their evening shift at Moorgate. There was only a year between them in age and they had worked for the police in Warwick for some time before coming back to Cornwall. Their mum had hated them living so far away and when she found out Carter Security was recruiting, she had phoned Mark to arrange an interview for her boys.

Mark had been intrigued and when they had arrived together, he had interviewed them together and offered them a job together. Mum had been very pleased.

They answered all of Dunbar's questions together and when the interview was over he drove away with a box full of scones made by Mum.

He slowly worked his way through everyone else on the list and came up with nothing that caused any ripples of unease. Mark had been right in saying how thorough his vetting system was.

And so, Dunbar began to work his way through his colleagues. This was harder. Some of them didn't like being called to account, while others were only too happy to comply. But, he found nothing.

The only ones left in the melting pot appeared to be family members and friends. He felt sick at the thought but knew he couldn't ignore any avenue. These people had to be visited and interviewed but with the funeral one day away, he decided to postpone the distasteful task until it was out of the way.

The morning of the funeral was a bitterly cold but sunny January day. Everyone waiting around outside the crematorium was shivering. The funeral cortege arrived on time and slowly the room filled. Freda had been popular; this was mainly through her many years of service to the medical practice and her involvement in a number of community activities. She would be missed.

Brenda was just holding up. She was having great difficulty accepting that Freda was gone. Even the strong support of Ken and her family simply wasn't enough. At the end of the service, she went to the coffin with Ken with an arm round her waist holding her firmly. Brenda placed a simple red rose on top of It.

'Sleep tight, Freda,' she whispered. 'Safe with Jack now.'

The obituary in the local newspaper had asked that all mourners wear something red and almost everyone had embraced that. Mark sported the red and white striped tie requested by Freda and fastened it down with the gold tie-pin fashioned into the name Freda. The bright sunlight made the reds glow and Dunbar cast an appreciative eye over the assembled crowd. He smiled to see the colour and knew Freda would have loved it.

Again at Freda's request, the wake was held at the Pig and Whistle and was open to everyone. DI Dunbar wished she hadn't been quite so generous; a small crowd would have been easier to watch. He was scared but wouldn't have admitted it to anyone. Jess and the children were safely tucked away overnight in one of the large hotels in Bude and they had sufficient protection to cover everything. He had no worries about them. But he did have worries about the rest of the family. Once again, they had no idea what Treverick looked like, where he was staying, what he was doing. In short, they knew nothing.

The party to celebrate Freda's life finally broke up around eight o'clock and the entire family went back to Moorgate. Everyone looked drained. Defeated.

Pat was inconsolable. The events of the day, coming so soon after David's death, had been unbearable. Mark Carter had never left her side, sensing she needed extra support. Coping with their own grief, the others had been grateful. He followed Pat into the kitchen to help make tea and coffee and everyone else moved into the lounge. The Christmas tree had been hastily removed and everything had been returned to normal.

Except nothing was normal.

One man was singlehandedly trying to wipe out the entire family because he blamed a six-year-old child called Amelia for all the miseries of his life.

Pilot stood at the large window wondering where the hell they went from here. He hated his children being away from their home without Lauren and him, yet it had been the only option they had.

Mark and Pat carried the drinks through and everyone took one. Very little was said until Lauren spoke.

'We can't let him win. That's what we're doing; sitting here as though the world has come to an end. Okay, we've lost someone wonderful, an outstanding person but of all of us, Freda is the one who would have said stop being miserable. Get on with your lives and get this man out of them. Am I right?'

'You're right,' Pilot said with a sigh. 'But can we do it tomorrow? I'm so bloody knackered, emotionally and physically, and I don't think I can do anything about anything tonight.'

They all laughed at his miserable face and eventually the evening became more typical of evenings spent together. Eventually the Hillside residents returned home, Mark returned to his flat above the office in Padstow and Pat, Dawn and Josh went to sleep without the much-loved family member they had cremated.

And everyone felt relieved that Treverick hadn't tried anything.

The children arrived home bursting to tell their parents about the wonderful bedroom they had shared the night before. Only Grace understood that the reason was because children couldn't go to funerals and it was Aunt Freda's day.

Grace was very clingy towards Lauren and so Jess was given the day off and their mother spent the whole day playing with all three of them. They painted, did jigsaws, had a picnic in the lounge at lunchtime and then, while Noah was having his afternoon nap, she taught them how to sew on binca, something she remembered from her own junior education.

The girls loved it; two little mats were saved in a drawer for completion in the future and they went to bed that night feeling happy to be back home with Mummy and Papa even if their lovely Aunt Freda wasn't there anymore.

Treverick watched as the lights went out at Hillside and knew his Angel was there. He could wait, but not for much longer.

He had watched the funeral from a distance through binoculars and hadn't seen anything of any of the children. It just served to confirm what he had been told. The children were holed up somewhere else for their own safety. The protection around them for that journey was too strong, so he had ruled out the possibility of taking her from Bude.

Yes, he could wait.

For a short time.

Chapter 35

Josh finally managed to persuade Jess that she needed a night away from Hillside, that they needed to eat at Rick Stein's place in Padstow and that Aunt Freda would wholeheartedly approve.

She agreed with a grin on her face and they arranged to go out on the Thursday night. Josh rang Mark and explained what was happening and asked if they could go without one of his protection detail and Mark laughed at him.

'No.'

'No?'

'No.'

'Well, that's an in depth conversation. Why not? I can protect Jess.'

'And what if you need to protect yourself as well as Jess? And can you stop a bullet? We know he's got a gun and isn't afraid to use it. You take protection, Josh. No arguing. He'll be discreet and he'll be in his own car. I'll organise with the restaurant that he sees you safely ensconced and then I'll grant you a small concession. He'll wait in your car for you until you come out. That way if you suspect anything is not quite right you'll know exactly where he is. There'll be no argument on this, Josh,' he warned.

Josh sighed. 'Okay. I suppose one day Treverick'll be dead and we will be able to get back to living a life that normal people have.'

Mark laughed at him once again. 'Stop being so melodramatic and enjoy your night out. Just one thing,

Josh, and I'm being really serious now; if this develops into anything with you and Jess, don't become complacent. Always make sure somebody knows where you are – either one of my men, myself or the police. You know we'll get him eventually and these precautions will come to an end, but for now they're so important.'

Josh turned to Jess who had picked up most of the conversation from his reactions.

'We'll have a bodyguard.'

She smiled.

'As long as we're safe, does it matter?'

Jess looked stunning. She had saved the grey silk dress and with her dark hair and grey eyes, she became the centre of attention the minute they walked through the door of the restaurant. She had been the centre of attention for Josh the second he had seen her walk into the lounge at Hillside.

Sam had followed Josh's Mondeo and they had parked in the car park, at opposite ends. The restaurant was obviously busy. He escorted them inside, checked where they were seated and then took Josh's keys. He went back to sit in the Mondeo and wait. There'd be no bombs, remotely detonated or otherwise, fixed to this vehicle.

He sat quietly for half an hour and then locked the car before leaving it to circumnavigate the car park. He returned to the car satisfied he had seen nothing to worry him and pressed the key fob to unlock the central locking. He was about to get in when he spun round to the words,

'My name's Treverick.'

The gun was aimed at Sam's head. His thoughts and actions froze. His left arm hanging by his side, his right arm extended towards Treverick.

'Arms by your side,' said Treverick and Sam breathed an inward sigh of relief. He brought his right arm down and carefully pressed the heel of his hand against his jacket pocket, activating the alarm requesting assistance. Other operatives would hear it; Treverick was oblivious.

'We're going to wait here until they leave the restaurant,' Treverick said, 'and then it's anybody's guess as to how many of you die. I'm not bothered about killing you but if I have to, I will. It's Josh Thornton I'm after and he's heading off to join great Aunt Freda tonight. Now get in the car, son.'

Sam moved away from the door and turned round to open it. Out of the corner of his eye, he was aware of another car entering the car park and driving slowly as if looking for a space. He thought he recognised Luke and Dom Stones but wasn't sure.

'I said get in,' Treverick growled and Sam ducked his head and slid behind the wheel. Treverick opened the back door and as he bent his head to get in the car, he saw two men get out of the car that had just driven in.

'Bastard,' he said and fired the gun. Sam slumped forward on to the steering wheel and Treverick turned and ran. He leapt over the small stone wall surrounding the car park and turned right to head for the harbour area. Luke flagged down a second car that had just turned into the car park and hastily explained to Jim Brooks what had just happened. Together they went over the wall where Luke had seen Treverick go and they ran, knowing that he would have had an escape plan in place long before the evening's activities.

Dom let Luke go and he went over to the Mondeo. There was a lot of blood spattered on the windscreen and all over the front seats. No movement from Sam. Dom got into the passenger side and felt for a pulse but couldn't find one.

His first call was for the ambulance; his second call to his boss. The ambulance was there in five minutes but Dom knew it was too late. Sam was gone.

Mark arrived at the same time as the ambulance and went straight into the restaurant to get Josh and Jess out of it. Josh saw him walking from the entrance towards them and knew something was bad.

He stood, placing his napkin on the table.

'Mark?'

Mark moved behind Jess' chair and eased it away from the table. She stood up.

'Let's go.'

'But I haven't paid...'

'It's taken care of. Go.'

They walked to the exit trying not to look like naughty children who had been caught out doing something wrong.

'Mark, what's wrong? What's happened? It's not Grace...?'

'No, it's not Grace. Treverick is here, he was in the car park. Now, get in this car.' He indicated a Toyota that had pulled up in front of them. 'You're going straight back to Hillside and ask Lauren if it's okay if you stay there tonight. I'm sure she can find a settee for you. And some food.'

'Where's my car?'

'Crime scene. Now go.'

He spoke to the driver. 'Linc, don't stop for anything. You'll be waved through by the officers at the bottom of the drive; they've got your registration. Just keep going. We need these two inside the house.'

Josh and Jess climbed into the back seat and Josh put his arm around her and pulled her close.

'I'm so sorry,' he whispered. 'I wouldn't have put you in any danger...'

'I know,' she said. 'Mark is clearly on top of it, so let's just follow instructions. I'll make us an omelette or something when we get in. We can still have a nice night; we don't need a fancy restaurant.'

'Linc? Do you know anything about what's happened?'

'No, sir, I don't. I was told to take you to Hillside and stay there to augment the protection detail.'

Josh felt disgruntled. Why on earth was his car a crime scene? They arrived back at Hillside and Pilot was waiting to open the door for them.

'Inside,' he said and closed the door behind them.

'What's happened, Pilot? I've never moved so fast.'

'Not sure yet, Josh, but Mark said if it's not too late by the time everything is cleared, he'll call up. If not, it will be tomorrow morning. All I know is that you'll not be getting your car back in a hurry.'

Lauren came through from the kitchen.

'You two want something to eat? Mark said you'd only had a starter.'

'A sandwich?' Josh looked at Jess for confirmation and she nodded.

'Okay, I'll make some. Josh, the spare room is made up for you. I understand Mark wants you here tonight. He says to tell you they've doubled the men at Moorgate so Dawn and Pat are fine but he doesn't want you out there. He suspects you're the intended target for whatever went wrong tonight, so he doesn't want you, in his words, wandering the countryside or drawing Treverick to Moorgate.'

'Target? Has Sam been hurt? Is that what it is?'

'We really don't know anything yet. Somebody - Dunbar, Mark or somebody else is bound to turn up at some point and tell us what's happened.' Lauren moved towards the kitchen. 'Now come and sit down round the table while I feed us. Pilot, wine I think.'

'I'll ring Mum, first. She'll be worried. God, what a mess,' and Josh moved into the hall to use the phone there. They could hear a muted conversation before he came back into the kitchen. His face was white.

'Mum seems to think Sam is dead. She overheard a conversation between the new ones who've just arrived and the ones who were already there. Pilot, what the bloody hell can we do? I feel so guilty now. And I actually asked Mark if we could go on our own! Jess, I'm so sorry. I've put both our lives in danger...' He knew he was babbling and didn't know how to stop.

Jess went to stand by his side and took his hand.

'Come and have a drink. We don't really know anything yet. Let's sleep on this and talk tomorrow. And, by the way, I went willingly. You didn't force me to go. Stop feeling guilty.'

Chapter 36

The next morning was a very sombre one. Pat and Dawn had arrived very early and had shared breakfast with the Hillside residents. By nine o'clock, they had been joined by Dunbar and Mark.

Dunbar was clearly in a place that said, "don't trifle with me." He had been hauled over the coals that morning and was in no mood for any arguing with the extended family of the Farmers.

'Okay,' he said. 'Here's what happened last night. Sam Marks was killed by a bullet to his brain, his blood spattered all over the windscreen and front seats of the Mondeo. His wife is distraught. She's seven months pregnant and they've admitted her to hospital. They're hoping to stop the early labour, keep that baby safe until the due delivery date but it's not looking likely.

'Now, is there anybody here who doesn't understand just how serious your situation is?'

The anger in his tone was palpable and nobody spoke.

'Right, here's what's going to happen until we finally catch the bastard – or kill him. You will go nowhere. I am closing down Moorgate. Lauren, can you accommodate everybody here?'

Lauren nodded, almost afraid to speak. She'd never seen Dunbar so angry.

'Then do it. None of you are to move from here. All groceries can be delivered and if you need medical help, we will organise with your doctors to make home visits. Are you all with the same medical practice?'

Everyone nodded.

'Josh, Dawn, Pat – you three will be escorted back to Moorgate to pack whatever you will need. This means we can free up protection to give more here. I can't stress enough just how important it is that you don't go outside. He has at least two guns. He shot Freda with a rifle but it was a handgun that killed Sam Marks. I'm leaving you with Mark now. He'll answer any questions. I've things to do. I'll be back later. I need to re-interview each and every one of you. Last night's events confirm a suspicion and I need to start with all of you. Pat, a police car will be here shortly to take all three of you back to Moorgate. Leave the place securely locked and alarmed, and make sure you bring everything you need; medication, clothes, books. You won't be allowed to go back until this is over.'

His short staccato sentences showed just how angry he was and Pilot stood to escort him to the door. Dunbar turned once more and faced him.

'Didn't it sink in at all, Pilot? Stay away from all doors and windows if you want to live. He's stepping up his campaign to get Grace back and he'll kill you all if he has to. Everybody except Grace. I'll leave you to imagine what he wants to save her for.'

He slammed the door behind him and there was a concerted swoosh of air as he left. It seemed as though everybody had been holding their breath while he was speaking.

'Pilot...' Lauren looked at him with tears in her eyes. 'That poor woman – her baby...'

'Hush,' he said and pulled her close. 'There's nothing we can do. I know it's not the ideal scenario but if she's seven months, the baby stands a good chance of surviving. I'm sure Mark will keep us informed.' He turned to Mark for confirmation.

He nodded.

'I will. But don't think I've gone soft on you. I agree wholeheartedly with everything Dunbar has just said. I've lost two of my best men now, Alan and Sam. I won't lose anymore. If you ask to go out accompanied, the answer will be no, so get used to it. You stay in this house at all times. You will have three men in the house and three men outside. They will work a shift system so that there will be different ones here but here they will be. Josh, I felt I was in a bit of a battle with you last night. I appreciate that you wanted time on your own with a very attractive young lady but that put both of you in grave danger. There will be time for romance when all this is over. And it will be one day, but for now, you're going nowhere. Sorry Jess, but Treverick will see you as part of this family now, so I can't even ask if you want to leave. It just wouldn't be safe.'

Jess answered quietly.

'It's my choice to stay, Mr. Carter; I'm not staying because you say I have to. These children have become my world and yes, I would literally take one of Treverick's bullets for them. Let's hope none of us has to.'

He nodded, took out a roll of paper and spread it on the coffee table.

'Now, I realise you don't know all of my operatives so this is a sort of crib sheet. This is the rota for who will be on duty at what time and whether they're indoors or outdoors. These are their photographs so that you can identify them. Always check their badge ID when they come on duty and if a problem occurs, tell one of them. I don't want somebody having an exploding appendix because you've been scared off from doing anything. The telephone, of course, isn't out of bounds, but no doctor is going to get in here unless he comes in escorted by one of us. Your first port of call is one of my men for everything.'

It was the roll of paper that was the final straw. Everyone realised just how important a piece of paper it was and Pilot was the first one to pick it up.

'I'll make copies of this' he said. 'We all need one, and we need to study the faces. We know Treverick can change like a chameleon and we don't want him getting in here unchallenged. We have to put a name to a face. Properly.'

'Now you're thinking like a pro,' Mark said. He tugged on his purple silk tie. 'And now, may I have a cup of tea, please? This is thirsty work. We can talk more, maybe a bit more quietly, over a drink.'

Lauren and Jess went into the kitchen and Jess crossed to the window. She lowered the blind and then went to switch on the light.

'He can't see us with the blind down,' she explained.

''Thank you,' Lauren responded. 'We're all going to have to start thinking like that. And thank you for what you said about the children. It's a comfort to know that there are so many of us watching their backs but you spend more time with them than anyone, so thank you.'

They carried the drinks through to the lounge and placed the two trays on the coffee table. They could hear the photocopier going in Pilot's office and Lauren took his drink in to him. She pulled down the blind and switched on his light.

'The electricity bill will go up, but we'll be alive,' she smiled.

Lauren had to put Dawn and Pat into the same double room that Dawn had shared with Freda and Josh was moved back into the box room he had occupied before. The camp bed wasn't ideal but the room wasn't big enough for a single bed.

It became something of an adventure for the children; they now had lots of adults to play with.

Dunbar made good on his promise and arrived the following day to begin his interviews. He concentrated on the newcomers to the family, Dawn, Josh and Jess. It soon became very clear that he was barking up any tree but the right one. He completed the interviews with all of them and then left to repeat question Mark's men. He made no apologies for his overbearing manner towards the family and kept a formal attitude throughout.

Eventually, Dunbar arrived back at his office feeling disgruntled, and out of sorts. They were no further on with this investigation than the day Grace had knocked on the Wainwrights' red door. All he had to show for his team's efforts were four dead bodies; he had no hesitation in including Freda in the tally. Without Treverick's bullet, she would still be alive. He sat down at his desk and picked up a report that had been marked for his attention. It confirmed that Matthew Shaw was indeed Ronald Treverick's son. He had never doubted it for one minute but legally they had needed the proof.

He picked up the phone and rang Marcia. She answered almost at once.

'Hi, Kenny,' she said.

'It's DI Dunbar, Marcia.'

She sounded flustered. 'Oh... sorry, I was expecting a call back from someone else.'

He laughed. 'Clearly. Would his name be Kenny?'

'Yes.' She sounded embarrassed.

'I just wanted to let you know that the DNA result shows that Treverick is unquestionably Matthew's father. I'm sorry.'

'No need to be sorry, DI Dunbar, I knew. I don't need a piece of paper to tell me. Treverick was the only person it could possibly have been.'

'Will you tell Matthew?'

'I already have.'

'Oh?'

'I thought it was for the best.' Now she sounded evasive.

'Right. Er... well, that's all I rang for. If you need any more information, you have my number. You may get a witness call up at some point in the future.'

'You caught him then?'

'Not yet. But we will.'

He put the phone down and stared at it. There had been something not quite right. Her tone had been offhand; she hadn't been like that before.

He dismissed it with a shake of his head and pulled some more paperwork towards him. He needed to go home and the sooner it was finished and filed, the sooner he could get off. Perhaps a new day would bring some advancement. He could only hope.

As he turned the corner to park up outside his home, he thought again about Marcia Shaw. She had definitely been offhand; could she possibly have been in contact with Treverick? Maybe another trip to Wadebridge might be in order. He locked the car and went through his front door.

He kissed Fran, said,

'Hello, wife, I'd like food,' and was asleep within five minutes. It had been a long day.

Chapter 37

Newspapers were delivered to Hillside by seven o'clock and by 7.05 am Dunbar was getting his first phone call of the day.

'Have you seen the papers?'

'Pilot? And good morning to you.'

'Have you seen the papers? There's an article by somebody called Kenny Raines. It's an interview with Marcia Shaw. Headline is *I had a love child with Ronald Treverick.*'

'Shit! The silly cow! I knew there was something wrong, something she was hiding when I spoke to her yesterday.' He groaned. 'That's all we need. It was irrelevant before. The information gave us no leads; it was no help at all. In actual fact, the only people who knew about this young lad were you and Lauren, his mother and myself. And now, this damn journalist and the rest of the public. It was as irrelevant as that. It's not even been passed on to my team. Now he's going to know something as big as this and what will that do to him? He's possibly going to go after his own child as well.'

'What will you do?'

'God knows. Go and get the paper for a start, then we'll take it from there. Thanks for the heads up, Pilot.'

He disconnected and leaned back on the kitchen chair. Fran wrapped her arms around his shoulders from behind and kissed the top of his head.

'It'll be over one day,' she whispered.

'You reckon?'

'I reckon.'

Dunbar called his team together and went through the information he had on Marcia and Matthew Shaw. He spoke for quite a while; he wanted them to have all the facts, but when he got to the end DC Johnson spoke.

'Does this help, sir?'

'Not at all. I suspect she's been well paid for this article and it will be a one-day wonder. However, Treverick will be aware of this by now. What really bothers me is if he likes little boys as well as little girls. Our evidence so far points to little girls only, but who knows? I'm going to Wadebridge after this meeting to talk to her again. Sarah, you'll go with me, please. This silly woman has put herself and her son into danger for the sake of a few quid and her fifteen minutes of fame. And I'm damn sure she doesn't have the Farmer-size fortune to pay out for protection. Right, I'm dealing with this issue along with Sarah. You all know what you're doing?'

There was a chorus of yeses and Dunbar stood. Sarah followed him into his office and waited for him to speak.

'I could quite cheerfully strangle her.'

Sarah nodded.

'Know exactly what you mean.'

'But why? She seemed like a nice young woman when I met her. What on earth can she be thinking of...?'

'Let's go and ask her, sir.'

The journey didn't take too long; traffic was light at this time of year. He pulled up outside Marcia Shaw's house with some difficulty; there were several journalists milling around obviously waiting to get a photo or speak to her. After knocking on the front door, they waited patiently for some sign of life. He bent down and called through the letter-box, telling her it was DI Dunbar. There was absolutely no reaction.

There was a shout from across the street, and Dunbar turned to see a tiny, old woman waving at him. 'You a copper?' she asked.

'Yes I am, madam,' he called.

'Then come here.'

Sarah followed him across to where the old lady waited for them and she hustled them inside her home. It was beautiful. Cushions were on every surface and the colours in the rugs glowed and matched perfectly the shades in the wallpaper on the fireplace wall. Lamps and candles lit up the gloom caused by the overcast skies outside and Dunbar looked around appreciatively.

'Sit down,' she said.

'Well...'

'Cup of tea?'

He nodded weakly. 'Thank you.'

'And you, young lady?'

'Thank you. We both have milk, no sugar.'

She disappeared into the kitchen and returned a few minutes later with their drinks and a plate of biscuits.

'Right, now get that down you and we can talk. My name's Poole, Mrs. Take your time because I reckon that lot out there will be gone soon. They'll give up. Some of them have already gone. And I've got something for you.'

She handed him an envelope that said DI Dunbar on the front. 'She popped it through my letterbox some time during the night. I can't tell you what time cos I'm a bit deaf, like, and I didn't hear her. I found it when I came down this morning. There was a little note pinned to it that said, "*Keep this till DI Dunbar comes*." ' She reached across and picked up the plate of biscuits. 'Eat,' she instructed. 'They're all homemade.'

And so they ate. Dunbar finished his snack and then slipped on a pair of latex gloves before opening the envelope. He realised he was probably being overcautious but didn't want any nasty surprises inside the envelope.

'How did you know it was from Miss Shaw?'

'We look out for each other. It's not the first note she's put through my door. If she's expecting a parcel or something and she's going to be at work she drops a note through and I look out for the van. I look after her place if she goes away – we watch out for each other. Has she done something bad? Why are all that lot out there? They've been banging on her door and hanging around all day. It's a good job you had your uniform on, Miss, or I'd have thought you were one of them vultures.'

'You've not seen the newspapers, Mrs. Poole?'

'No. Can't see too clear these days so I have the evening news on the telly instead of reading about it. Will she be on that?'

'Possibly.'

He took out the piece of paper and read through it quickly before putting it back inside the envelope. Nestled in the bottom was a key.

'It looks as though she'll be away for some time, Mrs. Poole. I'm going to leave you my number and when all that lot have disappeared, if anything out of the ordinary seems to be going on across there, can you call me, please? Don't approach anyone, not for anything. Just ring me.'

She nodded. 'I hope Marcia's ok, and Matthew of course.'

He handed her his card and they walked towards the door, thanking her for her hospitality.

'Give her my love if you speak to her, will you? I'm going to miss our little chats. And that little lad ran errands for me.'

'I'm sure she'll be back. She's just taking some time away for now. Listen to the news tonight. Thank you, Mrs. Poole.'

They went back to the car and Dunbar handed her the letter. 'I couldn't read it and digest it in there, so look at it, read it out to me and let's have your thoughts on it.'

Sarah smoothed out the letter.

DI Dunbar – I'm sorry if I've upset you but I believe I did the right thing. I was paid quite a lot of money for my interview and I've explained to Matthew exactly who is father is and why we have to go live elsewhere. In England, Matthew will never be rid of the link to Treverick, so we're leaving. Nobody will know us where we're going and that's how I want it. I have taken everything I want from my house but I am leaving you a key just in case you should need to go in. I don't know what will happen when Treverick reads that article but I do know he will be able to find that address. Thank you for your kindness and I hope you catch him soon. Marcia and Matthew Shaw.

'Short and sweet, but you were wrong to give Mrs. Poole false hope. She's definitely not coming back, ever.' she said.

'You think she's done the right thing?'

There was a moment of hesitation. 'Absolutely.'

'Why? Treverick didn't know anything about his son...'

'Didn't he? You're sure about that? And she's scared. She's looking out for the most precious thing in her life and doing what's right for him. She's obviously thought about the fact that she's told you – and you're possibly the only person she's ever told – and realised the enormity of this secret. She doesn't know who you might have shared it with and I actually think she's done a very brave thing.'

'Only Pilot and Lauren knew apart from me and out of everybody attached to this case I would say that the three of us are definitely the people who don't fit the criteria for accomplice to Treverick.'

She laughed. 'Maybe you're right. This really was the biggest red herring, wasn't it? All it did really was confirm what his name was ten years ago.'

'Until now it was a red herring,' he said grimly. 'Who knows what will happen after this.'

They arrived back at the station and began to work on their reports. The mood in the big room was sombre. They all felt they were getting nowhere and everyone was repeating work, going through witness interviews, potential sightings that had cropped up after the initial television broadcasts; they searched for anything they might have missed or dismissed first time round.

Just after six o'clock, Dunbar decided to call it a day. He popped his head round the door of the main room and told everyone to have an early finish.

'Be back here for eight tomorrow. Keep thinking about what you've been checking and we'll have a brainstorm first thing.'

Chapter 38

So, he had a son. He could vaguely recall the girl – that was where he thought he had lost his wallet and she had confirmed that for him in the interview with the journalist. He wondered what she had called the boy but knew it wouldn't be too difficult to find out.

He might have to take a little careful trip to Wadebridge and see if he could find her house again; get a look at this son. Ten years old and he hadn't known.

It was a long article and he reread it several times. He didn't want to miss anything. It briefly occurred to him that if he had known about this child, his life might have been different but he quickly dismissed that thought. His mission to take Angel had been solely about payback to Amy Thornton. Killing her on their wedding day hadn't been enough; using his son wouldn't have done anything to assuage the anger he felt towards the Farmers and Thorntons.

He carefully cut out the two-page article and folded it tightly. It fit into his wallet with a squeeze but he needed it with him. Maybe he could have a chat with this Kenny Raines; maybe he knew where this tart was living with his son. Maybe.

It was time for a change of appearance. Now he had to look professional; time to darken his hair, wear dark glasses maybe, small moustache. Time to track down Kenny Raines.

Life was stressful at Hillside. Having everyone under the same roof to keep safe was a good idea in theory but in practice, it had its flaws. There was a lot of people traffic. Brenda and Ken kept very much to their own wing, realising very early on that the fewer people in the main part of the house, the better. Their main visitor was Grace.

She had developed a real affinity with her great Nan and frequently popped in to show what she had been doing with Jess. Most of the stuff centred around Harry Potter, which left Brenda a little wrong-footed as she had never read the books but she loved to hear Grace fill her in on the stories.

'I'm going to have to read these books,' Brenda announced one day after admiring a picture that vaguely resembled a unicorn but was assured by Grace that it was something called a patronus. Never having come across such an animal before, she asked if she could borrow the first book.

'I'll get it now, Nan Brenda,' the little girl said excitedly. 'This is the one Sarah read to me in hospital. And don't be scared when Harry is rescued, will you?'

She ran from the room and Brenda looked at Ken for support. 'What have I let myself in for? I read romance and classics,' she said.

Ken laughed. 'I don't know, my love, but one thing's for sure, this'll be nothing like Jane Eyre.'

He didn't care what it was like; this young child was working the miracle with Brenda that he hadn't been able to do. She could bring a million patronuses (patronii?), if she wanted, as long as his Brenda was reverting to her normal happy self.

He really smiled two days later when Brenda asked this very precious great granddaughter for book number two.

'Now don't be scared by anything will you, Nan Brenda? You just call me if you are.' And then she hesitated for a moment. 'Or Granddad Ken. But he's not read them, so he'll not really understand...'

And so, at the age of seventy-seven, Ken Buckingham began to read Harry Potter, just one book behind his wife of eighty-seven. And they both began their recovery from the death of Freda in a way that Freda would have found hilarious and would have wholeheartedly agreed with.

The breakfast meeting a couple of days earlier had done nothing to help. Dunbar was still going through the vast amount of reports and interviews. Nothing made him stop and think that something was amiss.

He decided to take advantage of a fine February day and check on things at Hillside. He would once again take Sarah with him. She had said on the way back home from Wadebridge, how much she missed Grace.

They ran the gauntlet of the police car at the bottom of the drive. The young officer had checked his identification even though he had recognised him instantly but then had told him to open the boot, Sir.

Dunbar had smiled and complied with the request before completing their journey up the drive.

'Sarah!' Grace squealed her name out loud and they all laughed. 'Come and look at my room!'

Sarah looked to Dunbar for permission and he nodded.

'I'll give you a call when I'm ready to go.'

Jess gathered up the other two children and they all went upstairs. Dunbar looked around.

'Are Ken and Brenda free?'

'They'll be reading. Grace is educating them,' said Pilot.

'You want them here?' Lauren looked puzzled.

'Yes, if they're not napping or anything. Don't wake them, if they are. I just want to try some thoughts out with you, a bit like our brainstorming session we had at work. It didn't produce anything very much there, but you're closer to the action.'

'I'll get them.' Dawn stood and walked over to their rooms. She knocked and walked in. They were both reading, and Brenda looked up with a smile.

'Hello Dawn. You want something?'

'Jake Dunbar's here and if you're up to it he wants you to join the rest of us. If you don't want to, I can tell him you're asleep.'

'Don't be silly! Of course, we'll come through. I'll just put my broomstick away. I've been playing Quidditch.' She put her bookmark in and stood slowly. 'Could do with borrowing his wand though to magic these aches and pains away.'

They followed Dawn through to the main lounge and all six sat around in a semi circle facing Dunbar.

'Okay, these are my thoughts. As you all know, I've re-interviewed all of you and I don't mind telling you I concentrated specifically on Jess. She's the newcomer to the family. I also paid particular attention to Dawn and Josh because they were, initially, part-time members of the family.'

Dawn looked angry so he hurried on.

'Stop glaring at me, Dawn. I'm only doing my job and this evil man has to be caught before he kills anyone else. And I can tell you that you all passed with flying colours. Please tell Jess, won't you?'

'Passed what?' It was Pilot's turn to look puzzled and angry.

The detective looked around at them all. They had suffered so much loss they deserved some answers.

''You all passed, so my theory of an accomplice doesn't fit any of you.'

There was temporary pandemonium. Eventually the noise subsided and Pilot said,

'Accomplice?'

'Before I go into details I must tell you I have absolutely no proof that he isn't working alone. I may be barking up the wrong tree, clutching at straws or any other cliché you can think of. However, I didn't come to this conclusion on my own. Somebody else did which made me look at it more carefully.' He nodded towards the stairs and the sound of the children's laughter. 'Sarah suggested it one afternoon in my office.'

Pilot had now stopped looking angry but the puzzled expression was still there.

'But there's never been any suggestion he could be involved with anyone else. Surely something would have surfaced by now?'

'And nothing has except for one thing. He seems to know exactly what you're doing, what we're doing... he's getting information from somewhere. I'm not saying this accomplice had anything to do with the awful acts committed on your daughter, Pilot, but I am saying he may have linked up with someone connected to this case.'

'And do you have any idea at all who it could be?'

'None. My whole team has been going through report after report after report; nothing has shown up. We have checked and double-checked everyone on the police team, everyone on the Carter Security team and everyone here. In about an hour, there will be a team of experts here to do a sweep for listening devices around your home. But if they're here, I have no idea how he managed to place them. This brings us back to the accomplice theory. However, gut instinct tells me that it isn't bugs and that's because this house is never empty, there's always someone here.'

He turned to Pat. 'We're going to do the same at Moorgate, Pat, so I'll need your keys. I'll return them as soon as we're finished. We know he managed to get into your house, so if anywhere is bugged, that would be the better option.'

She nodded.

'Of course, Jake, I'll never forgive myself if you find anything at Moorgate. It means our home is the reason David died. That's unthinkable.'

'Pat, I don't think we'll find anything. It really is just ruling it out so we can move on to the next possibility. I believe somebody close to you is passing information on to him. I don't know why. I don't know how. We've checked everybody's bank accounts and there are absolutely no strange payments – in fact, after I'd checked the accounts for the constables on our team, I wanted to have a whip round for them! This doesn't rule out that Treverick might be paying somebody because as we all know he's one smart cookie and could be paying them in cash but openly there are no payments.'

He was finishing speaking when he took his mobile phone from his inner pocket. He glanced at the caller.

'Excuse me, I have to take this.' He moved across to the patio doors and outside on to the paved area. Instantly Martyn Pearson moved towards him and stood with his back to him, surveying the surrounding area.

He listened for some time without speaking and then said,

'I'll go straight to the Cathedral. Inform DI Garside that I'm on my way.'

He went back inside and asked Lauren if she would mind calling Sarah down as they had to go.

'Everything all right?' Pilot asked. Dunbar looked angry.

'I can't say at the moment but we have to go now. Sorry Pilot, can I leave you to accommodate my de-bugging team, please? And hand Pat's keys to them. I hope I don't have to tell you that you don't go with them...'

'Don't worry,' Pilot laughed. 'That message is well and truly engrained in our brains.'

Sarah came downstairs and looked at her boss. He nodded and said,

'We have to go.'

Once in the car, he began to speak. 'We're off to Truro Cathedral so if there's anybody you need to tell that you're going to be late home tonight, do it now.'

'No, sir, there isn't. People have stopped expecting me home full stop. Why are we going to the Cathedral?'

'We have a body. Fortunately the DI on the scene has linked this body to our investigation and has contacted us.'

'So we know who it is, sir?

'Kenny Raines, the journalist who wrote the article about Treverick's son. This is going to be a bad one, Sarah; he'd been tortured before he died. All we can hope for is that he didn't have the information Treverick wanted which is the whereabouts of Marcia Shaw. Because I don't doubt for one minute that this is the work of Ronald Treverick, not for one minute.'

He drove in silence for most of the way and Sarah allowed herself to relax and relive a most enjoyable afternoon with Grace. The little girl had blossomed and while there were still big gaps in her education, she had clearly made huge strides in catching up. It was all down to Jess and her infinite patience and Sarah felt so much better for spending an hour at Hillside.

She had no idea what faced her at the Cathedral; she just hoped the journalist hadn't suffered too much. Torture was obviously another sideline of Treverick's that they hadn't come across before – she hoped Marcia and Matthew Shaw were safely out of the country but more importantly she prayed they hadn't disclosed their destination to Kenny Raines.

Chapter 39

Truro Cathedral is an imposing grey edifice of a building. Stunningly beautiful, it dominates the landscape and every day it attracts visitors from near and far. Today, it boasted crime scene tape.

Dunbar and Sarah entered by a side door and were met at once by DI Pete Garside. Pete and Jake had risen through the ranks together and had been friends for a considerable number of years. Dunbar had never seen him look so ill at ease.

'That bad, is it?' he asked.

Garside nodded.

'Oh, it's bad. Both ears gone, all fingernails gone, several teeth missing and both eyes. He either was a brilliant bloke who wouldn't give up the information or he simply didn't have the information. Either way, he's paid for it with his life. He's been left round the back of the restaurant and we do have CCTV of him being dumped in the doorway there. The chef found him. He's still throwing up.'

'So, Treverick doesn't care if he's seen now.'

'Apparently not. He's sending you a message, mate. He's going after his son. Does anybody actually know where they are?'

'I don't think so. I can't imagine Marcia would have told this journalist; she just went. I'm the only one she contacted to say she was going and she definitely didn't tell me where she was going.'

'Right. Come and see the body. As you can imagine, it's a mess. He brought it in a white van, stolen yesterday from Indian Queens. We're doing the forensics on it as we speak.'

'He left it?'

'Uh huh. Dumped the body through the back doorway of the restaurant, closed the van door and simply walked away. There's a brief case in the van, good quality, empty. He looked like a smart city gent so I'm assuming the briefcase was just for effect; that was obviously how he persuaded Raines to talk to him. The CCTV is pretty clear but it doesn't show us much. The action took approximately thirty seconds and he'd gone, out of range of the camera. Raines' eyes are in his left coat pocket. His ears, fingernails and teeth are in his right coat pocket in a plastic bag. Our forensics chap seems to think the eyes were removed after death but he'll know more after the post mortem. Lovely chap, your Treverick.'

Closely followed by Sarah, Dunbar walked through to the area that was busy with police personnel. Sarah already felt sick and she hadn't seen anything other than Garside's face; that had shown her enough.

The body was slumped in the doorway, carelessly cast aside for anyone walking down the side road to see. The head was in an unnatural position, forced into staring up into the sky with eyes that couldn't see. His hands were bloodied along with the whole of his head where the ears had been sliced off and the teeth removed. At this point they didn't know if the teeth had been knocked out or forcibly removed.

If Kenny Raines had known the information Treverick wanted, he had put up a fight to maintain his integrity. He had probably realised from the beginning that he wasn't going to come out of the situation alive but he had been a brave man to tolerate the intense pain that had been inflicted on him. Dunbar hoped he had been unconscious for most of it but he doubted it. There would have been no point carrying on with the torture if he hadn't been able to feel it.

Sarah just stared. She had never seen anything like this. Six years of being on the Force hadn't come close to preparing her for this abomination. She said a small prayer to God. It helped her.

Dunbar moved her away from the body and led her towards a seat.

'Sit there,' he said. 'I don't need you yet. You don't have to look at this. They have taken photographs already, so they should be moving him soon.'

He was as white as Garside had been when they arrived.

'Thank you, sir,' she said and sat down. She took a packet of mints out of her pocket and offered one to Dunbar. 'It helps combat nausea, sir,' she said and he took two.

Dunbar went to speak to Garside and asked him if Raines' family had been informed. Garside nodded.

'Yes. We sent someone round as soon as we knew who he was. His wallet had been left in his inside pocket.'

'Where does he live?'

'Wadebridge. According to his wife, he knew Marcia Shaw from their teenage years. He hadn't seen her for a long time and she had rung him out of the blue and offered him the story. We haven't spoken to Mrs Raines properly because I figured you might want to do that, but I didn't want her hearing anything on the news. I had to let her know he's dead. He had a helluva scoop that all the big papers wanted after he broke the news, but my God, he's paid for it. The poor wife is absolutely distraught. I don't think they've been married very long. They haven't any kids, according to my man.'

There was a flurry of activity and the body was zipped inside a body bag and removed from the premises. Immediately, the forensic team went to work taking samples, more photographs with the body not present and generally working to provide Dunbar and Garside with anything they might want.

Two hours later, they were on their way home. Sarah didn't speak - couldn't speak. She didn't think she would be able to sleep that night either. Dunbar asked her if she wanted to get some food but she just shook her head. Did he want her to throw up in the front of the car?

He dropped her off at home and told her not to come in till lunchtime. She just nodded and said,

'Goodnight, sir.'

He drove home and tried to eat the meal Fran placed in front of him but was unsuccessful. He moved various bits around the plate until she removed it from the table.

'It was a bad one, then?'

'The worst.'

The last time she had seen him like this was when he had attended a hit and run in which two young children had been mown down. His face had been the same then.

She handed him a whisky and placed the bottle in front of him. 'Let's watch a movie,' she said. 'We're not going to sleep much tonight, are we?'

Chapter 40

Dunbar walked into the station just before eight o'clock next morning and met Sarah coming down the stairs.

'Lunchtime already is it?' he asked with a smile.

'Couldn't sleep,' she mumbled. 'Could you?'

'No. Couldn't eat, either.'

'So now what?'

'We find him. Amy Thornton, Alan Shimwell, David Farmer, Freda Andrews, Sam Marks, Kenny Raines – we have to find him. And let's never forget what he did to Grace. She'll have to live with that for the rest of her life. There's no escape from him for that poor little girl.'

'Did they find any listening devices at Hillside and Moorgate?'

'Nothing. So, this takes us right back to the accomplice theory. And let's face it, Sarah, there's only the two of us that's really buying into that.' He sighed. 'It's so bloody frustrating. What price gut instinct? It's proof we need.'

Dunbar left Sarah to carry on down the stairs and he headed up to his own office. He pulled out the reports once more and started to read through them. There had to be something somewhere that didn't sit right and his plan for the day was to find it. The vision of a man who had been brutally tortured had haunted him all night; sleep hadn't come until the early hours and then he was awake at six o'clock. No sudden inspiration was going to appear; this had to be down to plodding police work not just from him but the entire team as well.

The tired detective pulled out the report on Grace that captured so much of what she had said from the second she staggered into the Wainwright's home to the day she left hospital for the Farmers. He pulled his yellow notepad towards him and began to make notes, forming a kind of timeline of everything listed.

An hour later, he did it again but this time he used Sarah's report of her daily visits with the little girl.

And then he repeated it with Karen Eaves' psychiatric report, noting dates and times.

It was fast approaching lunchtime and Dunbar decided to go to the pub and get a sandwich before building any more links. He was tired and emotionally exhausted. Grace's own words were harrowing and for that alone he wanted to kill Treverick.

Descending the stairs to ground level, Dunbar didn't hear the phone on his desk ring and the answering machine pick it up.

He sat alone in the pub, repeatedly pushing his dark hair back from his forehead. He was battling a headache that threatened to become migraine level. His cheese and pickle sandwich and the half pint of shandy that followed it went down without him tasting them.

Having walked down towards the harbour, Dunbar now sat on the harbour wall and stared out to sea. Although he didn't know it, he was in the same place that Amy Andrews and John Thornton had sat so many years ago when they had talked about walking straight across the oceans to America. He remained there for some time, letting his thoughts drift in the lukewarm March sunshine. No heat to it yet but it wasn't unpleasant for all that.

His headache began to subside and he briefly closed his eyes. Fran had tried to talk him into taking a couple of days off, to have a break, but he knew that wasn't going to happen. Time enough to rest when Treverick was dead.

He jerked himself awake. The object of the exercise was to catch Treverick, not to kill him. He had to stop thinking about him dying. The man had to be punished, had to do the actual dying in a prison cell.

He stood, stretched out his arms and fastened his coat. The sun had disappeared behind a cloud and it had become suddenly chilly. He walked back to his office and climbed the stairs up to his office. He saw the red light flashing, noted there were two messages and sat down at his desk. He pulled a pad towards him and pressed play.

Hello Dunbar. I saw you yesterday at the Cathedral. Just thought I'd check in with you today because I didn't think it was a good idea to get too close to you as you were busy. I did a good job on him, didn't I? It's a pity really that he didn't know anything. So now I'm thinking maybe you do. Or have you told your wife? Fran, is it? Maybe I'll ask her. Anyway, I'll call some other time. I just want to see my son.

Dunbar left his office at a run. He jumped into his car and fumbled to get the key in the ignition. His hands were trembling, his heart pounding; she had to be safe. He switched on the lights and siren and sped through the town centre until he reached St.Merryn.

Fran had been working voluntarily at the church three days a week for a number of years and was an expert on the church history. He knew she wouldn't answer her mobile phone, she said it was rude to have a phone ring when she was telling a visitor something of interest about the church.

Tidying some leaflets in the entrance to the church, Fran looked up with a smile, expecting to greet a tourist, not her husband.

'Get your things,' he said. 'Don't make a fuss. I need you to come with me.'

'Was it you making that awful racket with your siren?'

'Yes. Now come on.'

'No. Not without a damn good reason, Jake. I've another hour yet before Janet gets here.'

'Do you want me to arrest you?'

'Don't be ridiculous.'

'I'll arrest you if I have to, Fran. Now go and get your coat and bag. You're leaving. I'll explain in a bit. Tell them you need some time away, family matters or something. Now, do I get the handcuffs out?'

She glared at him and walked towards the room set aside for staff members. He followed her.

'I can get my own coat,' she snapped.

'No, you can't. Welcome to my world, Fran.'

He stood by her side while she explained she wouldn't be in for a few days and then they returned to his car.

'I'll follow you,' she said. 'Where are you going? Back to the station?'

'Yes,' he said and held open the passenger door. 'Get in, and make it snappy. We're vulnerable out here.'

'But ... my car...'

'I'll get Johnson to pick it up. You'll have it back tonight. Get in the bloody car, woman!'

They spoke very little on the way back. Dunbar said he wanted her to listen to something before making any smart Alec comments.

She could tell he was scared; she had never seen him scared before. He was always in control, always the one she turned to when *she* was scared. *He* was the one who removed spiders, who killed moths when they threatened to come within ten yards of her. He was her rock.

He ushered her out of the car, looking all around him the whole time. He breathed a sigh of relief when they were in his office. He helped her remove her coat and hung it on the coat stand. He took her in his arms, held her close and kissed her.

The applause from the main office where several members of his team were working was sustained and raucous and he looked through his partition window at them with a grin.

'Sit here,' he said to Fran. 'I need one or two more in to hear this. Won't be a minute.'

He went out into the outer office and asked them all to collect in his room. Sarah was the first to move and grabbed a note pad and pen.

Eventually eight people crowded into the tiny place and they all waited expectantly, puzzled. A DI's wife in the office?

'Right, everybody, I need you to listen to this. The call came in just as I left for my lunch. I listened to it as soon as I got back and then I went to get my wife from St. Merryn. She is hearing this for the first time as well; she has no idea why she's sitting in my office and she definitely has no idea why I threatened to arrest her in St. Merryn church.' He smiled gently at her. 'You'll understand in a minute, Fran, but I apologise if you felt harassed.'

He pressed the play button and Treverick's voice filled the room. Dunbar heard a gasp but not from Fran who went white and looked at her husband.

'Now,' he addressed his team members, 'I could waste public money by having this call traced back to a phone but it will do no good. We know Treverick by now. This will be so far from where he's staying it will be of no use to us at all. This phone message isn't going to help us at all except put us all on high alert, I hope.'

'What about your wife, sir? How can we help?'

'Thank you, Johnson, but you can't – oh, other than by getting someone to run you out to St.Merryn church car park and collecting her car. She's not going to need it for a bit but I'd like you to bring it back and park it in the police car park here. Before you get in it, Johnson, get on the floor and have a good look underneath. Check under the bonnet and in the boot. If there's anything at all that you're not happy with, we'll get the bomb squad out to check it over. I'd rather you were wrong than dead.'

Andy Johnson nodded, signalling he understood. Fran handed him the keys.

'It's a red mini, Andy. Registration is on the key ring. It's a bit dodgy getting into second gear. Just be aware. Oh, and there's a warning light comes on and stays on but I'm sure it's all right.'

Dunbar looked at her.

'What warning light?'

'Oh, don't fuss. It's nothing new. It's been coming on for a few weeks.'

Johnson grinned.

'This is like listening to my girl friend. It'll be the oil light, I guarantee it. I'll have a look sir, and if it's oil, I'll put some in. And I'll check the water.'

'Thank you, Andy. Right, off you go all of you. Remember, this is the first time we've had this sort of communication from him and it feels as if he's stepping things up a notch. Be extra vigilant.'

They all left the office and Sarah squeezed Fran's shoulder.

'Trust him,' she whispered. 'We all do.'

She smiled in acknowledgment and then turned to Jake.

'So now what?'

'New York?'

She stifled a squeak. 'Really?'

'On one condition, Fran. You tell nobody other than Kate that you're going – and I mean absolutely nobody. When you speak to Kate, tell her your life is in danger and she mustn't tell anybody that you're flying over to her. I have to trust you will be safe there but I can only concentrate on my job if you follow my instructions absolutely to the letter.'

'Of course. When do I go?'

'I'm booking your ticket now. You're going to be on the next available flight. There's just one issue. No luggage.'

'What?'

'If Treverick is watching our house, I don't want him to see you wheeling out a suitcase. He would just follow us to the airport and find out where you're flying. You would be easy to trace. Take that big handbag you're so fond of and pack it with things like, oh, I don't know, stuff you'll need on the flight. You and Kate are twins, for heaven's sake, so I'm sure she can find you some clothes for a couple of days till you can get out and buy some. Just use the credit card that you refuse to use, sweetheart, and get what you want. It could be a long trip but as soon as we have him, you can come home. I'm so sorry this has happened, Fran. I try to keep work away from you...'

'Hey, it's fine. I'm a little confused as to why only Kate can know but I can live with that.'

'We believe, or at least Sarah and I believe, that Treverick has an accomplice. We have no proof but he seems to know our every move. That's why you can't tell anybody. We don't know who is giving him information.'

He handed her the receiver. 'Here, ring Kate. And then I'll book your ticket.'

Chapter 41

He drove Fran to Wadebridge, pulling up on the High Street. He waited, the ever-dutiful husband, while she went into one of the shops situated in a courtyard. She carried on walking through to the back alleyway that led out of the courtyard and walked down the road to the taxi rank. Twenty-four hours later she was in America.

Dunbar continued to sit in the car for three quarters of an hour after dropping off his wife at the shops, continually checking his watch and peering through the car windows as if looking for her. He had no idea whether Treverick was watching or not, but he had to keep up the pretence for as long as possible that she was just on a shopping trip. Eventually he got out of the car, walked into the courtyard of shops and went into each one as if trying to find her. He then went back to his car and drove off. He had given her around an hour and a half head start, he hoped.

The text from her that said

'At Cheltenham xxx'

told him that she was at Gatwick and through into the departures lounge. He had booked her to travel business class and mentally wished her God speed. His text back to her simply said 'Enjoy xxx'. He knew it would be some time before he saw her again.

It felt bleak at home. He wasn't sure how to handle it; they hadn't really been apart for all of their married life – the odd couple of days if he had to attend conferences but no extended time, as this was promising to be. It was a spur of the moment decision that made him book into a hotel. He realised he probably wasn't going to eat now;

Fran enjoyed cooking, he didn't. And just how much fish and chips or pizza could one stomach absorb? He also didn't relish the idea of having to check out every little noise in their three hundred year old cottage in case it was Treverick. A three hundred year old cottage has plenty of strange noises.

He picked one of the hotels near the police station, packed a bag and moved in that night. He would text Fran with his location when she contacted him to say she was safely at Kate's apartment.

Then he slept. Deeply.

His next contact with Fran was when she sent a text saying *credit cards are good xxx*. He smiled to himself and sent one back that said *don't use wisely xxx.* She was as safe now as she could possibly be and he put her on the back burner in his mind. He needed to concentrate on his job now and without the worry that Treverick's threat had created, he felt better equipped to do that.

As he was dropping off to sleep in the comfort of the hotel he had realised that in all the panic of getting Fran from St. Merryn and the subsequent organisation of her escape, he hadn't given another thought to the second message on the answering machine.

When he arrived in his office feeling much more like himself, he glanced at the red light. It showed two messages.

He pressed the first one and it was from Mark Carter; he explained it was just a courtesy call, just checking in with him and asking if there was anything further they could be doing. He said there was no need to get back to him, and just to be aware that he was there if he was needed. Dunbar actually liked Mark and his ties and he certainly appreciated the intelligence of the man. That message was timed three minutes later than the Treverick one.

He pressed the play button again to hear and then delete the final message. It was timed at 3 am and it was from Treverick.

She's gone then. But she can't stay away forever, can she? And just remember, DI Dunbar, there's nowhere in this world that's out of my reach. You've protected her for the moment but if she knows where my son is then she's got that information from you. I'll leave you to think about that one, Jakey boy.

He put a finger up to the answering machine and quietly said 'Fuck you, Treverick, fuck you.'

The rest of the day was spent comparing the lists he had been making when he had been catapulted out of the office to get Fran. He would miss her very much. He was in the habit of bouncing thoughts off her and she always seemed to know the right thing to say to him.

Just as he decided to stop for the day, his phone rang.

'Dunbar,' he answered.

'Jake, he's rung here.'

'Pilot? You're saying Treverick's rung?'

'Yes. Lauren answered and she's in pieces now.'

'I'll be there in fifteen minutes. In the meantime, get Lauren to write down as accurately as possible everything he said.'

He picked up his coat and was out of the office and in his car within a couple of minutes. He went through the usual 'Good evening, DI Dunbar. Pop your boot, please' and then headed up the drive to the house. Within seconds of parking his car, one of Mark's men appeared and stood by his vehicle.

He showed his ID and was accompanied to the front door. Pilot let him in and they moved through into the lounge.

Lauren's eyes were red but she appeared to be composed.

'Did he ring on the landline?'

She nodded and handed him a piece of paper.

'This, as far as I can recall, is the conversation. It was very short. He just wanted to frighten me. This is something new, Jake, isn't it? We've not heard him speak before, or at least not since he was Brian Lazenby.'

'Yes, it's something new,' he agreed. 'He phoned me twice yesterday, both answer phone messages. In my case the first one issued threats against my wife and the second one acknowledged I had got my wife to a place of safety, so he was coming for me.'

Lauren gasped. 'Your wife! But...'

'Don't worry. She's safe. He's trying to find his son. He thought my wife might know; he thought I might have told her where Marcia Shaw and the little lad are. If only. I have no idea where she is but she did us no favours selling this to the press. That death in Truro Cathedral yesterday; did you hear about it?'

Pilot nodded.

'No details though, just that there had been a body.'

'It was where Sarah and I had to rush to when we left here. The body was Kenny Raines, the journalist who wrote the article. Treverick obviously disagreed with his writing about him.'

He gave them no further details; enough was enough. He looked at the piece of paper Lauren had given him. It had been a short conversation but she had written each side of it down.

Treverick call 4.17 pm approx.

Me: Hello?

T: Is Lauren there, please?

Me: Speaking. Who is this?

T: A friend. Angel's Daddy.

Me: What?

T: You might know me as Ron.

Me: No.

T: Listen to me, sweetheart. Angel belongs with me, just as my son does. I have money. Lots of money. Would you like to sell her back to me? I'll take care of her. (Some laughter here). If she comes back to me, I'll not kill anyone else. If she doesn't, Brenda is next.

Me: You evil, fucking pervert.

I slammed the phone down at this point. Apologies for my language but you asked me to be accurate in what was said.

His accent was sort of Northern, but not like Ken's is Northern. It was maybe more North East, Tyneside area, but with a touch of poshness to it. Sorry I can't be more explicit. He definitely didn't sound anything like Brian Lazenby.

He looked at Lauren.

'Thank you. This is very good. I'll have it transferred to a witness statement and then next time I see you it will need checking and signing. I'm sorry this had to happen to you, to all of you, but he's not shooting guns down a phone. If all he did was make phone calls, I wouldn't be half as concerned. What worries me now is why he is suddenly doing this? It can only be that he thinks it will rattle us even more. He's trying to mess with our heads but phone calls are amateurish compared with what he's already done. I just need you to put it in perspective, Lauren, and see it for what it is. Try not to dwell on it and carry on doing what you're doing.'

She flashed him a half smile; it was a good job he couldn't mind read.

'I'm not going back to work. I'm staying at the Old Custom House so if you need me, ring me on my mobile. And, Lauren, don't hesitate. If you need me for anything, call me.

The drive back down into Padstow took very little time and although Dunbar enjoyed the hotel restaurant meal, his mind wasn't on eating. Treverick had now moved into playing mind games but he was fully aware these threats couldn't be ignored. If he said he was going to target Brenda, then Brenda he would definitely be targeting. Luckily, she very rarely ventured beyond the confines of their own wing but he needed to speak with both her and Ken before much longer.

He slept fitfully; while the bed was ultra comfortable, Dunbar's brain was not. Facts, figures, theories, span round and round in his mind, preventing him from sleeping.

He was in his office early; he had given up on sleep by five o'clock. Coffee didn't help; Sarah popped her head round the door and asked if he wanted one but he declined with a smile. He'd had two already.

He stood and walked to his window that overlooked the car park. He could see Fran's mini, the car that now had some oil and water in it and was probably breathing a sigh of relief. He must remember to check it for her in future.

He surveyed the scene below him for quite some time allowing his mind to slow down. When Sarah popped her head round his door it brought him out of his reverie.

'Sorry, Sarah. Can I help? Was just thinking...'

'You can take this phone call, sir. It's Jeanette Yardley and she's got some information for you.'

He moved to his desk and picked up the receiver.

'Jeanette? DI Dunbar.'

He listened for a minute and then said 'I need to come and see you.'

He put down the receiver and called Sarah back in. 'We're going out at three o'clock. This could be the break we've been waiting for.'

Chapter 42

By 3.30 pm they were walking through the front door of Jeanette Yardley's home. She greeted them with a smile and said the coffee was almost ready. They followed her into the lounge and sat in the two armchairs while she disappeared into the kitchen to get the drinks.

'This is lovely,' Sarah whispered to Dunbar.

He nodded. 'She certainly has an artist's flair for colour. Very peaceful atmosphere, isn't it?'

'It's how I'd like my new place to be,' she said. 'I'm moving into a new flat within the next month.'

'We're paying you too much then,' he said with a laugh.

Jeanette arrived to break up the banter and sat down facing them.

'So,' she began, 'I saw him. I saw Treverick or whatever he's called now. Apparently he changes his name frequently?'

Dunbar nodded.

'You're sure it was him?'

'Definitely. I don't know where he's living because I couldn't hang around any longer watching him. I daren't go to find a policeman or ring you because I thought he might have disappeared by the time I got back, so it was a strange sort of situation. I just stayed watching him for as long as I could and then I had to leave for a doctor's appointment. I'm so sorry.'

'Didn't you have your mobile phone?'

She shrugged. 'I don't have one. Until that day I've never needed one,' she sighed.

'Right. Tell us what happened, Jeanette, from the beginning.'

She paused, gathering her thoughts before speaking. 'I'd been off work poorly for a couple of weeks and was starting to feel better. That's why I had the doctor's appointment yesterday evening; he wanted to see me before giving me the go ahead to go back to work. And it's why I was in Padstow during the day instead of on my flower stall. It all boils down to my illness, really. I wouldn't have seen him at all if I hadn't had this infection.'

Again, she paused and they waited without speaking.

'I decided to make a day of it doing some sketching around Padstow and I got there about eleven o'clock. It was a bit cold at first so I did some doodling to get my fingers warmed up and then I went down on to the harbour to sketch figures. I like doing landscapes but they come to life if they have figures in them and that's what I enjoy doing, faces and figures. I sat for an hour or so and then became aware of a man standing just behind me. I didn't take much notice at first because it happens a lot – people like to watch artists. Sorry, am I talking too much?'

Dunbar shook his head.

'Not a bit. If only all our witnesses were as articulate! We need the full picture; sorry about the pun.'

'He stood there for quite a while and he actually unnerved me a little bit, partly because I couldn't see him and partly because he didn't move at all. He just stood and watched me. I kept rubbing out bits because he was stopping me concentrating and then suddenly he moved. He went as far as the next bench along and sat staring out across the sea. But as he left, he came into my vision and I knew his face. I had already drawn it, after all.'

She shivered, and then carried on. 'He has the sort of face that can change expression easily but I knew him. I didn't know what to do. As you well know, there's never a policeman about when you want one,' she glanced quickly at the two officers, 'so that was no help to me. I had no idea where the nearest phone box was, so first of all I packed up most of my stuff so that if he moved it would only take seconds for me to throw everything in my bag and follow him. It was him, DI Dunbar.'

'I don't doubt it for a minute. Did he move?'

'Not at all. He just sat there.' She handed her sketchpad over to Dunbar and he showed it to Sarah. The drawing was a picture of a man they instinctively knew was Treverick. His face was at rest, and he was clearly in a contemplative mood. His hair was now dark and the beginnings of a moustache showed. Dark glasses rested on his head.

'But then I had the best luck,' she continued. 'The sun came out. It actually became quite warm, warm enough for me to take off my jacket. And so did he. He had the tattoo visible for about ten minutes before the sun went back in and the skies darkened. He put his coat back on and sat there still staring out across the sea. And then this happened.' She handed over another sketch.

It showed Treverick closest to her drawing position and another man at the side of him. There was no face to see, he wore a hooded sweatshirt and the hood covered his head, concealing his features.

'They talked for ages but I couldn't see anything other than what you're seeing there. His jacket, by the way, is a Fat Willy's one. I couldn't get all of the logo on the drawing but everyone in Cornwall knows Fat Willy's surf shack. It's a sort of dark blue, but it's not as dark as navy. I had to pack up and go because of my appointment and they were still sitting there. But they were deep in conversation and had been all the time from the second man's arrival. After my appointment, I ran back down but they'd gone. I worked on the picture last night making sure it was as accurate as anybody could get it and then I rang you this morning. I'm really sorry I had to leave the area. I was only away about half an hour and in that time they'd disappeared. A later appointment time, and I would have been able to watch where they went.'

'Just out of curiosity, Jeanette, if they had walked away while you were there, what would you have done?'

'Followed them,' she said. 'I wouldn't have been able to help myself. And I think it's because I know what this man's done.'

There was silence in the room for a moment. Both Dunbar and Sarah looked at Jeanette and she said,

'What? What have I done?'

'Nothing, thankfully,' Dunbar said drily. 'Now listen to me. I went to Truro the other day to, of all places, the Cathedral. A body had been discovered down one of the little lanes that surround the building. That body had no ears, no fingernails, very few teeth and no eyes. And no heartbeat. Who do you think killed him?'

Her face visibly blanched. 'No!'

He pushed relentlessly on. 'Yes, indeed. That man had been tortured for information, information he couldn't give because we believe he didn't have it. But whether he'd had it or not, Treverick would have killed him. Make no mistake about that. So what I'm really saying, Jeanette, is what do you think he would do if he had any inkling at all that you were trailing him?'

'Sorry. I promise not to follow him. Ever. But what do I do if I see him again?'

Dunbar wanted to scream. She didn't seem to be getting the main issue; there was no more dangerous man than Treverick and she didn't seem able to grasp that.

'Why would you see him again?'

'I draw around Padstow all the time. Why shouldn't I see him again? You see, DI Dunbar, I am actually the only person who has seen him and who knows who he is so it makes a lot of sense for it to be me in Padstow looking for him.' She grinned at him. 'But I promise not to follow him. Don't forget he thinks I'm one of the local artists, which I am – he watched me for ages. So why shouldn't it happen again that he comes and watches what I'm doing? My question is, how do I get hold of you?'

'If I get you a phone,' he said tiredly, 'you'll be able to get me. I can't instruct you not to go but I would rather you didn't.'

'I don't want a phone.'

'It's only until Treverick is behind bars. I'll have it back then.'

'Okay. I have Tuesdays and Wednesdays off so it will be next Tuesday before I'm on the harbour again – and that's only if it's not raining. There's not much point drawing in the rain.'

'No, I can see that,' he said with a smile. 'But I want your solemn promise that you will do nothing except either ring or text me.'

'Text? You might have to teach me that one. And of course, I promise. I just hope he comes again because let me tell you this; I've never seen him down there before and I go there a lot. Let's hope he enjoyed his trip out yesterday and he wants to do it again.'

Dunbar organised with Andy Johnson to take the mobile phone to Jeanette and to stay with her until she was fully conversant with it. It had been programmed with his mobile number and to save confusing her it was the only number in it.

He laughed when he received her first text,

I'm no longer a text virgin!

He just hoped he was doing the right thing giving her the phone. Part of him wanted her never to see Treverick again; the other part hoped she would.

Chapter 43

'This is so frustrating.' Pilot was standing by the patio doors, staring outside. The weather was starting to warm up now and he enjoyed getting the lawns ready for the summer. The sit and ride lawnmower was a big part of that enjoyment. Surely, something would happen to unearth Treverick soon. Get him out of their lives forever. But Pilot knew this was wishful thinking and that the man could never be completely out of their lives; he'd killed so many of his family. And Grace would never be free of him. They had difficult issues to deal with in the future; things that would have to be explained to her in great detail and she would always know just how different she was to Olivia. They looked very much alike facially but Olivia wasn't far off Grace's height despite being nearly four years younger. Grace's early years of undernourishment would always be an issue although she had grown an inch since her arrival at Hillside. She needed to grow many more.

He saw Dunbar's car pull up outside. The policeman used to ring to check that they were in before coming to see them; now he knew they were in. After the tirade he had directed at them, would they dare go out? Pilot waited until Jay King, Mark's man of the day, moved across to the door and then he went to open it.

'Jake. Good to see you. You just after a cup of coffee or imparting information?'

Dunbar looked at Pilot then laughed.

'Do you have any idea how like your father you are, Pilot? Because I can tell you, sometimes when you speak it's like he's in the room with me.'

'Well! Where did that come from? It never occurred to me I was like him.'

'Oh you are. Looks, language, sense of humour – just like him. Is everybody available?'

'Would we dare to be anything other than available? You have news?'

'A little bit. Something to show you to add to your collection of rogues gallery portraits of Treverick. But this one I can't make public because he would guess where it came from and that would put my informant in considerable danger.'

Pilot nodded. 'No problem. I'll get everybody here.'

They opted to sit around the dining table and before Dunbar passed around the photocopies of Jeanette's drawing, he explained what had happened as briefly as he could. They already knew about his first contact with her so he just told them about her trip to sketch in Padstow. And then he took the copies out of the folder and passed them around.

'This,' he explained, 'is how he looked two days ago. He doesn't know we have this and I am deliberately not making this public. As I explained to Pilot, it would put the artist in a lot of danger but it would also highlight the fact that we know how he looks now. He would immediately change his appearance.'

They all remained silent as they studied the picture. Pilot spoke first.

'Are you sure it's him?'

'Definitely. He took off his jacket when the sun made the air quite warm and guess what's on his right arm?'

'Beautiful.' Lauren breathed the word quietly.

'So why did your artist sketch the other chap?' Josh lifted his head and looked at Dunbar.

'He came and sat with him and they talked virtually nonstop for nearly an hour. He's the one I want you to look at. Does anything about that drawing make a connection in your brain? The way he's sitting, the angle of his head, his clothing; is there anything at all?'

'But it's only a sketch,' said Brenda.' How accurate can it be?'

'Just treat it as a photograph. Believe me, if she says this is how it was, this is how it was. She is uncannily accurate in her drawing skills, an amazing artist. We're so lucky he went to her flower stall.'

'Is that a Fat Willy top?' Josh asked. 'Pilot's got one. It's quite distinctive, darkish blue.'

'Huh!' He snorted. 'I definitely have got one but when a certain mate called Josh arrived from the States he borrowed it and it doesn't seem to be in my wardrobe anymore.'

Dunbar felt cold. He didn't want to think the obvious. 'Is it here?'

Josh looked at Pilot.

'I thought I'd given it back to you.'

'No, but I'd kind of like it back,' he grinned. 'Nip up to Newquay and get your own.'

Josh stood and moved towards the stairs. 'I'll see if it's in my wardrobe then,' he said sheepishly.

Pilot looked at Dunbar and didn't like what he was seeing on his face. 'Jake, half the population of Cornwall has a Fat Willy tee shirt or sweatshirt. 90% of the tourists go home with one. It's Cornwall's biggest export. Just don't get too excited that this is some sort of clue. Even my kids have Fat Willy hoodies.'

Josh came back downstairs.

'I don't have it, honestly. Are you sure I didn't give it back?'

Pilot looked puzzled. 'I'm certain. The last time I saw it you had it on when the two of us went to buy some Christmas drink.'

And then Dunbar interrupted.

'So it would have been at Moorgate when Grace's present was left there?'

Josh nodded. 'I guess.'

'Okay. That's all for now. But if you can both have a thorough search, please, and if it does turn up let me know immediately.'

He stood to leave. 'Study this picture. Make sure you know what he looks like now. And you're all still grounded,' he said firmly.

His unease continued all the way back to the station. Pilot? Josh? Could the mysterious figure be either one of them? Surely not?

This opened up another possibility. Maybe it hadn't been Treverick who had breached the defences at Moorgate to leave the gift; maybe it was someone else, someone with more reason to be there legitimately.

He called Sarah into his office and they sat and stared at the picture. He explained his thoughts and she looked up at him.

'I know we're right, sir. He has somebody facilitating his activities, someone in the know: and someone who has access to Moorgate. Possibly access to Hillside as well and that's a scary thought.'

'Maybe he does have access to Hillside but he'd be hard pushed to get by the protection that's in place up there. Moorgate was easy with only one man on duty.

Hillside has more protection officers than people living there.'

Sarah gathered up her papers and walked to the door. 'Sorry, sir, but I have to ask this. Do you really suspect either Pilot or Josh?'

He shook his head. 'No. Initially maybe, but they genuinely had no idea where the sweatshirt was. Apparently, Josh had borrowed it because they'd brought limited clothes with them. As far as Pilot was concerned, Josh still had it and I actually think Josh was quite put out that it now seems to be missing.'

'I'm glad you said that. I don't think I could bear it if it turned out to be a family member who's helping him. Why would they do that?'

Sarah went back to her work-station feeling disgruntled and out of sorts. Although it wasn't definite that Treverick was in the Padstow area, the sighting of him near the harbour was a positive step. Finding him wasn't going to be easy.

Dunbar stared out at the main room where several of his team were working on different things. It was a good team; they needed very little instruction, came to him if they needed advice or direction – yes, a good team.

In his meditations on the current issues, a name suddenly jumped at Dunbar that startled him in its intensity. Amy Thornton. Everything that had happened to this beleaguered family had at the heart of it a woman called Amy Thornton.

The attack on her as a child had kept Treverick at the forefront of everything. He hadn't been a particularly clever child but his years of imprisonment had certainly improved his brain-power. It had also bolstered his deviousness. He had planned out his entire life around getting back to Amy.

Dunbar wasn't sure if marriage to Amy had been the ultimate goal or if it had just been to kill her. In the end, both had happened.

But, Amy had touched so many others' lives. John Thornton had loved her once, of that Dunbar was sure. Dawn and Josh had come into her world after John's death and Pat had been friends with her since they were eleven years old.

It seemed like she was the central pole in a maypole, and all the ribbons danced around her. The Lauren ribbon now had three little extensions attached to it.

He mulled all this over, knowing he was missing something. Missing somebody.

He stood up abruptly and called into the main office as he left for the day.

'I'm going home,' he said and they all looked at him as if he suddenly started reading the Bible or the Koran. Going home?

'I need some time out' he said, somewhat sheepishly when he saw their expressions. 'See you all tomorrow. Anybody need me before I go?'

There was a chorus of '*no, sir*s' and he headed down the stairs. He was confident that if they needed him for anything they would ring. He drove back to his hotel and parked the car in the car park.

He didn't go in. Dunbar walked down to the harbour and looked around. Jeanette had seen him purely by chance; perhaps he could be lucky too.

He sat staring out to sea for quite some time but then walked slowly back to the hotel feeling chilled to the bone. No sighting today.

He went up to his room, opened his briefcase and took out some papers. He had been reading them for five minutes when he started to fall asleep. He slept soundly through the afternoon, woke up briefly around ten o'clock and then went back to sleep. His telephone woke him at just after five and he answered it automatically.

'Dunbar.' It came out as a growl.

'Sir? It's Martyn Pearson, Carter Security. We've had an attempted break in at Moorgate.'

'Have you caught anybody?'

'No, sir. We just have a minimal protection detail here and we patrol the perimeter of the property most of the time. On our third check tonight, we found the side door open. It wasn't open half an hour earlier. We have one key and it's for the back door because that leads into the kitchen and that's our base when we're not patrolling. The side door has been opened with a key.'

'Have you checked inside the property?'

'Not yet. I rang you as soon as we saw it.'

'Stay where you are. If this is Treverick, we know he has at least two guns. Don't walk into gunfire. I'm calling for armed officers. They'll be there within minutes. I'm coming over now.'

'We're outside the open door, sir. We'll stay here until you tell us otherwise.'

He put down the phone and cursed. What the fuck was Treverick doing? He must know nobody was inside Moorgate, that they were all resident at Hillside now.

He picked up his phone again, called for armed back up and then set off for Moorgate.

He found Martyn Pearson and Gerry Williams still by the open door.

'No sounds from inside,' they confirmed. Within a minute, the armed taskforce arrived and Dunbar stepped back, taking the two Carter men with him.

'Let's leave them to it, now,' he said. 'They know what they're doing.'

All three of them walked back to the car and leaned against it. They watched the activity around and in the house but Dunbar was troubled. He knew there would be nobody inside so why had this happened? Was it just Treverick winding them up, keeping them on their toes? Or had he thought they would bring some of the protection over from Hillside, leaving them vulnerable? But nothing would make Dunbar leave that child in a vulnerable situation. Nothing.

An hour later, calm had been restored and most of the taskforce had left. Dunbar had requested two of the armed men to remain until midday and having rung Mark and asked for one other man to supplement the two already there, he felt his job for the early hours was complete.

He drove over to Hillside and filled Pat in on what had happened overnight. He ached for this woman. She looked so flattened by life; losing her very much loved husband, turned out of her home, control of her life wrested away from her. She was beaten.

'But why?' she asked. 'What on earth can he have gained from that? And where's he got my bloody key from?'

'I don't know where he's got it from but I've seen the door and it definitely wasn't opened by force. We've checked your CCTV and the camera shows him unlocking the door, and, we assume, keying in the alarm code. This explains how he got in last time.' Mentally he corrected himself. It explained how *someone* had got in last time. 'And I don't know why he's done it. I had a couple of theories; one was that he wanted us to pull some security people from here to check out Moorgate, leaving everybody here under-protected and vulnerable. Or, that he is just showing us that he's in command and can have us running round like headless chickens while we try to work out what he's playing at.'

Grace came downstairs and walked over to them.

'Nan Pat, are you okay?' Her face looked troubled and Dunbar marvelled at this child who had experienced so much and yet had turned into one of the sweetest kids he had ever met. He knew this was mainly down to Lauren but guessed Jess had played a massive part in that rehabilitation.

'I'm absolutely fine, sweetheart,' said Pat and held out her arms, to give the little girl a cuddle.

'But he's done something else, hasn't he?' she persisted.

'What?'

'Ronald. What has he done this time? Has he killed someone else? Is this all my fault?'

Pat looked flustered. 'Of course it's not your fault, Grace. He is a truly bad man but he's not a bad man because of you. He has always been a bad man. He was a bad man for many years before you were born, so please don't have thoughts like that. None of this is anything to do with what you did or didn't do, it's his fault entirely.'

Grace turned to Dunbar. 'Is that true, Jake?'

He smiled at her.

'Of course it's true. And, young lady, don't let me hear you query anything that your Nan Pat says in future. Of course, she's right. She wouldn't lie, especially to you.'

Grace looked down at the carpet. 'Sorry, Nan Pat. Sorry, Jake.'

Adult eyes locked and Grace moved to go back upstairs. 'Tell you what, though,' they heard her mutter. 'If

I ever see him again I'll kick and kick and kick until he's dead. Dead like Granddad David and Aunt Freda. Dead.'

Chapter 44

On Tuesday it rained, and Dunbar breathed a sigh of relief. He knew it meant Jeanette wouldn't be playing Miss Marple and going down to the harbour to sketch. Although she had promised not to follow if she saw Treverick again, Dunbar wasn't altogether convinced she would stick to that promise. He had decided that if the day were fine, he would go down and sit in Fran's car on the harbour road. He couldn't risk leaving Jeanette there on her own. Effectively, the rain had stopped that plan.

He pulled his chair closer to his desk and switched on his computer. There was an email with the post mortem report for Kenny Raines and he read it through carefully.

He had been alive when his ears, teeth and fingernails had been removed. His heart had stopped at that point, unable to take any more. Treverick had then removed his eyes. Just for effect? Dunbar did note that Kenny Raines' days might have been numbered anyway. He had had a brain tumour.

He closed down the file and sat staring into space, unsure where to go next. He walked into the main room and looked around. Everybody ignored him, each busy with his or her own work.

'I'm going out for a while.'

Nobody reacted.

'Sarah! I'm going out!'

She looked up guiltily.

'Oh, sorry, sir. I was busy...'

'I just wanted somebody to be aware. Ring me if I'm needed. I'm going down to the harbour area.'

'Okay, sir.'

Dunbar shook his head as he left the room. Sometimes he felt unappreciated.

He parked his car on a back street away from the harbour then walked down the sloping cobbled lanes until he reached the harbour wall. There were usually two or three artists in this area, sketching or painting. Today was pretty bleak and the only person braving the bad weather was an elderly male photographer. He nodded at the man. His camera hung around his neck while he used his hands to frame the view he wanted.

'Not a good day for it,' he said conversationally.

'No,' the man agreed, 'but I want a dark picture. I am entering a competition and the subject is sunshine and storm. I'm going to have a go at mingling two pictures, same view, different weather conditions. The wife thinks I'm mad.'

Dunbar laughed. 'She's not with you, then?'

'Not likely. Now last week, when I was getting the sunshine one, she was right here with me, eating her ice cream and reading her book. Bit of a fair weather wife, she is.'

'When were you here last?'

'Friday, was it? Nice day. Even had a couple of people sketching. Not today, though,' he said with a laugh.

'Are your pictures still on that camera?'

'Yes. Until I get this collection of stormy ones I just keep them all on. These digital cameras are brilliant for that. It was a bit different back in the day when we had to use film.'

Dunbar took out his warrant card and showed it to the man. 'Can I look through the pictures, please? Let's go and have a coffee, out of this rain.'

'Oh. You think I've got something in particular?' The man looked bewildered. He followed Dunbar across the road and the detective ordered two teas.

'My name's Eric, Eric Merton.' He shook Dunbar's hand. 'Let me show you how to view the pictures. I haven't downloaded any yet so these are what I've taken over the past four weeks or so.'

He pressed a couple of buttons on the back of the camera and handed it over. 'Just touch the plus button to move on to the next one, the minus to move back.'

Dunbar began to go through the pictures and paused when he spotted Jeanette on one. She was sketching, head down in total concentration. It was difficult to see much detail because the photographs were tiny. He knew he needed to see them in much greater detail.

'Eric, I'm sorry to have to do this to you, but I need to take this camera back to the station and get one of my tech team to download all the contents so I can see them properly.'

Eric sighed. 'My competition...' he said.

'Don't worry. I'll have it back to you tomorrow,' Dunbar assured him. 'But there may be follow up questions if I'm unsure of anything.' He took out his notebook and wrote down Eric's address.

'Right,' he said. 'That's that sorted. I'll give you a ring tomorrow as soon as it's released back to me. I'll take care of it, I promise. Now drink up. You want a doughnut?'

He signalled to the waitress and she brought across a selection of cakes. Half an hour later, they shook hands and Dunbar watched as Eric walked back to his car.

The camera was in a navy blue waterproof case and Dunbar put it around his neck. He didn't want to run the risk of dropping it and damaging it before they'd got the pictures on to a computer for viewing in detail.

He started to walk back to his own car and suddenly veered off to the left and up a slight incline to the Carter Security offices. He pressed the intercom and heard Mark say,

'Come in, Jake.' A buzzer sounded and he went through the door and into his office on the right.

Mark stood and walked round to the front of his desk.

'This is unexpected, DI Dunbar. What can I do for you?'

'It's Jake, Mark. This isn't an official visit. I just called in because I was in the area. Thought there might be a coffee in it.'

Just for a second he thought Mark looked uncomfortable but then the look disappeared.

'I'll need to pop up to the flat in that case. Just hold the fort, I'm out of milk. Won't be a minute. If the phone rings, answer it – I seem to work on the assumption these days that it will be connected to the Farmers.'

He walked out of the office, turned right along a small corridor and through the door at the end marked *Private*.

Dunbar was aware that Mark lived above the office; his dedication to his business and his men was outstanding. Being so close to any information he might need at any time was commendable. It was also damned handy when you ran out of milk.

Mark was back within about a minute, crossed to the coffee machine where there was a pot keeping warm and poured two coffees. He handed one to Dunbar and took a sip from his own cup. His tie, a glorious tartan in shades of red and pink, reflected in the white porcelain of his coffee mug.

'Taken up photography, then?' He nodded towards the camera Dunbar had placed on his desk.

'As if I have time. No, it's just some photos I need to have downloaded. I'm heading for our tech team when I get back.'

'Can I help?' If it's urgent...'

'No, you're ok, thanks, Mark. Although visiting you here isn't official, that camera is. I'll save it for the boys; they might need to do a bit of enhancement and suchlike.'

'Okay, the offer's there if you need it. So, are we any further on?'

'No. We know it was Treverick breaking into Moorgate but have no idea why. We got him on CCTV going in and coming out. I'm assuming he's taken something from the house, unless it was just an exercise in winding us up, committing us to yet more resources for this damn case. I tell you, Mark, without the Farmers stumping up for the costs for your protection, I don't know what would have happened. We couldn't have covered them in the way that you have.'

Mark shrugged. 'Lauren is Amy's daughter. And John's, of course. Why wouldn't I protect them? And just so you know, the profit on this job is minimal. I have to cover costs but I'm not doing much more than that.'

'Think much about Amy?'

'Every day. I played a pretty big role in John's death, you know. That sort of thing sticks with you. I know it was a heart attack but she got me into that bedroom and orchestrated the whole bloody thing with John catching us there. I was like a lamb to the slaughter. Naive.' And then he laughed. 'How stupid must I have been? I can still feel Freda's wrath now. And yet Freda and I came to an understanding as the years passed; I think she realised just what had happened that day. So before you ask, I was a little bit in love with Amy Thornton, maybe even more than a little bit. In a strange way, I also came to admire Brian Lazenby. Never in a million years would I have thought he was Treverick. To be perfectly honest, up to the point when they talked marriage, I always had an inkling he was gay, or at the very least bisexual. In the end of course, he was simply a rapist.'

'And a murderer. Let's not forget he killed Amy.' Dunbar paused, momentarily deep in thought. 'He's killed one or two more since then, but the net's closing now. We've a lead that will take us to him, I'm sure of it.'

'Want to talk it through?'

Dunbar shook his head. 'I can't. It's not clear enough in my head just yet. I need confirmation of a couple of things before I can definitely say it's a good lead.'

'Well, anytime you need us, pop in and we can give support as and when.'

Dunbar finished his coffee and stood, pushing his chair away from the desk.

'Thanks, Mark. I'll be in touch.' He picked up the camera and moved towards the door. 'See you soon.' He paused outside Linda's office door and contemplated knocking to say hi but decided against it. It would only disturb her if she were on the phone.

Mark buzzed him out of the front door and he walked around the side of the building. It was a quicker route to his car and he walked past the red door that was the direct entrance to Mark's flat for those times when he didn't need to go through the office. He stopped and looked at the picture of Treverick attached to the door, asking people if they knew him. Maybe he should have dropped in the new picture of Treverick, the sketch drawing done by Jeanette.

He decided to bring one next time he was in the area and to stress it was for Mark's eyes only, not general consumption.

A minute later, he was leaving the harbour area and driving towards the police station. He handed the camera over, asking for the pictures as fast as possible and within fifteen minutes he was looking at them on the computer screen.

Slowly, Dunbar worked his way through them all. Most of them were views, but occasionally he would add people to the scene in front of him. He particularly liked one with two children who had climbed up on to a concrete base and were looking out across the water through a telescope. Their positions were perfect, the sunshine on the water was perfect and the picture captured everything about Padstow that he loved.

And then he saw Jeanette again. It was the photo with her head down, beautifully capturing the artist at work. Her concentration on what she was doing shone out of the photograph; it was a breathtaking study. He looked at it intently for quite some time but there was nothing to show Treverick was anywhere in the vicinity.

The next one was taken five minutes later according to the digital record of the time at the bottom of the picture and again showed Jeanette, this time with her head lifted up and staring out across the water. Standing behind her were two people, a man and a woman. Dunbar didn't feel that they were together. They were both looking over Jeanette's shoulder at her work, but they were either side of her, not side by side. It was Treverick.

He looked up as he heard a knock on his door and called,

'Come in.'

A young man popped his head around the door and held out a brown envelope.

'From Tech, sir. They've printed out all the photos for you now.'

'Thank you.' He reached across and removed the envelope from his hands. 'Thank them, please. It's so much easier with real photos.'

'Yes, sir.' He left with a shake of his head. So much easier with a piece of paper? Some of these bigwigs were just dinosaurs...

Dunbar took the A4 sized glossy prints out of the envelope. There were about forty in total. He pushed his screen to one side and laid them out chronologically, according to the times recorded in the bottom corner of each picture. He thanked the Lord for expensive cameras.

He then separated the views from the people, taking care to keep them chronological; he didn't want to have to sort them out should it become necessary. He put all the views back into the brown envelope and labelled it.

He was left with eleven photographs all containing the people who had either visited Padstow over the past four weeks, or who lived there.

He took a deep breath and pulled the first one towards him.

Chapter 45

The fourth one was the one with Jeanette sketching, head bent, oblivious to the surrounding area. He looked at it carefully using a magnifying glass, inspecting every inch of the photograph. It was a good picture; the sun bounced off the white of her drawing paper and cast a warm glow over the entire scene.

He put that to one side and pulled the next one towards him. This time Treverick was clear; he had on the clothes that Jeanette had depicted in her drawing. He didn't recognise the woman at all and he scanned her more carefully than he did Treverick. In the end he decided there was nothing linking them together and he felt sure Jeanette would have mentioned her presence if in fact they had conversed or sat together.

The sixth picture told him everything he needed to know. The man sitting with Treverick on the bench was nearest to the camera; Treverick was also in focus with Jeanette slightly blurred and a little more into the distance.

The man's face was slightly turned towards the camera and therefore not hidden by the hood.

Dunbar had all the answers now.

Dunbar put the camera into a carrier bag and went down to his car. He needed to speak with Eric Merton before the final act could take place. He drove fast along the familiar route to St. Merryn. Last time he had driven like this it had been because he feared he might find his wife dead at the end of the journey. This time, it was because he needed to bring down the curtain on the many years of hard work, he and his team had carried out.

Eric came to the door as soon as the car pulled up and welcomed his guest.

'Good to see you again, DI Dunbar.'

'And you, Eric. I've brought your pictures to show you and I need you to think about anything you may be able to tell me about a couple of them.'

'No problem. Come through here, we can spread them out on the kitchen table. My wife is making us a drink.'

Dunbar handed him the camera. 'Returned with many thanks.'

He took the large brown envelope containing the people pictures out of his briefcase and sat down. Eric's wife placed cups of tea in front of them and disappeared with a book clutched in her hand.

'Reads all the time,' Eric said with a grin. 'She just leaves me to get on with whatever I want to do. At our time of life we're comfortable like that.'

'It's a good stage to be at,' Dunbar agreed. He pulled out the pictures and fanned them across the table. He had put post-it notes on the two photographs that had shown a man and a woman behind Jeanette and then the two men on the bench.

Pointing to Treverick, he said, 'Do you know this man?'

Eric shook his head. 'No, but I know the artist. Not by name but she's out there quite a lot in the height of the season. She's only been a couple of times lately but it's not been warm enough to wield a pencil, has it?'

'It definitely hasn't.' He reached inside his briefcase again and produced the picture that Jeanette had drawn of the two men on the bench. 'She drew this.'

Eric Merton looked at it and whistled. 'Well! This is wonderful. What a talent this young lady has. I'll look at her with different eyes next time I see her.'

Dunbar took back the sketch and put it away before continuing. 'That drawing was just to show you what led me to you. I came down to Padstow yesterday specifically to make sure she wasn't there even though I knew she wouldn't attempt to draw in all that rain. And you were there, instead.'

'I'm pleased I could help but I'm even more pleased to get this back.' He patted the camera inside its protective carrier bag.

'Please don't wipe any photos off it,' Dunbar said. 'I know my tech team will laugh at me and tell me they've downloaded this and downloaded that but if they disappeared, it wouldn't help our case.'

Eric pulled the other tagged photo towards him. He looked at it for some time before pushing it back towards Dunbar.

'I feel as though I know him.' He tapped the second man on the bench.

Dunbar shifted in his seat and picked up his mug of tea. 'Really?'

Eric stared at the picture and then pushed it away. 'It's in my head somewhere but it won't come out.'

'Okay, just think about it and if the name comes to you, call me. I will need you to come down to the station soon, preferably tomorrow, to make a statement. It's really just to validate the photos were taken by you. Will it be okay if I send a car for you about ten o'clock tomorrow?'

Dunbar was mindful that Eric was around seventy years old and he didn't want to push him too much.

'That will be fine. I'm always up by about six.' He turned to the pictures on the table that hadn't had post-it notes attached. 'They've turned out really well, haven't they? Look at this one. These people leaning on the harbour wall are all wearing different shades of blue. That was the reason I snapped that one, but I had to do it pretty quickly before they all split up and spoilt the composition.'

Dunbar picked it up and looked at it. 'It would never have occurred to me to look for something like that in a photo,' he said admiringly. 'But you're right. It's a blue picture: the sky, the sea, the people, really quite spectacular. I envy your ability to see something like that.'

'But I can't catch crooks. Each to their own, DI Dunbar, each to their own.'

Eric looked at the other pictures and then said 'I know her.'

'Who?'

'That woman there.'

Dunbar took the picture from him and looked at the figure Eric indicated. He could only see the back view of the figure but thought he also knew who she was; he needed Eric to continue the conversation.

'Who is she?'

'I don't exactly know her as in being able to put a name to the face, but she left the area with both of these men.' He pointed at the two men on the bench. 'I'm sorry if I'm not being very helpful...'

'Eric, I could kiss you. You're confirming lots of different angles for me. Everything you've told me today will need to be in that statement tomorrow.'

He stood and shook Eric's hand before gathering up the pictures. 'Please thank your wife for the tea. The car will be here at ten o'clock for you tomorrow.'

He left St. Merryn and headed back to the station. It was time to get organised.

Chapter 46

The following morning, Dunbar called the team in for four o'clock and they went through the details of what was to happen before dawn. Nobody yawned; alertness was part of their DNA when a result was expected. They knew just how important this day was going to be, what reports would be needed, who would be accompanying Dunbar on the early morning activity; nobody queried any part of it, recognising that Dunbar was showing real genius in these final hours of such a long investigation.

Some of the team were to stay behind; he chose the older members, the ones he called his brainbase. They were skilled in acting efficiently, digging up information and basically being the back-up for the more active younger members of the team.

At five o'clock, with dawn not yet breaking, they met up in the car park and quietly moved towards their designated vehicles. The armed response unit was already there and Dunbar checked that everybody was in communication with everybody else. They all confirmed their codes and Dunbar then put them into quiet action mode; no talking unless it was deemed necessary for their own safety.

The vehicles were parked quietly on the side streets and without fuss; a lone dog walker stared in astonishment then hurried home, keen to get out of the way. He had seen the armed response vehicle.

They followed the instructions to the letter and moved into position. Dunbar signalled to his DC who had been trained to use the Enforcer, that he needed to lower his eye protection and place his gauntleted hands ready for the swing of the battering ram.

The armed officers stood close by ready to enter the premises as soon as the door was breached.

In a low voice, Dunbar said,

'Go!'

DC Craig Lomax, a huge 6'7" mountain of a man, swung the Enforcer. The door gave way after one swing and Dunbar shook his head in admiration.

Within seconds, there was uproar. The noise was horrific as six armed men took over the operation closely followed by Dunbar.

They burst through the bedroom door that was partially open and

pointed guns at the two men struggling to surface from their sleep. Treverick moved his hand towards the nightstand where a handgun was clearly visible; the first man through the door raised his gun and shouted,

'Armed police! Stop!'

Treverick didn't stop and the bullet entered his head; blood and brains spattered all over the pristine white bedding, up the wall behind the bed head and turned the beige velour of the bed head into a dark red river.

The strangled scream from the other side of the bed and the absolutely devastated expression on the man's face was something to behold. His head was covered in blood and he tried to wipe it from his eyes with only limited success. Dunbar stepped into the room once the handgun had been secured and looked at the figure now kneeling on the floor, leaning on the side of the bed and trying to reach the body that would never move again. His sobs would have been heartbreaking if Dunbar hadn't known all the facts.

He stepped forward. 'Mark Carter, I am arresting you on suspicion of being an accessory to murder. You do not have to say anything. However, it may harm your defence if you do not mention when questioned, something which you later rely on in court. Anything you do say may be given in evidence.'

Mark continued to lean on the bed, seemingly unable to move. His moans became louder and Dunbar stepped forward to pass him some clothes.

'Get these on, Carter, or I'll take you as you are.'

Mark looked up and tried to stand. He was clearly struggling; his grief was threatening to completely overwhelm him. Blood and brains dripped from his body and he tried ineffectually to wipe it away.

Dunbar turned to one of his officers.

'Okay. Put the handcuffs on him, I've warned him we'll take him like this.'

The DC stepped forward and Mark took the trousers from him. He put them on, his white, grief-stricken face all the time looking at Treverick. He was handed the shirt from the bedside chair and fumbled as he buttoned it up.

'No tie, Carter,' Dunbar growled. 'We'll only take it off you at the station.'

He was hustled downstairs and Dunbar breathed a sigh of relief. It had gone as smoothly as he had hoped; he had always been prepared for the fact that Treverick might be killed when it was time to arrest him but it would have been good to see him die in prison.

He now turned his attention to Treverick. Death had been instantaneous; the top of his head had disintegrated in quite a spectacular fashion. He could hear the pathologist coming up the stairs and he shook his hand as he came through the door.

'You've finally got him, Jake.'

'Yes, Don, finally got him. It's a pity he had to die; I'd have liked my day in court with this one. I'll leave you to it, now. I witnessed everything that happened so I'll get back and fill in my report. He was warned not to touch his own gun and he still went for it.'

'Killing by cop?'

Dunbar shrugged.

'Could be. Wouldn't like to say. I know it was the whole prison thing that set him off on this journey. He blamed his first victim for putting him in prison so when we came in like the wrath of Zeus he must have known it was over. He never hesitated after the warning. Just carried on going for the gun.'

'Okay, leave it with me. Now get out, you're contaminating my crime scene. Oh, and well done, Jake. It's been a long time coming, but that little girl is safe at last.'

Dunbar went back down the stairs and round to the front of the building. The crime scene tape extended to cover both doors and Dunbar knew there was one last thing to tidy up.

He left four men at the scene and called for Sarah to accompany him. They climbed into his car and he drove once again towards St. Merryn; he turned off before the town and headed for Harlyn.

Linda Chambers lived with her mother in a small, whitewashed cottage; the garden was starting to look very pretty with daffodils and primroses bringing it to life after the long winter.

He walked down the path with Sarah following closely behind him. His knock was loud and it was Linda who answered it.

She imploded as soon as she saw who it was. Her face turned grey and she choked back a sob. She crumpled to her knees and her head sank.

'You'll not be going into work today, Linda. You're coming with me. I think we need to have a chat. You haven't got a job anyway. Carter Security just went into voluntary liquidation.'

She said nothing; he helped her to stand and as she climbed into the back of his car with Sarah, he saw Linda's mother pull the net curtain to one side and look out. They drove away with her eyes still on them, following the car until it was out of sight.

Chapter 47

'Is he dead?' There was anguish in her voice. 'He has to be dead or else...'

'Or else what, Linda?' Sarah asked. She could feel the shaking coming from Linda. She was one terrified woman.

'Or else he'll kill my mother,' she sobbed. 'I couldn't do anything. He's destroyed everything since Friday.'

'Look, Linda,' Dunbar said from the driving seat, 'don't talk now; wait till we get to the station. Your mother is safe.'

There was a long low moan from Linda who cried quietly to herself all the way back to the police station.

Sarah booked her in and then went to join Dunbar in the interview room with her. She heard Dunbar say WPC Sarah Millar had entered the room and she sat down by his side.

'Okay, Linda, tell me what you know.'

She screwed the tissue round and round in her hand and gulped.

'I know very little except Treverick was in Mark's flat above the office. I went to work as usual last Friday.' She paused while she gathered her thoughts. 'I went in a bit earlier than usual because I had lots of work piling up on my desk. Mark seemed to be going through a phase of passing everything on to me. I worked out rotas for Hillside and Moorgate, stuff like that and all things he used to do.'

'When did you start your employment with him?'

'He came to see me at home – just like John Thornton did all those years ago. It was in May last year. He said he needed a PA because the work was building up and would

I like to work for him? I said yes straight away. I've always liked Mark.'

'And what were your duties.'

'Everything really. As you know, I had the little office across the corridor from Mark. He set up an intercom between the two rooms so that he could just call me if he wanted me and everything worked brilliantly. When I first started, I did all the invoicing, sending out of letters, photocopying – the usual sort of office work. I was basically my own boss. He was out a lot because of the situation up at the Farmer's homes and he trusted me to just get on with it. Which I did.'

She gulped back tears that threatened to overflow again.

'And what was different about last Friday?'

'It was sunny for a start. As I said, I came in early and then just as I was going to have my packed lunch, a potential new client came in. Mark had gone out – I think up to Hillside but I'm not sure – so I took him into my office, talked him through our rates, showed him our references from other clients and had a very pleasant hour getting him on board. He left about two o'clock and I decided to take my lunch down to the harbour. I sat on one of the benches down there. It was lovely in the sunshine. I actually ate my lunch before walking along the harbour to come back here. If I hadn't done that I wouldn't have seen them.'

'Who?'

'Mark and Treverick. They didn't see me at first but I could tell they were deep in conversation. I actually think it was an argument because there was a lot of hand waving and pointing, but I couldn't tell what they were saying. And then Mark saw me.'

She stopped for a moment and asked if she could have a drink of water. Sarah left the room and returned a couple of minutes later with a plastic beaker of luke-warm water.

'Sorry, it's tap water,' she apologised and smiled at Linda. She hoped Dunbar was seeing what she was seeing; this girl was terrified and it wasn't of the possibility of a prison sentence. It went much deeper than that.

Linda took a sip and continued.

'Mark went deathly white. He stood up and for a second I thought he was going to fall over. That was the point I realised who the other man was. They moved to either side of me and Mark spoke first. He said, *"Shall we go back to the office, Linda?"* I nodded and then Treverick spoke. His words were flat.'

'Flat? What do you mean?'

'Emotionless. Totally spaced out. He said, *"My gun is in my right hand pocket. Don't make me use it."* I freaked, I tell you. I walked back to the office with a man either side of me and they took me round the side and up into Mark's flat.'

She looked at Dunbar, her face a mask of terror.

'I've never been so scared in my life. Treverick grabbed hold of me and dragged me over to the settee by my hair. Chunks of it came out and the pain was bad. He forced me face down and then twisted my arm up my back. I need to stand up to show you. Is that ok?'

Dunbar nodded and Sarah stood at the same time. She moved round to Linda's side of the table and said,

'Can I help?'

Linda nodded and took her left arm out of the sleeve first. She then slid her jacket carefully off her right arm. She had on a flimsy white blouse and Dunbar could see the bruising through it. He winced.

'I'm sending for a doctor, Linda. This needs documenting.'

'Nothing's broken, DI Dunbar, just my spirit. He hurt me so much and Mark just stood by and watched it happen.'

She leaned forward and took her hair out of the pony-tail she was wearing. As it cascaded around her face, it revealed bald patches and angry red weals on her scalp.

'Are you okay to carry on? I can have a doctor in here in two minutes.'

'I'll be fine. All of this really is nothing because after he'd finished hurting me and I was laid on that damned settee like a quivering jellyfish expecting to die any minute, he played his coup de grace. He said that if I said anything to anyone about what had happened, or the fact that I had seen him, he would kill my mother. Please, DI Dunbar, is he dead? I have to know.'

He nodded. 'Rest easy, Linda. He's dead.'

She crumpled as the relief of hearing that statement washed over her. 'And Mark?'

'In custody. You can relax. Had you really no idea Treverick was there?'

'Not at all. I've thought and thought about it since Friday, trying to remember when Mark changed. Because he did. One minute he was on top of everything, organising the rotas, visiting the families of Alan Shimwell and Sam Marks and then just after we had all that commotion with Father Christmas being Treverick, he changed. Now I stop and think about it, I guess that's when Treverick moved in. But they must have been in contact before – you don't just walk up to a man who is in a high-flying position as Mark is and say hey, I know I'm a murderer but can I stay at yours because I've just lost my flat. My head's spinning with trying to remember pointers, maybe things I could have picked up on but the biggest way Mark changed was that he kept nipping up to his flat at odd times during the day.'

'Linda,' Dunbar frowned. 'Did it not occur to you on Friday to come and tell the police what was going on?'

'No, it bloody didn't.' There was anger in her voice. 'For a start I was in horrific pain. All I wanted to do was get home to my mum, make sure she was safe. And to be honest, DI Dunbar, you've not exactly handled this case very well, have you? A lot of people have died. I know I've done nothing wrong but I sure as hell wasn't going to risk my mum's life by going to you. I dealt with everything the best way I could. If you want that doctor to take pictures of my injuries, that's fine, but then I'm going home. I need my mum.'

'I'll get the doctor now, Linda. I will need a statement from you but we can do that another time. All I ask is that you ring me if you think of anything else. And just for the record, I never thought for one minute that you were involved. We've known for a while that Treverick had an accomplice, because he was two steps in front of us all the time. We just never considered it might be Mark Carter. And logically, he had to be the one. You two are the only people who knew the movements of all the security people and I'll be honest, I didn't know that you did the rotas. I thought Mark did it all.'

He stood. 'Think you'll be okay tomorrow to come in and sign that statement?"

She nodded.

'The doctor will take you to a much nicer room than this. I want you to be examined properly, Linda, so if you've missed anything out, anything that he did to you, you must tell him.'

'He didn't rape me, DI Dunbar, if that's what you're asking. He likes little girls and big men, it seems.'

'Sarah, stay with Linda, will you. See that she gets home safely and go in with her. Talk to her mum, make sure she understands that Linda needs some TLC at the moment.'

Dunbar smiled at Linda and left the interview room. He went to his office and made himself a coffee. The bruising down Linda's arm and along her shoulder showed just what pressure had been exerted and he knew he had to calm down before interviewing Mark Carter. He sat at his desk and picked up the phone.

'Pilot?' Hi, it's Jake. Listen, why don't you take Grace and those other two little darlings of yours down to play on the swings? It's over, Pilot, It's over. Is Iain Dunne there? I need to speak to him and send your protective detail away. He needs to go and look for another job.'

Chapter 48

There was pandemonium at Hillside. Iain had spoken to Dunbar and was looking shell-shocked. He explained to Pilot that it appeared to be Mark Carter who had passed information on to Treverick and that Treverick was dead but beyond that, he knew nothing.

'So I'm going, Mr. Farmer, along with everybody else. I'm not sure what we'll do yet, but I'm just so glad your little one is safe now. It's been a pleasure being stationed here and meeting your lovely family. I'm taking a couple of weeks off while I think what to do. We might know a bit more by then as well.'

Pat looked at her son.

'Does this mean we can go back home? We've imposed on you for long enough and I need my own home.'

'Best let me check with Dunbar first. Don't forget the last person inside Moorgate was Treverick, so he might want to have it all checked out first.'

She nodded. 'You're right. And I'm not altogether convinced Josh will want to go back to Moorgate.' She nodded towards the settee where Josh was sitting by the side of Jess. 'The lad is smitten, methinks,' she grinned.

Dunbar looked at Mark Carter through the two-way mirror of the interview room. Gone was the smartly dressed man he had always known; in his place, an unhealthy-looking, blood-spattered, shrivelled individual, every part of him shaking. Dunbar walked into the room and didn't offer to get a doctor for him.

He switched on the recorder, said the names of the people present and asked Mark if he required a solicitor.

Mark declined and Dunbar began the interview by asking him to confirm his name and address. Mark mumbled his address without looking up.

'And this is the address where Ronald Treverick was killed by police action this morning?'

He nodded and murmured, 'Yes.' His head stayed down.

'When did you first meet Treverick?'

'February 1974. He came to film John Thornton at that time. He was known as Brian Lazenby.'

'And when did you get together this last time?'

'He rang me when Angel left him.'

'Grace. She's called Grace.'

He shrugged. 'She was Angel for seven years.'

'Tell me the story, Mark. It will be better for you when this goes to court.'

'He rang me. I met him. We fell in love. End of story.'

'Not quite. I have questions. Firstly, why did you meet with him? Why didn't you just tell me?'

'I believed I could convince him to stop. I really got to know him when he was with Amy and I liked him. I thought I could help him move away and the whole thing would stop. We talked and talked when we did meet up and I saw another side to him that I trusted. He convinced me that what he was doing, what we were doing, was right in every way. I don't expect you to understand...'

'Too damn right I don't understand. Why did he wait so long to move in with you? Why did he have to live in a caravan and then that awful little flat above the grotto?'

'He also had a tent between the caravan and the grotto. He didn't want me to be in any danger. And he said that if things went wrong, I wouldn't be drawn into the endgame.'

'So why did you both go down to the harbour last Friday?'

Finally, Carter lifted his head.

'The sun came out. Simple, really. He changed his appearance a bit and went down there first. I followed soon after and we sat on the bench for quite a while. Did Linda tell you? He thought he'd done enough to scare her into not speaking to you.'

'He had. No, it wasn't Linda. Remember the camera? You're all on it. And I had no idea it was you until I saw the photo. We guessed there was an accomplice. There had to be one, but I never thought for a second you would be that stupid. What were you arguing about?'

'He wanted me to speed things up and leave Angel vulnerable. You'll have realised by now I was passing information on to him. I thought it was too soon.'

'I just want to back-track a little here. When he rang you after Grace ran away from him, what convinced you to meet up with him? You knew what he had done, what he was capable of. So what was it that attracted you to a paedophile and a murderer?'

'Just one thing, Jake.'

'DI Dunbar.'

'Just one thing: Amy Thornton. She was the one thing we had in common. I loved her and in a twisted kind of way, so did he. He just mentioned her name and I was lost. We were lovers within a week of that first meeting. It wasn't just a physical thing. In ordinary circumstances, I would have spent the rest of my life with him. And now he's dead and I'm covered in his blood.'

'You'll be in the shower shortly.'

Again, he lifted his head. 'I'm pleading guilty. I don't regret anything, I loved Ronald and I'd do it all again;

whatever you end up charging me with, I shall plead guilty. Angel has suffered enough and I don't want her having to relive it all.'

Dunbar stood. 'Get a solicitor, Mark. Get a solicitor. We'll speak more after you've had a shower and something to eat and drink.'

He left the room and walked up the stairs back to his office. He had phone calls to make, people to see and he needed personal time out. He leaned back in his chair and closed his eyes.

EPILOGUE

Grace and Olivia rolled over and over down the grassy bank; Noah watched them, delight on his face. He held up his arms to his Mummy and she lifted him up.

'No. Noah,' she said gently, 'you're not quite old enough to do that, yet. Just watch your sisters.'

Grace ran back up the bank followed by a panting Olivia.

'Can Papa take us to the swings in the park, please, Mummy?'

'Papa's at work, sweetheart. Maybe we'll have a walk down later, after Noah has had his afternoon nap.'

'Is it still safe?'

Lauren laughed. 'As long as you're with either me or Papa or the two Nans or Josh or Dawn or Jess or Granddad Ken, you'll always be safe.'

And then Grace asked the question she asked every day.

'Is he dead, Mummy? Is Ronald dead?'

'Yes, my love, Ronald is dead.'

Dunbar was sitting in his office when the phone call came through.

'DI Dunbar, it's Marcia Shaw.'

He hesitated, not quite knowing how to respond.

'Hello?'

'Hello, Marcia. How can I help you?'

'Is he really dead?'

'Yes.'

'So Matthew will inherit anything he's left?'

Dunbar put down the phone and just stared at it. A flashback to Kenny Raines' body hit him and he knew he could never speak to her again. God help that little boy with a mother like that.

He pulled his computer towards him and looked at Eric's photographs one more time. He had a temporary flashback moment and shivered.

What if?

What if he had accepted Mark Carter's offer of help in downloading the photographs?

The End

Acknowledgements

My grateful thanks go as always to my family who patiently listen to me trying out different avenues in the plotline, who get texts and emails at odd times and who just as patiently respond to my requests for instant answers.

Individually I have to thank

- Erica Cheetham, who was the first one to read Beautiful and who read the first 50,000 words of Angel for me when I was starting to doubt; her words were inspirational.
- Cerys Kitchen, my twelve year old granddaughter and proof-reader for her attention to detail; let no typos go undiscovered!
- Karen Tighe, for her brilliant feedback and nagging.
- Siân and Kirsty Waller, for their unswerving support.
- Bloodhound Books for their commitment to a seventy-year- old author. Thank you, Fred and Betsy, for your belief in me.

There are many people who I haven't named individually who have, in some small way, kept me strong. You know who you are – the people who have written fantastic reviews, helped with publicity and quite a huge chunk of thanks goes to the United States reading public who have helped a British writer climb the charts over there to quite dizzying heights!

25199967R00198

Made in the USA
Columbia, SC
31 August 2018